D0375643

AS IMPORTANT AS BREATHING

Carly continued chattering. "I cook breakfast. Pancakes. With butter and maple syrup."

Evan's face was inches from hers. She didn't recall his moving closer, but he was suddenly close enough for her to notice that his pupils were very, very wide, rimmed with just the thinnest band of sky blue.

"With butter and maple syrup," he repeated her words in a low, warm voice as if he wouldn't mind having her served that way.

She opened her mouth to speak but never got that far. His lips met hers, and all mental activity ceased. Her autonomic nervous system, in charge of basic survival functions like respiration and heart rate, also seemed to be in charge of kissing, which, at that moment, was as important as breathing. Carly found herself falling into a deep kiss with Evan—a full-frontal, lip-on-lip, tongue-in-mouth, hands-roaming, toe-curling kind of kiss.

My Red Shoes

Liana Merrill

ZEBRA BOOKS
Kensington Publishing Corp.
www.kensingtonbooks.com

For Ron,
my lucky charm,
with whom all things are possible,
without whom not much matters.

ZEBRA BOOKS are published by

Kensington Publishing Corp.
850 Third Avenue
New York, NY 10022

All Kensington titles, imprints, and distributed lines are available at special quantity discounts for bulk purchases for sales promotion, premiums, fund-raising, educational, or institutional use.

Special book excerpts or customized printings can also be created to fit specific needs. For details, write or phone the office of the Kensington Special Sales Manager: Attn. Special Sales Department. Kensington Publishing Corp., 850 Third Avenue, New York, NY 10022. Phone: 1-800-221-2647.

Zebra and the Z logo Reg. U.S. Pat. & TM Off.

ISBN 0-7582-7893-5

First Printing: June 2005

10 9 8 7 6 5 4 3 2 1

Printed in the United States of America

Chapter One

Well, hell.

Carly woke up in bed wearing a blue bathrobe. A quick check underneath revealed nothing—no clothes, no underwear, nada—which wouldn't normally give her cause for alarm, except that while the bed was hers, the bathrobe wasn't. No fairy tale she'd ever read, at least not the happy ever after kind, had a scenario where the fairy godmother replaced the gorgeous silk party dress with an ugly plaid bathrobe. All in all, she felt she had just cause to feel a bit uneasy.

At least, she thought, closing her eyes and slipping eagerly back into the womb warmth of unconsciousness, she wasn't lying in the middle of a chalk outline with a bunch of forensics guys snapping her picture and taking hair samples. A couple of hours later, she slowly tuned back in to see if life was any better.

Well, hell.

An aerobics class was pounding away on her frontal lobe and her mouth was as dry as a package of Pixy Stix. Refusing to acknowledge her hangover in hopes that it would get the hint and go away like an uninvited guest, Carly rewound the tape to the night before. How she lost her clothes and who had brought her home was a mystery, although she was fairly sure that she could cross alien abduction off the list. That only happened to yahoos out in the middle of the desert, not to people partying in the Hollywood Hills.

Her last clear memory was of herself innocently sipping a cocktail at her best friend Dana's birthday party. She cast around for even a tiny glimpse of what had gone on the night before, but netted only a few flashes of flaming torches and flying mangoes. No leads there. Moving on, she wondered how she and her clothes had parted ways and what or, more probably, who had caused the rift. Despite her nakedness, Carly sincerely doubted that she'd been defiled. Every other time that had happened she'd woken up feeling pretty damned good. This morning she just felt damned.

Surveying her surroundings, she found her purse lying on the nightstand next to her. That was a relief. At least it hadn't skipped town with the rest of her clothes and shoes.

Shoes! Oh, my God! Where are my shoes?

Shooting from the bed like Seabiscuit out of the starting gate, she careered around the room in a mad search for her shoes. Seconds later, the contents of her stomach threatened to fly out with the same kind of frantic urgency. After a purgative trip to the toilet, Carly stood underneath a hot shower, forehead leaning on the cold white tile, and contemplated her loss.

These weren't just any old pair of shoes. They were her lucky shoes, the ones she'd worn to her first audition, the ones that had landed her her first real part—the voice of a vegetable in a grocery store commercial. (Not the lead tomato, but supporting artichoke wasn't bad.) It was the role that had launched a thousand commercials. Ever since then, the shoes were *de rigueur* for any important audition.

The cherry-red heels weren't the most expensive shoes around, but they did for her what a $50,000 sports car did for a man with a comb-over. Wearing them, she was Carly Beck, voiceover actress: cool, sexy, and successful. Without them reality reigned and she was merely Carlotta Rudolph, loser. A short, nervous nobody, always the last person left holding the lit cartoon bomb right before it blows.

"Dana, it's Carly. Pick up the phone! Pick up . . . pick up . . . pick up . . ." Every fifteen minutes for the last hour, Carly had left the same pleading message while she tore apart her house.

"If I have to hear this message one more time," a groggy voice interrupted, "I think I'm going to have to have you killed." Dana was not known for being at her best when she woke up in the morning, or in this case, the afternoon. Other than that, she was really quite a nice person to have as a friend.

"I can't find my shoes!" Carly wailed, ignoring the threat.

"So what? Buy a new pair." A soft pop followed by a whooshing sound came through the phone line, no doubt a Diet Coke, Dana's nonalcoholic drink of choice.

"I can't find my *lucky* shoes!"

"Oh, honey," Dana said, now sympathetic. "Not your luckies."

"Yeah, my luckies."

"I'll be right over. Do you have any aspirin?"

"Yes, but it's baby aspirin," Carly said, heading for the bathroom. "I think if you take eight it's the same as two regular. But stay put, I'm coming over there. We need to go over your house with a fine-tooth comb."

"Great." Dana's response was unenthusiastic. "I'll notify the boys at search and rescue. They haven't been by in a while."

The two women sprawled on Dana's cranberry sectional sofa couldn't have been more mismatched. Where Carly was small and sleek with short dark hair, Dana was tall, buxom, and blonde. Carly could just hit five-six—with three-inch heels and liberal use of volumizing mousse. Dana slouched in at five-eleven in bare feet. A gamin and a Vikingess. An Italian greyhound and a golden retriever. They had been friends since college: Dana was the adventurous, ballsy one; Carly the thoughtful peacemaker. They laughed a lot, bickered constantly, and cried on each other's shoulders—as close as friends could be who couldn't swap clothes.

The living room was surprisingly clean despite the madcap goings-on that had gone on, and on, the night before. The caterers had done their best to clean up any party detritus, but numerous champagne corks and the odd glow-in-the-dark party favor still popped up like stale Easter eggs.

It had been Dana's second annual thirtieth birthday bash, the celebration to end all celebrations, until the next one, of course. Carly, too, was looking down the barrel of thirty the coming spring, but she was leaning toward something a little more sedate—like reading a book on a sugar-sand beach with a masseur and cabana boys in attendance.

Shall I apply more sunblock, querida? Perhaps loosen the strings on your bikini?

Why yes, Enrique, I am feeling a bit restrained.

The vision vanished, leaving behind the fading scent of coconut oil and a growing sense of foreboding. If her shoes didn't make an appearance soon, she could kiss that fantasy good-bye and settle, instead, for a nice ice floe inhabited by a couple of walruses tossing her herring.

The women had searched the high and the low of Dana's Tudoresque two-story house to no avail. The remains of Carly's clothes had shown up in the guest bathroom shower stall, the wet heap of pale pink silk resembling a pile of drowned rose blossoms. The shoes, however, were still AWOL. They did find an abundance of bottle caps and even one leftover guest snoring comfortably on a lounge chair by the pool. Adjusting the umbrella to prevent a sunburn, they left a can of Red Bull and a bag of tortilla chips by his side.

Dana shoved the remains of their In-N-Out burgers into the carry bag and put her size-ten feet up on the ebony wood coffee table.

"Okay, now that I can think," she said, popping back a fistful of baby aspirin and sucking them down with a mouthful of chocolate shake, "when was the last time you saw the shoes?"

Taking a deep breath, Carly hoped that french fries could somehow be classified as a brain food. She glanced over her friend's shoulder and stared at the giant French movie poster of Elvis that dominated the far wall. *L'Amour en Quatrième Vitesse* it read, the Gallic version of *Viva Las Vegas*. Surely Elvis, *le roi du rock et roll,* would understand the importance of shoes, blue suede or otherwise.

"The last thing I remember, while I still had shoes, was standing at the bar talking. Then it fades to black until this morning when I woke up in bed wearing a ratty blue robe."

"Hey, lay off the robe," Dana said, getting her back up. "That was a souvenir of my last love, Jean-Paul."

"Jean-Claude," Carly corrected, wiping down the coffee table with her napkin and tossing it into the bag.

"Whatever." Dana shrugged. "I loved him."

Carly rolled her eyes. "I've got a huge audition on Monday that I'm going to blow if I can't find my shoes. Now what?"

"We call everyone who was at the party," Dana offered.

"Are you kidding me?" Carly asked incredulously. "The entire drinking-age population of Los Angeles was there. Why not just throw another party and announce it over a bullhorn?"

Despite her hangover, Dana actually looked interested.

"Don't even think it," Carly said, giving her a warning look. "Besides, I don't want the world knowing I woke up naked and can't remember a thing."

"We come into this world naked and unknowing, my child," Dana replied solemnly. "We won't mention the naked part."

"No. They'll figure it out." Carly ran her hands nervously through her short, dark hair. "They'll assume I was naked. Everyone always assumes you were naked."

"I know I do." Dana took a final noisy pull of her shake. "At least your car's not stolen. How'd you get here?"

"I cabbed it." Her silver Audi could be clearly seen through the diamond-paned living room window. It was parked on the street, a breeze playing with a pink parking ticket tucked underneath the windshield wiper. She hugged herself and moaned softly. "I want my shoes back. They're my life."

"Don't worry," Dana said. "We'll get them back."

Carly leaned back, her hand slipping between the cushions. She pulled out a size fourteen man's brown, tasseled loafer. "Holy guacamole, who slept here last night? Bigfoot?"

Dana shrugged. "I wouldn't rule it out. Although, I wouldn't have pegged him for a loafer man. Hiking boots, maybe."

The frenetic jingle of metal tags announced the entrance of Daisy the Dangerous Dachshund. Tail wagging excitedly, the wiener dog headed straight for the sofa and snatched the shoe out of Carly's hand. It was about the same size and color as Daisy.

"Attagirl," encouraged Dana as her dog chewed energetically on the faux crocodile leather. "Never trust a man with tassels on his shoes."

"Tassels," Carly repeated slowly. The hitherto paralyzed cogs of Carly's brain let out a pained metallic squeal and began to turn. Moments later she let out a low moan. "Oh, Christ."

Dana put her arm around her friend's shoulder. "I take it men and tassels don't mix for you either."

Carly's face contorted in horror. "I know who has my shoes."

Dana looked in the direction of the loafer. The tassels, thanks to Daisy, were now a fused, lumpy, sodden mass. The dog stood triumphantly, one tiny front paw in the shoe as if she were trying it on for size.

"Bigfoot?"

"Worse, much worse." Carly's shook her head dejectedly as the missing memories reintroduced themselves. "I was at the bar talking to a bunch of people. We were discussing exotic dancers."

"It happens."

"We were wondering how they get their tassels to twirl in both directions at once. A couple of the guys suggested a field trip. But no one wanted to leave the free booze, so they sat around and talked about it instead. Then Martin, the Cirque du Soleil guy, thought it's like juggling, so he takes some limes from the bar and starts tossing them in the air in opposite directions."

"Why do I waste money on a band, with entertainment like this going on?" Dana asked the air.

Daisy, who was now busily hunting down champagne corks and dropping them into the cavernous loafer, looked up and arfed.

"Shhh," Carly scolded the both of them. "Let me finish. Soon we're all tossing fruit around. I'd just kicked my shoes off by the edge of the pool when I had to suddenly get out of the way to avoid an out-of-control coconut. Next thing I know, me and most of a fruit basket are floating in the pool."

"That explains the clothes in the shower and the

bananas in the Jacuzzi. I don't know what I'm going to say to the pool man."

"Same thing you told him last time." Daisy finished the cork roundup and climbed onto Carly's lap.

"So, what happened after the fruit toss?"

"One minute I'm swimming toward my shoes. Next minute, I am hanging over the water looking straight into Evan McLeish's stupid face. That's when I passed out. I feel darkness coming on just thinking about it."

Of all the unlikely rescuers Carly could have wished for, she would have taken Bigfoot over Evan McLeish. Sure, they were both tall and dark and dangerous enough to give any woman heart palpitations, but while Evan was by far the more handsome of the pair, Bigfoot probably edged him out on social skills. Evan was a gorgeous vision of manhood who spent his life surrounded by his own personal microclimate of arctic air, swirling gray mist, and brooding thunderclouds. The only thing missing was the sound of baying hounds in the distance. Heathcliff in black denim and Doc Martens—that was Evan McLeish.

"Oh, Evan," Dana said, dismissing Carly's concerns. "Just give him a call and your problem's solved."

Carly sat up, shocked. "I can't call him. It would be so humiliating!"

"Yeah, right. And being fished out of a pool, drunk and sopping wet, is so dignified? What? Were you wearing a tiara or something?" Both Dana and the dog gave Carly a look of curiosity mixed with disdain.

"You don't understand," Carly moaned. "I just can't. Besides, I don't even have his number."

"I do." Dana let out a small snicker. "What's the big deal, anyway, Tinkerbell? Is it 'cause he saw you . . . nek-ked?"

"You know," Carly paused and then shuddered, "I didn't even think about that."

"If it makes you feel any better, with that thin little slip dress you were wearing, after it got wet, everybody saw you naked."

"No," she grumbled, "it doesn't."

"I tried."

"Just kill me . . ." She knew she didn't make Evan's top ten list of Wonderful Women, probably didn't even make it in the top one million, but she hated to give him a reason to add her to the list of Women I Wonder About.

"C'mon, he's just a guy," Dana tried to assure her. "Besides, I think he thinks you're cute."

"No, he's not just a guy. He's a guy who maybe thinks I'm cute but absolutely thinks I'm as witless as a bread loaf, and as neurotic as some overbred, overpriced, ornamental dog."

"Hey!" Dana warned. "Not in front of the over-bred, overpriced, ornamental dog."

"Sorry, baby," Carly said, petting the dachshund. "Every time I see Evan, he's taking potshots at me for doing kitty litter commercials. And the cartoons! Don't get him started on the cartoons. I'm messing with the minds of America's youth, I tell you. Of the seven deadly sins, I'm right there between sloth and gluttony."

"More like lust and gluttony," Dana corrected.

"He hates me."

"Yeesh," Dana said, making a face. "Don't you think you're taking this a little hard? So he doesn't appreciate what you do? So what's new? I'm a sit-com writer, I'm used to people thinking what I do is crap. Let it slide."

"I can't!" She wrung her hands in frustration. "He makes serious documentaries. I make com-mercials for products nobody needs. He does it for art. I do it for money. That makes him a hero and me a ho."

"Take it easy, okay? Besides, he can hardly play Mr. High and Mighty," Dana argued. "You drive a sex-on-wheels sports car and he's got a piece of shit truck. You don't owe for anything but your house, and he's still paying for a snotty film degree from the University of Spoiled Children. Screw what he thinks. He's a jerk."

Carly gave Dana a warm smile. "You're a good friend, D."

Dana returned the smile. "Anytime, Tinkerbell. Your scum of the earth is my scum of the earth. I'll get scum's phone number for you."

The Audi slipped quietly into the garage located behind the small Studio City home that Carly shared with her cat, Odin. Her little white ranch house with light blue trim was once a duplicate of every other house in the tree-lined neighborhood. But that was in the forties, when the area was home to many of the burgeoning movie studios' laborers and stage workers. Many decades later, it was still home to studio employees, but now they were ex-ecutives and highly paid production personnel. And the homes reflected it.

Whenever possible, all efforts were made to turn

the sturdy little postwar tract homes into mini-estates. Crowded together on half- and quarter-acre lots, the little cottages sprouted ever-growing boxes like architectural tumors on their backs as far as the zoning and easement laws would allow. Some dispensed with the original house altogether and built a new structure in whatever style caught their fancy—colonial, Craftsman, Toontown. Carly's was one of the few that remained basically untouched. By LA standards, where history is rented from a prop house, her place was vintage.

"Mrrrew?"

Carly locked the back door behind her, tossed her purse on the kitchen counter, and picked up her twenty-plus-pound feline.

"Hey, Odin. How's my little Nordic god? Hungry?"

The gigantic black cat purred his happiness like a fine German motorcar.

Carly opened the cupboard nearest the sink to peruse the cat treats. "We've got brown cubes, pink cubes, and orange cubes." She put the cat on the floor with an audible thump that made the glasses in the cupboards rattle.

Odin purred agreeably as he rubbed against her ankles. He had yet to meet a brand of cat food for which he didn't feel a deep and instantaneous affection.

The kitchen was small by modern standards with original rustic knotty pine cabinets and cheery lemon yellow tile counters. The refrigerator, food processor, and KitchenAid mixer were all modern, but the monster-sized white gas stove was straight out of Donna Reed's kitchen. A large double-hung window, trimmed with cherry print curtains, gave Carly a view of the street when she did the dishes.

Most nights she ate her dinner at an octagonal kitchen table with Odin curled up on one of the four chairs. The table and chairs were painted eggshell white, same as the matching buffet, which displayed her collection of blue and white china and provided a resting place for mail and the week's *New York Times*. The newspaper was a gift from her journalist father, who claimed that Los Angeles didn't have a real newspaper. Every week she attempted the challenge of the Sunday crossword puzzle, failed miserably, and threw it out. Once in a while, she completed the one in the *TV Guide* just to make herself feel like a Mensa candidate.

Carly dawdled as she fed Odin his treats one at a time in an effort to put off her call to Evan, but eventually the food ran out and the moment was at hand.

Chapter Two

It took her three tries before her spastic fingers finally managed to dial his number correctly.

"McLeish," he answered, his manner clipped and businesslike.

Carly's response was less impressive. She squeaked. A cartoon-worthy squeal of shock and horror. She had prepared herself for the digitized version of the man, not the real thing. For some reason, she didn't expect him to pick up. A dumb supposition based on nothing more than the fact that she didn't want him to.

"Hi, Evan, this is Carly Beck," she was going to say cheerfully into his machine. *"I wondered if you might know where a pair of my shoes are? They're high heeled and red. I seem to have misplaced them at Dana's party. If you do, please call me or Dana. Thanks!"*

This was Plan A. A breezy phone message that left him no choice but to call Dana since she wasn't going to leave her number. Sneaky? Yes. Cowardly? Definitely. Smart? Damn straight.

There was no Plan B.

Aborting her mission, Carly abruptly hung up and went to lie down for a while.

* * *

An hour passed before she got up the nerve to try again. Evan had her rattled and she hated it. She'd faced down jerks before, personally and professionally, but with him she always felt like an emotional weakling, a mere dandelion fluff of uncertainty trying to hold steady in a gale-force wind.

A year previously, Carly had had her first glimpse of Evan at a screening of her friend Gary's independent film. Evan walked into the lobby like he was leading an invisible army; head up, shoulders back, he didn't shuffle and he didn't fidget. He wasn't a kid, a guy, a dude, pal, or buddy. He was a man with a capital *Mmmmm*. Black hair, pearl-gray shirt, black jeans, black boots, he was the picture of monochromatic splendor. Except his eyes. The windows into his soul were vivid chips of Lake Tahoe blue. It was as close to seeing a sixteen-point buck enter a forest clearing as she was ever going to get. Carly never understood the appeal of hunting, but at that moment she really, really wanted to strap him to the front of her car and show him off to all her friends.

And her personal gift from the gods was tracking her as well. But, despite the predatory glint in his baby blues, Carly could tell that he was a catch-and-release-after-one-glorious-night kind of guy. Given her history of rat boyfriends, that was probably a good thing. Her relationships with men, she had found, generally did not improve with either time or proximity.

As mutual approving glances were tossed back and forth, Carly inventoried her overnight guest checklist: clean sheets, extra toothbrush, party pack of prophylactics. She was definitely set for a night of wonder and discovery, if only they could get past the ogling stage. Just then Gary came by to do the introductions.

"Evan McLeish, documentary filmmaker," Gary said with a flourish, "meet Carly Beck, actress."

On the last word Evan's eyes went from flame to iceberg blue.

Psych.

Carly felt like she'd been sucker punched. The disdain rolling off the cinema stud was thick enough to scrape off her shoes.

"I guess you must have mistaken me for someone else," she said flatly without extending her hand. "Well, have a nice life, Evan McLeish."

After that oh-so-unglorious first meeting, Evan would sometimes make a point of mistaking her for someone else. Anybody else. It was a mutual joke between nonfriends.

"Odin! Come here, baby." Carly needed some moral support. An answering meow preceded the cat by a few seconds. She picked up the full-figured feline and he began to purr with kitty abandon.

Carly hit the redial button with, she hoped, authority.

The phone rang once. *Please, don't be home.*

Twice. *Don't be home.*

Three times. *Don't.*

Four. *Yes!*

"You've reached Evan McLeish. Leave your name and number and I'll get back to you as soon as possible."

Beeeeeep!

"Hi, Evan," she said quickly, breathlessly. She had

to pause, inhale, and slow down. "This is Carly Beck. I was—"

There was an abrupt click as someone picked up the line.

"I was wondering when you were going to call." The brusqueness was gone. Now his voice was as inviting as warm chocolate cake. "Did you try calling a little while ago?"

"No," she said quickly, defensively. "Not at all."

"Hmm."

"Hmm, what?"

"Hmm, nothing."

"Hmm, something."

"You're being paranoid," he pointed out.

"You're being cryptic," she pointed back.

"Big word."

"Shut up." She slapped herself on the forehead the minute the words left her lips. *Stupid. Don't antagonize he who holds the shoes.* "Sorry."

"What's that noise?" he asked.

"What noise?" It was only a little slap.

"That throbbing sound, like a generator."

Odin. "Nothing. It must be this line."

"Hmm."

"Hmm," she echoed in frustration. She transferred the cat to the sofa cushion and started to pace. "What do you mean you were expecting me?"

"I had a hunch."

"What hunch?"

It takes two to tango, but talking with Evan was more like slam dancing in a shoebox.

"Why were you calling?" he asked.

"Why were you expecting me to call?"

"Do you want to hang up and try again?" he

asked patiently. "This conversation doesn't seem to be going anywhere."

"No." She wondered if he was laughing. She stopped pacing and listened hard for telltale quick breathing but heard nothing. Which was weird because she definitely felt like there was laughing going on on the other end of the line.

"Are you going to say anything?" he asked after a while.

Lucky shoes, lucky shoes, lucky shoes. "I think you have my shoes."

"Hmm."

"Please don't 'hmm.'"

"All right," he said agreeably, which was suspicious. Evan was never agreeable. "Why do you think I have your shoes?"

"Deduction. You were the last person seen in the vicinity of my shoes."

"I'll buy that."

"Thank you." Maybe he was going to be civilized about the whole thing after all. Her hopes rose. "Can I have my shoes?"

"What'll you give me for your shoes?"

Her hopes fell. "I don't have to give you anything," she said defiantly. "They're my shoes. They belong to me."

"Can you describe them?"

She tapped her foot. "Red leather, high heeled, size five."

"Sounds like them," he admitted. "Where's your receipt?"

"I don't need a receipt. They're mine."

"Sorry, no returns without a receipt."

Carly could feel his dastardly, dashing, devious

smile through the line. She hung up and called him all the names she wanted to scream into the phone but couldn't.

"You've reached Evan McLeish. Leave your name and number and I'll get back to you as soon as possible."
Beeeeeep!
"It's Carly." She drummed her fingertips on the arm of the sofa while she waited for him to come on the line.
"Ah yes," he said gravely, "the little mermaid."
"What do you want for the shoes?" She made a mental note to ask her accountant if ransom was somehow tax deductible.
"You. One night."
She blinked. "I'm sorry?"
"You won't be, I assure you."
Her nipples stood at attention like soldiers fresh out of boot camp. Two "ayes" against her one "nay."
She hung up.
Sucker punched, again. How did he do that? Take her from zero to sixty in a nanosecond? She hadn't forgotten their first meeting when she went from sixty to brick wall just as fast. The man had her coming and going. If she didn't watch herself, she'd end up totaled on the Evan McLeish Autobahn.

"You've reached Evan McLeish. Leave your name and number and I'll get back to you as soon as possible."
Beeeeeep!
"No," she said with finality.

Evan picked up the phone before she'd even finished the word.

"Why not?"

"I don't have to give a reason. Just, no. Name
your price, but not that."

"Dinner."

"Dinner?" she asked suspiciously. "That's it? Just
dinner? You go from one night to one dinner just
like that?"

"No, have dinner with me tonight and I'll tell you
how to get your shoes back. Simple."

"Simple. Right." As if that must be what he
thought she was. "Are you enjoying this?"

"Immensely."

"It shows. All right. Where? What time?"

Toluca Lake, nestled between Universal City, Burbank, and North Hollywood, was the longtime
home of Bob Hope, the actor, and Bob's Big Boy,
the restaurant (no relation, although they both
sported similar pompadours). Carly sat glumly in
a brown Naugahyde covered booth at Bob's and
waited for Evan to make an appearance. He was
late. Probably on purpose, the fiend.

Carly ordered a coffee from the waitress and
watched the door through dark glasses. She'd read
that gamblers often wore sunglasses to avoid giving
themselves away with their eyes. Apparently, the
pupil widens when it spies something good, like a
tub of full-fat cream cheese, and constricts to pinpoints when it sees something bad, like the slob
who just double-dipped in said tub. Perhaps dark

glasses would offer her the same protection. At the very least, they made her feel less vulnerable.

Evan walked in the door wearing dark glasses and carrying a thick manila folder. He was as ridiculously handsome as when she first set eyes on him, she noted with disgust. With his black hair, blue eyes, and angular features he looked like a secret agent playing a movie star or a movie star playing a secret agent. Unfortunately, Evan was that irresistible combination of dream and downfall that spelled trouble for her any way she looked at it.

"Sorry I'm late," he said, sliding into the booth across from her.

"No, you're not."

"Sorry or late?" He took off his glasses and blessed her with a brilliant smile that made her tummy flip and her pupils widen.

She wished he wouldn't do that. "Never mind. What's your deal?"

His dark brows gathered together in mock seriousness. "Tsk, not so fast. You make it sound so seamy and untoward."

"Taking people's shoes hostage is seamy and untoward."

The waitress reappeared and asked about their orders.

Evan spoke without consulting the menu. "A Big Boy hamburger, fries, and a cherry Coke."

"A hot fudge cake, fries, a side of ranch dressing, and a Coke." The regular. Carly had been ordering that particular gastronomic combination at different Bob's since she was a kid. A high-calorie panacea for all things sucky. And this situation was definitely sucky. Infinitely sucky.

"Okay, we ordered," Carly continued after the waitress had left. "Is that enough preamble for you, or do you want to wait until after the floor show?"

"You're not in a good mood."

"I forgot to refill my prescription for Xanax on the way here," she said sweetly. "I was hoping it wouldn't show."

The corner of his mouth lifted slightly and his eyes crinkled. He pushed the folder toward her. "Here, read this. Then we can make a deal."

Carly yearned to throw the folder into the air and let its contents rain all over the restaurant. Instead, she conjured up a vision of herself in her lucky shoes as she did a little flamenco number over the length of Evan's back. The crunch of bone underneath her pointy heels would be quite satisfying. She hung onto that thought and opened the folder. It held some photographs, a few Xeroxed pages of notes, and a script. The title page read "Fly Me to the Moon—The Life of Arlene Barlow."

"What does Arlene Barlow have to do with my shoes?" she asked, scanning the pictures of a slender blonde with large, sad eyes.

"Do you know who she is?" The unsaid words "you big fat dummy" hung in the air between them.

Carly allowed herself the sneaky luxury of rolling her eyes behind her sunglasses. "Yes, I know who she is. Arlene Barlow, jazz diva around the fifties or sixties. Disappeared at the height of her career. So, do I know who Arlene Barlow is? Can I have my shoes now?"

"Yes, you know who Arlene Barlow is," he admitted, none too gracefully. "No, you can't have your shoes."

The food arrived, and they set their differences aside for a few minutes. Hot fries have a short window of opportunity when they are at their zenith of delectability. Only fools let their fries grow cold and Carly was no fool. She pushed her coffee aside and dipped a fry into the ranch dressing.

"Catsup should be the only condiment allowed on a fry," Evan pronounced like a king to his court.

"I'll remember that next time I have you over to the house."

"That would be nice." Evan gave her one of those "I'm a great guy" smiles she knew he used to camouflage his true, evil nature.

"Come on, Evan. I don't have time for this. What does Arlene Barlow have to do with me and my shoes?"

"I want you to narrate my documentary about her."

Work with Evan the Terrible?! Are you out of your freaking mind?! "You want me to do some work for you? You've got to be kidding."

"Actually, no." He looked serious. He sounded it, too.

"Uh, I don't know if you've noticed, Evan, but I sell breakfast cereal and fee-free checking accounts. I also do cartoon voices for earthworms and space aliens. I don't do narration."

"I think you'd do a great job." He still looked serious.

"Okay, what's going on here? I think you just said something nice about me." Carly moved her plate of fries aside and started in on her hot fudge cake.

"No, I mean it," he said with disturbing sincerity.

Carly wondered how long he could keep it up. It was so against his nature. "I want you to voice my film."

She shook her head. "My spidey sense tells me I wasn't first on the list. Something's not right here."

A couple and their baby took the booth behind Evan. The man had his back to Evan and held his baby over his shoulder as he rubbed its little back. The baby looked as grumpy as Carly felt.

Evan let out a breath and paused. He seemed to be weighing his options. "Okay, I'll be honest. I originally had someone else in mind, but he didn't work out."

"James Earl Jones wasn't available, huh? You know, I get more jobs that way."

He made a sour face at the same time as the baby. "I've already recorded the narration with someone else, but I wasn't happy with the results. His voice just felt wrong all the way through. I thought it might be better with a woman."

"There are lots of women who could do this." Carly spoke to the baby. It was easier.

"Not as good as you."

Carly shook her head. "I don't get it. Since the day we met, you've gone out of your way to make me feel like some kind of creative biohazard. And then, suddenly, I'm the only one who can voice your film? I'm not buying it."

"Let's leave the past behind and start again," Evan said magnanimously. "Whatever I've led you to believe, I never once doubted that you were talented. You would be great for this."

He was almost pleading but not quite enough for Carly's taste. Perhaps, if he got down on his knees and did some Oscar-caliber groveling, she might think about it. He could start by kissing her feet, then he could move on to oral sex. The baby shot the back of Evan's head a dirty look for her.

"Right," she said to the baby. Glad to have an ally.

"You've got a great voice and, frankly, I think it's going to waste. This is a chance to put something real—"

Carly's eyes shot lightning bolts over the top of her sunglasses.

He caught himself and restarted. "To put something really different on your résumé. You're a pro—I need that."

"There are lots of other women who would love to do this. I could name half a dozen right now."

"Not as good as you."

"You already said that."

"Not as free as you."

"Ah, I see. Blackmail." Carly took a sip of her Coke and felt the drink sizzle all the way down to her stomach. "I voice your film for free and I get my shoes back. No go, babycakes. The union won't go for it, my agent won't go for it, and I won't go for it. End of story."

"Don't tell me you took the money for doing that pet adoption PSA I kept hearing all last summer?"

"Of course not! That was a public service announcement. Those shelters don't have the money for something like that. I donated it back like everybody else does. . . ." Her voice trailed off as realization hit her.

"Exactly."

"Shit." Her eyes weren't giving her away, but her mouth was making up for it. "Quinn isn't going to give up his agent's commission for a documentary, and I won't ask him to."

"I can deal with that."

"No." A busboy, heading their way with a pot of coffee, thought she was talking to him and veered off to the next table.

"Why?"

"Because."

Evan let out a deep breath and stared at her the way he did the first time he saw her. All raw energy and pure will.

"*Think about it*," he said in a voice that seemed to reverberate around the room and reach all the way down to tickle Carly's toes. He wanted this badly, very badly. Everything about him said so. From the way his eyes gripped hers through her glasses, to the intensity of his breathing, to the tautness of his body as he leaned in toward her. He was like a pit bull straining against a cheap leash.

Carly felt pinned to her seat. Three words. How he managed to grab the attention of every molecule in her being in only three words was incredible. *He could sell cancer with a voice like that.*

At that moment the baby let out a belch in surround sound stereo right next to Evan's ear.

Way to go, little guy. Carly beamed at the now very relieved little cherub.

Evan's eyebrows rose but otherwise there was no reaction to the toddler's sonic outburst. He stood up and tossed enough cash to cover both their meals plus a generous tip on the table. "I'll call you in a few days so we can figure out a schedule."

"I'm not doing it."

"I'll call you."

Carly scraped up the last of her hot fudge cake and stared at the folder Evan had left on the table. She took off her sunglasses and rubbed her temples. Hostage negotiation, it was becoming clear to her, was not a "learn as you go" sort of skill.

The Thai food restaurant was not far from the production offices on Gower Avenue where Dana worked. Catering to the nearby studio crowd, the trendy dining spot was fast, cheap, and always crowded. The two friends often met there for lunch when their schedules allowed. The celery colored walls were covered with framed headshots of actors, famous and almost. Above the cashier, a black lacquer shelf held a framed picture of the king of Thailand, a glass of water, and an orange.

"So," Dana mumbled around a mouthful of pad thai noodles, "how was your audition?"

Carly's pained expression said it all. She had attended the audition with as much enthusiasm as a visit to the gynecologist. Without the supernatural help of her shoes, only her sense of duty to her agent made her go. She didn't want to make him look bad just because she had lost her mojo.

"No joy, huh?"

"Powderpuff toilet paper," Carly said morosely as she tried to eat her chicken satay delicately off its wooden skewer without poking her eye out. "I'm ending my career with toilet paper. I should just sell my house and buy a Krispy Kreme franchise."

"I'll be your first customer." Dana poked her fork into Carly's plate of stir-fried chicken and baby corn. "So how'd it go with Evan?"

"Just as bad." Carly poached some shrimp curry in retaliation. "Not only does he have the shoes but he's holding them hostage as well, the dirty bastard."

"Funny, he doesn't look like a kidnapper."

"Well, he certainly is, believe you me." Carly paused dramatically. "He made me meet him for dinner."

Dana held her hand to her breast in mock horror. "The swine!"

Carly shot her a look that bounced right off.

"So what's he want? Stocks? Real estate? Money? Paper or plastic?"

"I wish. No, he gave me two propositions." Carly leaned in. "Me or my voice."

"Huh?"

Carly's eyes roamed the restaurant. On any given day, friend or foe could show up. Satisfied neither was around, she continued. "Well, by me, he means me, Carly Beck. I think his words went something like, 'You. One night.'" Just repeating the words made Carly grip her fork a little tighter.

"Whoa," Dana said, thoroughly impressed. "That's pretty hot."

"Dana, I am not exchanging sexual favors for shoes," she whispered fiercely. "Not even for my lucky shoes."

"Yeah, I know. But it sounds so sordid when you put it that way. I can't think that sleeping with Evan would be a hardship."

"I don't know why you have to take his side." Carly put her fork down.

"I'm not, I'm on your side. Don't pout. *Mi* scum *es su* scum, remember? Even if he is drop-dead gorgeous scum. Now, what about your voice? He doesn't want you to do phone sex, does he?"

"Only you would think of that." The waiter, a slim androgynous young man with lips and eyes like a fashion model, arrived to clear their plates and take their dessert orders. Carly waited for him to leave before she continued. "By my voice, he means he wants me to narrate his latest documentary."

"Not as fun as the first idea, but not awful either."

"For free."

"No fucking way." Dana had been known to make bad choices at many things, but business was not one of them. "Who does he think he is? You tell that son of a—"

"I did."

"Good."

The boy waiter returned with two orders of mango slices and sweet rice.

"The sex thing, well, I can understand that," Dana said. "But free work. That's beneath contempt. That's just low."

Carly shook her head at her friend's skewed take on things. "So asking for sex isn't offensive but free voice work is?"

"Well, yes. The sex, you know, that's a win-win. But free work? Nuh-uh. What an imbecile. And I thought he was cute."

Carly took a bite of mango. "I think I might do it, though."

Dana eyed her with interest. "Do *it*?"

"No, not *it*." Carly made a face. "Voice his film."

"This is blackmail or extortion or something like that."

"Probably. But listen, those shoes are the key to

my career. Without them I'm doomed. I know everyone thinks that lucky charms aren't for real. But I swear to God, those shoes are. They're all I've got between me and total loserdom. Until I get them back, all I can hear is this Haunted Mansion voice telling me that I'm a big fat failure."

Dana covered Carly's hand with her own. "Get a grip, Carly. You're not a failure. How could you even think that? Lucky charms and horoscopes, they're just for fun—a psychic serving suggestion, if you will." Dana paused a moment to enjoy her own wit. "What really counts is hard work, determination, and believing in yourself. To thine own self be true!" Dana's earnest blue eyes looked compassionately into Carly's downtrodden brown ones. "And fuck 'em if they can't take a joke."

Carly had to laugh. Her friend was full of life-affirming aphorisms that were never going to appear on plaques at the Hallmark store. "Yeah, well, as much as I'd love to believe you, the truth is those shoes changed my life. Nothing goes right without them. All my life my mother has been telling me what a loser I am and she was absolutely right until now."

Carly's mother didn't have a positive opinion of life in general and of her eldest child in particular. Judith was always the first to see the storm clouds gathering on the horizon and, therefore, was the herald of all things doomy and gloomy—Nostradamus as played by Joan Crawford.

"Now I've finally got it going," Carly continued with a desperate sigh. "I can't go back to what I was before, Dana."

Dana, who'd witnessed more than one of Judith's

tantrums, nodded. "You won't. But as much as *Vogue* would like to convince you otherwise, Carly, shoes do not make the woman."

"They make this woman," she answered, pointing to herself. "If I can't get my shoes back I might as well give it all up and commit myself to a life of sin and debauchery right now."

"Amen," Dana agreed heartily. "Let's start this afternoon."

"Shoes first, debauchery later."

"So you're gonna do the film."

"I think so."

"Wait a week. Then let's talk. You haven't even given it enough time for bad luck to look you up again."

Carly let out a bitter laugh. "Oh, it's back all right. Someone just charged three thousand dollars' worth of computer stuff on my American Express. Did I tell you you're paying for lunch? The bank machine ate my ATM card—Jesus, they want you to be so precise with those passwords. So I need to borrow some money, too."

Dana slapped a credit card on the table and pulled some bills out of her wallet. Carly struggled to pry open a tin of Altoids that wouldn't budge in the slightest. Determined, she kept working at it until the tin suddenly flew open, showering mints all over her lap and inside her purse.

Dana plucked a mint from the fold of Carly's shirtsleeve and popped it into her mouth. "Fine, do the film, but no freebies. Here's your counter offer. . . ."

Chapter Three

The Starbucks on Melrose wasn't Carly's choice. She would have preferred somewhere quieter and more fitting for dealmaking with the devil— somewhere like the morgue. Café au lait in hand, she chose a table on the patio, adjusted her sunglasses, and did some deep-breathing exercises. Bad idea. The fumes from the never-ending parade of cars that crept down the avenue left her light-headed and wheezy.

"Are you having an asthma attack or something?" Evan took the seat across from her and put his coffee down.

"No, I'm trying to avoid death by smog, if you must know." How had he gotten past her to get his coffee? She must have been really light-headed.

"You live in LA. Smog is an integral part of your metabolism. You need it to survive. If you were to leave and go somewhere like Nepal where the air is clean, you wouldn't last a week."

"So much for that Everest climb I was planning," she said with a tight smile.

"You're feeling feisty today." He eyed her grande cup. "Must be the caffeine."

"More like the company." She took a big gulp of

her steaming coffee and tried not to drop it as every taste bud on her tongue suddenly dropped dead. So much for bravado.

"Could you take off your sunglasses?" he asked. "I like to see the eyes of the person I'm making a deal with."

"Who says I'm making a deal?"

"Why else did you want to see me?"

Damn. Logic, she hated when he used logic. It was so . . . logical. She rubbed her numb tongue against the back of her teeth. The day's horoscope warned her that Mercury was in retrograde and not to enter into any contracts or agreements for at least two weeks or there would be dire consequences. Of course.

"You know, you're the most antagonistic person I've ever met," Evan said when she made no move to take her glasses off. "The first time I met you, you practically spat on me."

"That's only because you gave me the 'you suck, drop dead' look first."

"I did not."

"Even Gary felt the need to apologize for you," she said triumphantly. "He said that you weren't always such an asshole."

"Some apology. Nice to know who my friends are."

"We need to talk about my shoes."

He smiled benignly. "They miss you."

Sighing, Carly stared down at the day's footwear choice, blue square-toed slings with a medium heel. Blue to go with her dress and blue to match her mood, which had started out crummy and quickly degenerated to abysmal. She pined for her lost shoes, envisioning them tossed aside in a dark closet, alone and unloved. Her mind recoiled at the thought of her baby-soft, red leather heels being harangued and intimidated by his black, oiled leather thugs. The horror!

Carly shot him a baleful look. "Did you bring the photograph of them cowering in front of today's front page?"

He shrugged. "I don't get the paper."

Some kidnapper.

"Okay," she said, resigned to her fate. "I'll do it."

A satisfied smile unrolled across his face.

"But I name the time and the place. Monday nights are out because I've got read-throughs every Tuesday morning for *Compost Critters*. Same with Thursday because *Critters* records on Friday. Did you bring your date book?"

As her words sunk in, Evan's smile halted and something glittered behind his eyes.

"Gotcha." She took off her sunglasses and shot him a look like a hurricane warning. "You never thought I'd call your bluff, did you? This was all a big ruse to get me to work for free, wasn't it? Well, no way, buddy. If I do your film, I get more than my shoes back. I get a big fat credit and a percentage."

His pupils shrunk to pinpoints as his smile turned grim. "Makes no difference to me which option you choose. I get what I want either way, lady. How's tomorrow night?"

Anger and reason raced to see which one would get to drive her mouth first.

"Fine," she said, slamming her cup down. Anger was sitting in the driver's seat adjusting the mirrors. She picked up her briefcase and put her sunglasses back on. "My house. Eight o'clock. Don't expect me to feed you, so eat before you come by. Be polite, no garlic or raw onions. I'll do the same."

Without waiting for an answer, she stomped away.

The coupe shot up Highland Avenue like it was running on rocket fuel. Inside, Carly yelled obscenities in a high-decibel audio rampage. When she'd exhausted her English options, she ranted in tongues, words like *bundkuchen, fritto misto,* and *garam masala,* which were actually the names of some of her favorite foods, but they had a great ring to them anyway. By the time she walked into her kitchen, most of her fury had been dispelled, and her verbal arsenal had been reduced to the less witty and hardly creative "piss ant" and "fucking fuck."

It was only five o'clock, but she was already ready to fast-forward into oblivion. The bed beckoned and she obeyed. Wearing only a set of matching daisy-print undies, she crawled under the sheets. Carly's mother believed in thrifty plain white underwear. Carly's personal definition of luxury meant never having to buy panties in a three-pack, socks by the dozen, or bras for their durability. For her, a drawerful of happy, frivolous lingerie helped make up for a youth spent in sober, colorless underwear.

She awoke to the fitful ringing of her alarm clock, or what she thought was her alarm clock. Actually, it was her cell phone chirping valiantly through the thick leather of her briefcase.

"It's Carly," she answered.

"Where the hell are you? I've been trying to get ahold of you for ages!"

Quinn was not known for wasting time with salutations and sign-offs. Pleasantries were for friends. Quinn was an agent. The man was intelligent, shrewd, and aggressive, got in early, and left late. His success was measured by his powerhouse talent roster and his home in the Hollywood Hills, a Hanging Gardens of Modern Babylon kind of hangout complete with a terraced koi pond, rose arbor, and waterfall. Recently, tantalizing glimpses of it were to be had in a spread in *Architectural Digest*. Quinn's significant other, Glen, like the house, was never seen personally and, unlike the house, never photographed for public consumption.

"Hi, Quinn. What's up?"

"You've got a re-record in Santa Monica for that computer spot you did last week."

"Didn't they like what I did?" she asked, letting her paranoia leak out.

Quinn immediately caught the self-doubt in her voice. "Why shouldn't they like it? Did you suck?"

"No! I just wondered, that's all." She could almost hear the crackle of his synapses firing. Quinn did not tolerate losers.

"It wasn't you. There's a copy change, the megahertz or megabytes or megasomething. Nine o'clock sharp at Ocean Recording. Don't screw up." He hung up without saying good-bye.

Bundkuchen. She would have to match her previous read in her lucky voice with her present doomed-to-failure voice that was on the edge of hoarse from screaming for half an hour. Normally Carly treated her throat like the precious instrument that it was, but Evan's company and rational thought were having a difficult time coexisting in her universe. Grumbling at her own idiocy, she popped a cough drop in her mouth and headed for a steamy shower in hopes of soothing her pipes.

Carly had just finished her shower when the doorbell rang. Dana stood big as life in a red halter top, jeans, and stilettos, holding a pint of ice cream in each hand as an entrance fee. Ben & Jerry's Chunky Monkey for herself and Häagen-Dazs strawberry for her friend. Carly expelled a eucalyptamint-scented sigh and motioned her friend inside.

The walls of the living room were a pale Wedgewood blue with cream molding. A pair of French doors, draped in embroidered cotton voile, led to a small bricked patio lined with potted red geraniums. The blue and white toile couch faced a coffee table and flagstone fireplace. It was flanked on one side by a large sturdy maple rocker. Tucked in the corner was a blond wood armoire that hid a small TV and entertainment system. The art consisted of a quilt folded over the back of the rocker, tastefully framed photographs scattered around the room, and a charcoal study of nudes above the fireplace. It was a feminine space but easy on the estrogen.

Odin was sprawled on his back, a big black inkblot in the middle of the couch. He was bookended by Dana on the left and Carly on the right, both of whom were gorging themselves on ice cream.

"Thanks for the ice cream, Dana," whispered Carly. "My throat feels tons better."

"What happened to your voice?"

"I had a cow in the car."

"Does this have to do with the meeting with Evan?"

Carly made a mooing sound.

"Keep eating. We'll talk after you're done."

Dana opened the armoire, picked up the TV remote, and instantly Cartoon Network popped onto the screen. A couple of earthworms ambled up to a housefly and started up a conversation. *Compost Critters*, Carly's show, was on. She started to moo again, so Dana hastily hit the off button. Ten minutes later, everyone had finished their ice cream and were as happy as they were going to be for under five dollars.

"I have a date with Evan tomorrow night here at eight," Carly said in a lifeless monotone. She fiddled with the hem of her oversized T-shirt featuring Meerkat Marcy, a character she played on another cartoon, *Tails of Africa*. "I told him not to eat any garlic or raw onions for dinner."

Dana frowned. "What happened to the deal? What happened to my finely wrought, suitable-for-framing contract?"

"I blew it, Dana," Carly confessed miserably. "I got so mad thinking that it was all a bluff to get me to work on his film that I got kind of cocky. Next thing I know we've got a date."

Carly recounted her humiliating showdown with Evan while Dana shook her head in disgust.

"Okay, let me get this right," Dana said, fingertip on her chin, making an effort to comprehend the situation. "First you're insulted because he wants to sleep with you. Then you're insulted because he doesn't really want to sleep with you. And now he's coming over tomorrow night to sleep with you."

"Yes," Carly replied tersely. *Logic.* Everybody seemed to be overflowing with it recently.

"Are you really sure you need these shoes?"

"I just got an audit notice from the IRS."

Dana whistled. "Maybe he should come over tonight."

"He'll be over soon enough."

"Well, I must say, it couldn't have happened to a nicer girl." Her voice almost trilled with pleasure. Despite her brash personality, Dana was a romantic at heart. She had played matchmaker to quite a few tragic and unfortunate unions— and yet she remained cheerfully undaunted. "You and Evan McLeish shagging. Wow. He's not an easy catch. Many have tried, but few have succeeded."

Carly fell back onto the sofa. "You're totally off your nut."

"I can't wait to work this into my show!" Dana was the creator and head writer for a cable series featuring the antics of two beautiful women running a Harley repair shop. *Hog Heaven* was funny, quirky, and a ratings hit. It also borrowed shamelessly from Dana's life and, to their glee but mostly horror, the lives of her friends. Carly was never gleeful about being sitcom fodder.

"Don't you dare put this in your show! I will not have my life paraded around for America's entertainment pleasure."

"We're now being dubbed in Spanish, French,

and German," Dana informed her. "Oh, don't get your panties in a twist. No one knows it's you."

"Oh, right." Carly's voice was soaked with sarcasm. "No one would ever figure out that small, dark-haired Charlie and her mammoth cat, Owen, is me and Odin."

"Carly, you are so paranoid. Charlie's nothing like you. Just like Daphne and her dog, Iris, are nothing like me and Daisy." She cocked her head to the right and stared off into the distance. A sure sign she was thinking. "I think I'll have a customer steal Charlie's favorite bike. And I'll call him Ethan MacNeil. He'll be a photographer who needs a nude model for his portfolio."

Carly groaned. Had she been outside, she would have gladly thrown herself into traffic.

The Santa Monica Mountains stand three thousand feet above sea level at their highest point and separate the pedestrian San Fernando Valley from trendy West Los Angeles. Despite the hardly inconsiderable height, traversing the Santa Monica Mountains from one side to the other was referred to by Angelinos as "going over the hill," and always with a touch of weariness, as if a terribly trying and odious task was about to be undertaken. The trip was not unlike crossing the river Styx, but whether it was to or from hell depended greatly on which side one called home. But no matter where loyalties lay, everyone agreed on one thing. "Going over the hill" was a royal pain in the ass.

Despite an accident on the 405 freeway, Carly managed to make it from Studio City to Santa Monica with ten minutes to spare. She took pity on the parking valet, who was a minimum six feet tall with another four or five inches of bleached dreadlocks spiking off his head, and moved the seat back before handing him the keys.

In an effort to remain perpetually hip and to justify its outrageous hourly rates, the interior of Ocean Recording was an ever-changing showroom of style. Sometimes good, sometimes bad. The present theme was Brazilian Rainforest meets African Savanna. The carpet was zebra striped, orchids and bromeliads in vibrant neon colors bloomed everywhere, and spooky wooden carvings decorated the walls. An entire herd of cattle was no longer roaming the pampas because of a twelve-foot-long sofa that dominated the room. Assembled on it were the usual motley crew of actors, writers, and producers, wearing everything from Birkenstocks to Nikes to Guccis. Carly checked in, grabbed a vacant piece of cowhide, and waited to be summoned.

"Sunshine?"

She looked up at a scruffy-looking young man outfitted in board shorts, a Mr. Bubble T-shirt, and Tevas. His golden tan, sun-bleached hair, and broad shoulders bespoke many hours on a surfboard trying to catch the perfect wave.

"Dex!" Carly stood up and gave the wiry blond a warm hug that caught the attention of most of the males in the room. "What are you doing here?"

Dex had an easy, infectious grin that was hard to resist. "I work here now. Actually not here, at the Hollywood facility, but I'm training at this one."

"When did you leave Clipz?"

"About a month ago. I took a couple of weeks off,

drove down to Mexico, ate lobster, drank tequila, and surfed my brains out. Now it's back to the grind." He took her hand and led her back into the building. "You can wait in the kitchen with me."

Dexter James Holland III was one of the first people Carly had befriended in her voiceover career. He'd been the audio engineer on one of her early jobs, a commercial for doggie breath deodorizer. As it turned out, Dex was also just starting his career; naturally the fledglings had bonded from the start.

"You didn't tell me you got a new job." Carly took a seat at the small kitchen table.

Dex grabbed a couple of bottled waters from the fridge and sat down. "I tried to catch you at Dana's party but I guess you'd already left by the time I got there. My timing was totally off that night. Apparently, some girl fell in the pool right before I got there."

"Some girl?" Carly was pleased to know that the party headline was "Girl Falls in Pool," not "Carly Beck, Drunk and Disoriented, Falls in Pool."

"Yeah, I didn't catch the name, just that whoever it was looked really hot wet."

"That's a relief," she said thankfully, then corrected herself. "I mean, that she gets to remain anonymous."

"That's what Evan said. Apparently he was an eyewitness but he wouldn't say who it was."

"Evan?" she squeaked. "Evan McLeish?"

"Yeah. You know him?"

"Sort of." After tonight she'd be able to write a handbook on the guy. The thought made her tingly and nauseous all at once.

"When I first met him," Dex said. "I thought he was wound a little too tight. But once you get to know him, he's really pretty cool. I'm doing some freelance work for him right now."

"Don't tell me. Arlene Barlow?"

"Uh-huh. It's really good. I never really knew anything about her except that she disappeared or something like that. But after hearing her sing and seeing the stuff that Evan put together, I was blown away. I've got her whole collection now." The phone on the kitchen wall buzzed. Dex answered, then nodded at Carly. "It's time for your close-up, sunshine."

"It looks like the Mr. Bert gravy train is over."

Carly let this news wash over her as she stood in the waiting room of another recording studio, this time in North Hollywood. Mix N Match was as utilitarian as Ocean Recording was opulent. No designer anything stood in the circa 1980s waiting room. The gray industrial carpeting was as coffee stained and threadbare as the faded blue sofa that sat on top of it. A freebie calendar hung by a nail inexpertly pounded into the pine paneling. In the corner, a withered spider plant perched atop a bottled water dispenser. The room had slightly more charm than an auto repair shop.

For two years Carly had been recording television promos for *Mr. Bert Builds It*. The show was an arts and crafts extravaganza. There was nothing the fearless Mr. Bert wouldn't build and nothing he wouldn't build it with.

"Tomorrow Mr. Bert builds it with egg cartons! Don't miss it or the yolk's on you!"

"Shake a leg! It's sock puppets with Mr. Bert today at one!"

Hardly glamorous work, but it was steady and predictable.

"Did you just say what I thought you said?" Carly stared at the paunchy, balding man in front of her. He wore cowboy boots, faded jeans, and a chambray shirt over a black Grateful Dead T-shirt. "Say it isn't so, Tally."

"Sure looks like it." He slurped his coffee loudly before continuing. "It's not official, but I heard it from the show runner. It looks like Mr. Bert doesn't want to build it anymore. I'm gonna miss Mr. Bert. That was a nice gig."

"Me, too." Carly's heart sank.

"We can start in five," he said, heading toward the studio.

"Take your time. I've got nothing after this." Oh, how true those words were becoming. Carly plunked herself down onto the beat-up couch and called her agent.

"How was the revision?" he asked.

"Fine."

"Are you sure? You don't sound fine."

"No, it was great." She decided not to mention that her voice did not exactly match the original recording, as she had feared. But luckily, so much had changed in the copy that they needed to re-record the whole spot anyway, so matching became irrelevant. But Quinn didn't need to know that. He also didn't need to know about the imminent demise of the *Mr. Bert* show.

"Okay," Quinn said, unconvinced. "I don't have anything for you tomorrow, but I've got a few holds for Friday after the *Critters* session. I'll e-mail your schedule tonight. Maybe you should have a spa day tomorrow." He clicked off.

It was the closest thing to personal concern her curmudgeonly agent had ever shown her. She was touched and flattered. She also knew it wasn't a suggestion. It was an order.

The mahogany sleigh bed was the most fiscally irresponsible purchase Carly had ever made. And she didn't regret one penny of it. She hadn't even been shopping for a bed, but from the minute she saw it, she knew that therein lay her destiny. Or that it was her destiny to lie in it. Whichever. As with most irresponsible things Carly had been involved with, Dana was present at the time.

The friends had just become roommates, both struggling to get their careers going. They were surviving on ramen noodles, mac and cheese, and baked potatoes. Their entire food pyramid was made up entirely of starch and fat.

The bed barely fit into Carly's room since she had insisted on buying a king—a California king, a bed big enough to play field hockey on. Dana dubbed it "The Ponderosa."

Carly smoothed her hands across the creamy Egyptian cotton as she made the bed on the old homestead. The sheets had more threads to the inch than days in the year, felt like heaven, and wore like iron. This was certainly a twist on the old casting-couch routine—actress sleeps with director to get out of a film. She was finally going to get Evan between the sheets, she thought cynically, just not the way she'd planned.

Evan was certainly easy on the eyes and there was definitely an attraction between them that had exploded into existence the first time they met. He was smart, handsome, and possessed a kind of pulsing energy that reset all of Carly's systems to a matching rhythm. It was as if her body could tune to him with the accuracy of a laser-guided missile. She'd never experienced anything like it before with anyone else; the uncanny ability made her feel a little like a sideshow freak.

But physical attraction was only half the picture. As much as her body pulled, slobbering and panting, in his direction, her mind strained, screaming and gasping, in the other. Mentally, she recoiled from him, knowing that she was as much a person to him as a blow-up doll, as special as a No. 2 pencil.

The phone rang. Carly froze. *Evan? Had he changed his mind? Did he want to come over sooner? Yikes.*

"Hello?"

"Did you make an appointment?" It was Quinn.

"Yes." Carly rolled her neck, trying to ease the tension out of her muscles. "Facial, massage, paraffin hand and foot bath, the works. Tomorrow at two o'clock."

"Good. Everything that was holding for Friday after *Critters* went away. Nothing for Monday. Oh, and it looks like *Mr. Bert* might be going on permanent hiatus."

"Great." So the rumors were true.

"Also, you didn't get the Powderpuff gig. They're

going back to the drawing board. They want to try other animals. Maybe pandas or marmots. What the hell's a marmot?"

Carly sighed louder.

"What's the matter?"

"All this fabulous news isn't really helping my state of mind."

"Yeah," Quinn said, "but if I waited until after the massage, you'd need another one. I'd hate for you to waste your money. Try the eucalyptus steam room. I've heard it's good."

After Quinn's dismal news she went back to getting ready for her evening. A hot shower and a cold glass of wine later, Carly picked out an outfit.

Black heels, pearls, a curve-hugging black dupione silk skirt, and matching three-quarter-sleeve blouse with abalone buttons made up her ensemble. Underneath, she wore nothing but black lace and Coco by Chanel. Elegant but tough. Noirish, even. She looked like the kind of babe who would just as soon send you to heaven with a bullet as with a kiss, which wasn't that far off from how she felt about Evan.

Her hand hesitated over her makeup kit as she checked her reflection critically in the bathroom mirror. The woman she saw needed help; she always needed help. Her face, she felt, was uneventful and looked too young and vulnerable without makeup. Her left eyebrow sat a little higher than the other, which gave her a slightly cocky look. Not always a good thing. She didn't mind her hair on most days—it was short, shiny, and a deep, dark espresso brown. A couple of inches in height had been on Carly's wish list for years, but since puberty had long since passed, she figured height and accompanying jumbo hooters were no longer just around the corner. Resigned, she pulled out an eye pencil and tried to make the best of things.

With the exception of her dark-haired father, everyone else in her family was blond. Even her stepfather. And everyone else, step or otherwise, was tall. The men were sporty and rugged. The women were of the bombshell variety. Carly didn't just play with Malibu Barbie, her mother and sister *were* Malibu Barbie. Growing up in the land of the Swede and the home of the blond didn't do much for her self-esteem. She wasn't blind enough to think she was ugly; at best she thought she was pleasant. At worst, unremarkable.

She put on a minimum of makeup and test-smiled in the mirror. In a way it was freeing, she figured, not having the burden of beauty, not having to rise to the occasion at all times. Beautiful people were like ball players whose fans demanded a home run every time. Pleasant was, after all, quite pleasant. Low maintenance, too. She smiled again and threw herself a kiss.

Carly had a glass of mineral water and picked through a can of mixed nuts while she waited for the inevitable. She was nervous but thought she was holding together pretty well. Then the doorbell rang and the can flew out of her hands, spraying the counter and floor with nuts. Odin, who came to investigate the unexpected windfall, was sorely disappointed but tried a couple anyway.

Chapter Four

"Hi."

Evan, it seemed, had dressed for the occasion as well. He stood framed in the doorway wearing a navy suit and tie, pale blue shirt, and a smile that could make a prison matron giggle like a schoolgirl. He'd even swapped his normal workman's Docs for an expensive pair of dress shoes. In his hand was a bouquet of red roses.

"More like *High Noon*." Carly mustered up her own brand of lightning and flashed him her pearly whites. Meanwhile her insides were embattled in the old Bugs and Daffy routine. Cold logic demanded that she shoot him now. Sizzling hormones preferred to shoot him later. "Come on in. Meet the family."

Carly showed him into the living room and took the roses into the kitchen. She came back with them arranged in a cut crystal vase.

"Thanks," she said as she placed the roses on the coffee table. "Although you didn't have to. It's not like you need to smooth the way to the finish line or anything."

"It's sad that you think all nice gestures are bribes."

"Coming from you, they are certainly suspect."
Carly was surprised to see him wince. "Sorry, I'll try
to be on my best behavior from now on."

Odin padded in on large cat feet and heaved
himself onto the coffee table. Once convinced that
the roses were not suitable for feline consumption,
he turned his attention to Evan. For a moment, his
eyes turned to green slits of ocean glass and he
seemed to be eyeing Evan as if he were a suitable
kitty repast. After a full thirty seconds of his most
malevolent predatory stare, the cat yawned and
moved on to cleaning his fur.

"In case you didn't meet before," Carly said, gesturing to her pet, "let me introduce Odin, my cat."

Evan snorted. "Looks like a bowling ball in a fur
coat."

Her eyebrow shot up in extreme disapproval.

He looked at her. He looked at the cat. Outnum-
bered, probably outweighed, he conceded defeat.
"I just meant he was very . . . robust."

Carly smiled. Odin smiled. "You know, he was just
the littlest thing when I got him," she said proudly.
"They told me he'd probably be sickly, but he's
never, ever sick."

In response, Odin began to wheeze and gag. The
table shuddered as he writhed. The vase threatened
to topple. Waves, starting from his head and ending
at his tail, undulated down the length of his body.
His torso accordioned out and in on itself several
times. And then suddenly, he coughed. A slimy,
half-digested, fur-coated cashew was projected into
the air with a slight "foop." It landed wetly on
Evan's right shoe. That chore dealt with, Odin resumed cleaning the fur under his left armpit.

"Oh, my," Carly said in a small voice before she sprang from the sofa and ran to the kitchen to retrieve a paper towel. Quickly, she scooped up the offensive object and carried it to the bathroom for a quick trip to Santa Monica Bay. She doubted Odin's gift of a homemade hairball was on par with a bouquet of roses, no matter how heartfelt. She went back to the living room carrying a bottle of wine and two glasses. Perhaps a change of subject was in order. "So how's the movie going?"

Evan stared at the spot on his shoe where the cashew had landed. Carly peered at it, alarmed by what she saw. The spot looked different from the rest of his shoe—lighter, duller, like the cat's stomach acids had already begun to erode the smooth leather surface in the seconds before they were wiped away.

"Here." Carly thrust a full wineglass into Evan's field of vision. Without turning his head, he took it, drank it down, and extended it back. Carly refilled the glass.

"Thanks," he said, finally looking up at her. "It's a documentary, not a movie. There's a difference."

"You're right. Sorry." They were even. He insulted her cat, she insulted his film. She placed her glass on the table and sat down on the sofa. "So Dex Holland is working on the film?"

"Yeah. You know him?"

"We've been friends for ages."

Both he and his face said nothing. He just sipped his wine.

Carly waited for a reply, wondering if she'd said something wrong. "He's a really great engineer. Really fun to work with and lightning fast. He puts my demo reel together every year."

"Yeah?" Interest barely registering in his voice.

Boy, he really needs to work on his bedside manner.

"He hates doing demo reels but he's a whiz at it," she babbled nervously. "He charges people the moon to get them to go away but that doesn't seem to put anyone off."

"Really?" His eyes zeroed in on hers and held them tight.

Carly's breath caught.

"Really." She swallowed a mouthful of wine, set her glass back on the table, and continued chattering. "He raises his rates and, um, they just keep paying. Except me. I just cook him dinner. Actually breakfast. He likes pancakes. With butter and maple syrup."

His face was inches from hers. She didn't recall his moving closer, but he was suddenly close enough for her to notice that his pupils were very, very wide, rimmed with just the thinnest band of sky blue.

"With butter and maple syrup," he repeated her words in a low, warm voice as if he wouldn't mind having her served that way.

She opened her mouth to speak but never got that far. His lips met hers, and all mental activity ceased. Her autonomic nervous system, in charge of basic survival functions like respiration and heart rate, also seemed to be in charge of kissing, which, at that moment, was as important as breathing. Carly found herself falling into a deep kiss with Evan—a full-frontal, lip-on-lip, tongue-in-mouth, hands-roaming, toe-curling kind of kiss.

The peculiar achiness that had dogged her for

days, the feeling that her skin was on too tight, slammed into overdrive. Evan moved his mouth down her throat, alternating soft and hard kisses, warm and dazzling against her skin. A combination of excitement, anticipation, and plain old sweaty lust had her throwing her leg over his as she clenched her fists through his hair.

"Damn," Evan muttered, sounding surprised but pleased. Lying above her, he ground his hips against hers in response.

"Damn," Carly echoed and kicked her pumps across the room. A second later she heard the matching double thump of his shoes hitting the floor. He shrugged his coat off and let it fall to the floor. She grabbed his tie, loosened it enough to pull over his head, and tossed it over the back of the couch. As they tore at each other's shirts, buttons flew off like popped corn, showering the couch and floor. In the distant back of her mind, Carly hoped Odin wouldn't eat them.

Evan flicked open the front clasp of Carly's bra, releasing her breasts into his waiting hands. He squeezed them possessively, a self-satisfied, cock-eyed grin spreading across his face. He looked like a man who'd just discovered buried treasure and was making plans to enjoy every bit of it thoroughly and at length. "Mine, all mine," said the greedy glint in his eye. Carly's skin flushed and her nipples turned a rosy cinnamon as he rubbed his fingers against them. They buzzed with sensation at the slightest bit of friction, setting off pleasure bombs all over her body. Evan sucked her breast into his mouth and Carly envisioned herself going up in a churning ball of flame, leaving behind only some singed panties and soot marks on the ceiling. She arched her back, pressed herself against his mouth, and moaned like a porn star.

"Ahh . . ."

He moved on to her other breast.

"Ahh . . ."

His tongue circled her nipple.

"Ahhhh . . . chooooooo!" Carly's torso curled and whipped from the force of the sneeze. Her face bloomed crimson as she slapped her hand over her mouth. "Oh God, I'm sorry! Oh geez, I . . . ahhhh-chooo! I didn't mean to . . . ahhhh-choo! AHHHH-CHOO!"

Evan had let her go and moved farther and farther away with each sneeze until he was up against the sofa arm. He eyed her with growing apprehension as her sneezes got louder and more forceful.

"Are you okay?" he managed to ask between explosions.

Carly shook her head, unable to talk. She fled the room, her blouse and bra flapping like bat wings at her sides. Several minutes later, she returned with a box of Kleenex and a glass of water. Her bra had been reclasped but her blouse still hung open since all but the bottom button were missing in action. She sat down on the sofa and carefully sipped water. Her sneezing had stopped, at least for the moment.

"I'm really sorry," she said, sniffling. "I think I must be allergic to something you're wearing."

"Linen?" He tugged his shirt off and tossed it on the rocker.

"No, probably your soap or cologne. Don't worry. I took a Benadryl, so I should be okay in a little while. I usually only take half a pill but I think this calls for a whole one. Boy, I don't think I've ever—" A couple of quick sneezes cropped her sentence.

"I don't wear cologne."

"Maybe your aftershave."

"I don't use aftershave."

"Don't tell me you don't use soap either." She gave him a little smile despite the fact that her eyes and nose were dripping and starting to turn an unbecoming shade of Rudolph red. So much for elegant but tough. She crossed her fingers against a sudden attack of hives.

"Of course I use soap."

"What kind?"

"How do I know?" he snapped irritably. "Whatever comes in the giant multipack at the supermarket."

"Ivory. Get Ivory. It's unscented, no dyes, which is better for your skin."

"Please, no commercials," he muttered as he rubbed his temples.

"Okay, don't get so grumpy." If she didn't think it would make things worse, she would have laughed at the sight of the great Evan McLeish sitting on her couch, shoeless, shirtless, hair sticking out in odd tufts, his once-God-almighty erection reluctantly striking down the big top on his hopelessly wrinkled pants. God, he was a sight and she still wanted him.

"Are you going to be all right?" he asked after a few moments.

"I should be fine in about a half-hour." A handful of sneezes overtook her. Afterward, she smoothed her skirt and blouse as well as she could, then leaned back into the sofa and closed her eyes. Her blouse immediately fell open. "Don't worry. I plan to fully uphold my part of the deal."

"That's not what I meant."

"Yeah, right." She snuck a quick peek at him and found him staring at her breasts. She rearranged her blouse, holding it closed with her hand.

He noted her reaction but offered no apologies. "Are you sure you can take allergy pills when you've been drinking?"

"I'm not sure," she admitted thoughtfully. "But I only had one glass awhile ago and I just had one sip of the second one. So I think I'm okay. Although if I stop breathing, promise me you'll call 911."

"That's not funny," he said in a quick burst of anger.

"Sorry," she said, taken aback by his vehement response.

The minutes ticked by slowly until Evan finally broke the silence. "Can I ask you something?"

"Sure." Carly rolled on her side and tucked her legs under her. She peered at him for a moment through a watery curtain.

"Does closing your eyes help?"

"It doesn't stop them from tearing up, but it feels better. Was that your question?"

"No." He paused. "What is it about me that you dislike so much?"

"Oh." She dabbed her nose with a tissue, buying time to think. "You sure you want to talk about that now?"

"Why not?"

Okay, you asked for it. "Well, for starters, that's one of the things I really dislike about you."

"What is? That I'm honest?"

"No, that you think so little of me that you'd want to have this conversation right before you jump my bones."

"You were jumping, too."

"Yeah, but I didn't ask you for a list of character faults first. Come on." She opened one eye briefly. "I'm not a person to you, I'm an actress. Just a face with a voice."

"I never said that," he responded indignantly.

"Pretty-sounding wallpaper." She tried for a snort but could manage only a tiny snuffle. "That's what you told Gary."

"And you believed him?"

"He's my friend," Carly said, coming to Gary's defense. "Besides, he didn't have to tell me. Everything you do tells me. You despise me. You loathe me."

"Loathe," he repeated in a mocking tone. "Up late with the thesaurus, I see."

"There you go! You judge people you don't even know. I'm an actress, so my only interests in life are me, myself, and I."

"You're the one swimming half-naked at a party," he said. "If that doesn't scream 'notice me,' I don't know what does."

"It was an accident. I fell in."

Silence.

"You're a snob, Evan McLeish," she couldn't help but say. She wasn't using her head, but her brains had been sulking and grumbling "I told you so" since the kiss. "You only see what you want to see.

Yours is the only opinion that matters. You care more about people on film than in real life."

"It's all about the dollar to you, Carly Beck," he countered, matching her forthright tone. "You'd shill for beer and cigarettes, but you wouldn't even think about doing my film because there's no money in it. Look what you'd do for a pair of shoes."

She'd turned down work she found offensive and wouldn't hesitate to do it again, but there was no point telling him that. As far as she could tell, she could donate all her goods to charity and work with lepers for the rest of her life and that wouldn't change his mind one bit.

"Maybe we shouldn't talk for a while," Carly said quietly. Her eyes were tearing heavily, which she chalked up to a histamine reaction, not at all to the fact that she suddenly felt as shrunken and shriveled as a raisin inside. "I wouldn't exactly call this conversation foreplay."

Evan leaned back on the sofa, stretched his legs out and put his hands behind his head. He stared up the ceiling and scowled.

She twisted around on the sofa, showing him her back. As dates went, this one had gone from purgatory to heaven to hell, and the night wasn't over yet. Odin made his way to her side and cuddled up against her. She hugged him and waited for the allergy pill to chase her sniffles away.

They were all there, cold and clayey, with their stiff-legged gaits and angry eyebrows, drawing closer and closer.

"Nooooooo . . ." she whimpered, her voice small

and wispy in the night. Carly woke up trembling, eyes rolling, pillow clutched to her chest. God, she hated Gumby, and Pokey, and all the Blockheads.

Some people have nightmares about zombies or power tool–wielding maniacs. Carly's personal bête noire was Gumby with Pokey as the evil sidekick. She couldn't exactly pinpoint when Gumby came to be the bogeyman for her, just that he'd always given her the willies. In her mind, the ominous shadow of doom that fell across the wall would forever be pointy and off center. It had been years since she was last visited by the green specter. She took it as another sign that her old self was back.

She'd been made. Her secret revealed. Successful Carly Beck was going back to being Carlotta Rachel Rudolph, big-time loser. Soon the transformation would be complete. Her Audi TT Coupe would turn into a Dodge Omni. She would have to learn a trade, like palm reading or tattooing, and set up a booth down on Venice Beach. Forced to sell her home, she'd be obliged to move into a ratty apartment in Hollywood situated between a rent-by-the-hour motel and an all-night liquor store. The eligible men in her life would consist of people recognizable from episodes of *Cops*—and not the policemen. Good-bye Godiva, hello Hershey's.

The luminous readout on her alarm clock said 4:37 A.M. It took a minute for her mental faculties to calculate date and place. Then it hit her. Her head spun *Exorcist*-style to look at the other side of the bed and saw a shiny seal-black head of hair on the pillow.

It was Odin.

Where was Evan? For the second time in a week

Carly had no memory of how she had gotten to bed. Checking under the sheets, she was not surprised to find herself once again relieved of her clothing.

I see Paris, I see France . . .

At least she still had her underpants.

She remembered kissing Evan, that was for sure. Unfortunately, at that moment she couldn't sit and savor that particular mental sweet as much as she would have liked, so she wrapped it up carefully and tucked it away for later. Her memory lit briefly on her embarrassing allergic reaction and marched straight into the minefield of their last conversation. She flinched, recalling his hurtful summing up of her character. He didn't understand, he couldn't understand. Understanding would require empathy and thoughtfulness and a capacity for wisdom evolutionary years past Evan's present puny abilities. Given that, she told herself sternly, his opinion should carry as much weight as the disapproving hoots of a baboon. But damn, it still hurt.

Odin snored gently as Carly climbed out of bed, the wood floor cold and hard beneath her feet. She slipped into a pair of fluffy leopard fur slippers, threw on a chenille bathrobe, and stealthily did a perimeter check of the house. The bathroom was empty, as was the guest room she used as an office. When she got to the living room she found Evan fast asleep under the quilt, his long form folded into the couch.

Evidence of their aborted rendezvous dotted the room. The vase of roses, empty wine bottle, glasses, and box of tissues sat on the coffee table. Evan's jacket, with his tie stuffed in the pocket, hung on the back of the rocker, his shirt and pants folded over the arm. His shoes were neatly parked underneath the coffee table. Hers were left where they'd landed in front of the armoire. Her blouse, skirt, and stockings were haphazardly draped over the back of the sofa where he'd obviously undressed her.

She frowned at that, then grinned realizing that he, too, wore little to nothing under the quilt. The temptation to take a peek and even the score was almost overwhelming. If she thought he wouldn't wake up, she would have chanced it; instead she just watched him dream. He looked so damnably irresistible with his hair falling boyishly across his now worry-free brow, lips relaxed and pliant instead of pressed together in a grim line of displeasure. Gentled by sleep, he was beautiful enough to make angels contemplate a fall from grace. Carly liked him so much better when he was unconscious. She figured he probably felt the same way about her.

As her eyes stroked him for what she told herself repeatedly was the last time, Evan became restless and began to mumble, his words as intelligible as Odin's nocturnal meowings. Carly was about to tiptoe out when he called her name, once, then twice. Mutter, mutter, Carly, mutter, mutter. No doubt about it, he'd clearly said her name.

Curiosity tugged her closer as she crept nearer, leaning in, straining to hear. He rolled away from her, his words lost in the couch cushions. Carly scooted forward. Another few inches and she could have kissed his cheek. She could just make out her name. Suddenly, he spun back around, his hand flying through the air in her direction. Stifling a scream, she jumped back, arms windmilling madly as she tried to keep her balance. Eventually she won her fight with gravity, but just barely. Her heart pounded wildly, trying to break its way out of her chest. She'd broken into a nervous sweat, and the belt had come loose from her robe, leaving it hanging open.

Damn, she mouthed, afraid to even breathe as she watched him settle back into a dreamless sleep.

Carly ran from the scene, robe billowing, slippers flapping softly against her heels. She didn't even stop to shed her robe or slippers before jumping into bed and pulling the covers over her, disappearing like a rabbit down a hole.

No more nightmares followed Carly into sleep, so her transition to wakefulness the next morning was a little less dramatic than the night before. It was a little past ten when she got up the courage to roll over and check the pillow next to her. It was empty. The only clues that anyone had even been there were a really big cat-shaped dent and some stray black hairs. So far, so good. Hastily, she threw on shorts and a T-shirt and fished her slippers out from under the covers. She repeated her early morning rounds, checking the back of the house first before moving to the living room. Cautiously she made her way around to the front of the couch. It was empty except for her clothes still adorning the sofa back. Evan had left nothing behind but a man-shaped dent in the cushions and some stray black hairs.

Chapter Five

The girl behind the glass and steel reception desk at The Haven Spa Centre had hair as shiny as early morning sunshine, her eyes gleamed with health, and her skin was as smooth and dewy as rose petals. Swann wore a starched white lab coat and a sleek headset probably designed by the CIA. The pseudo-scientist delicately typed Carly's name into the laptop.

"A full day of beauty?" Swann asked, giving the subtle but unmistakable hint that anything less would have been woefully inadequate.

Carly returned the girl's critical gaze. She'd had a bitch of a week, her shoes were gone, Gumby was back, and she'd sneezed all over Evan while in the middle of the most sensually satisfying moment of her waking life. Yeah, she wasn't looking her best.

"Full day, yes," Carly said. "Does that come with the eucalyptus steam?"

Swann raised a finger in a time-out gesture and stared off into space while she tapped a button on her headset and whispered something cryptic about room twelve, her eyes steadily catatonic throughout her conversation. It wouldn't have surprised Carly to find out Swann was a computer-generated virtual babe. She resisted the urge to see if she could pass her hand through the girl's perfect forehead.

"Eucalyptus is one of the options," Swann said moments later, after reestablishing residence in her body. "Please have a seat and an attendant will collect you in a few minutes."

No sooner had Carly sat down than another lab-coated cover girl, also whispering furtively into her headset, brought her a cup of detox tea. It tasted like a mixture of licorice, orange peels, hay, and possibly wood chips. What, she wondered grimacing at the taste, was going to detox her from the detox tea?

A man entered the waiting room and approached the front desk, catching the eye of every woman in the room. A day of beauty would be wasted on him; he was already gorgeous. Marlboro Man material, he was tall, with broad shoulders and a lean build. Chestnut brown hair, rum-colored eyes, and a great smile completed the package.

"I'm a little late," Already Gorgeous said. He had a slight Western drawl that coated his words and slowed them down to a charming lope. "It's Baxter. Glen Baxter."

Carly's ears perked up.

Glen Baxter? Quinn's Glen Baxter? The man behind the man?

He took the seat next to her and was instantly handed a cup of tea. The other women in the room stared at Carly enviously. Oh, to bask in such radiance, their faces said.

"Excuse me. I don't mean to eavesdrop," she said softly. "But I heard your name was Glen Baxter."

He nodded and smiled in a neighborly fashion.

She hesitated for a moment, then plunged ahead. "Do you know Quinn Carey?"

The smile got bigger. "Yes, I do."

Whew. "I'm Carly Beck." She stuck her hand out. "I'm a client of Quinn's." She hated saying the words "my agent" out loud; it sounded so cliché, so Hollywood.

"Carly!" He bypassed her hand and gave her a bear hug. "I've always wanted to meet you."

"You have?"

"Quinn's told me all about you," he said. "He likes you a lot. You've got spunk."

"I thought he hated spunk," she said, astonished that Quinn would even mention her, much less say something nice.

"Naw. He just likes to pretend," he said with a wink as their names were called. "I'll see you on the other side."

Carly was lying on a table in a darkened room lit only by aromatherapy candles. Like a sacrificial lamb, she was basting in a delicate sauce of mint and eleven secret herbs and spices. A small fountain gurgled in the corner, the gentle noise a constant reminder that she had forgotten to pee before committing to a full body wrap. The door opened gently and was quickly shut.

"So do you feel fabulous or what?" a sonorous voice said behind her.

"Glen?"

"In the flesh." He came into view and took a seat next to her. He was wearing a white bathrobe and slippers. His hair was held back by a white chenille hair band, on his face was a thick green mud mask, and he wore what looked like aluminum oven mitts on both hands.

"Are you sure you're allowed in here?"

"Oh, it's okay," he assured her. "I told them we were married. So how do you feel?"

"Pretty good. The massage was terrific. The foot and hand paraffin thing was divine."

Glen waved his gloved hands. "Oh, I know."

"The brochure said this herbal wrap would suck the toxins and evil spirits from my body. Do I look exorcised?"

He pretended to scrutinize her aura. "Yeah, I don't see any demons lurking. Definitely demon-free."

Glen, it turned out, was a landscape designer with a penchant for cooking and big band music. He was also a dedicated fan of Arlene Barlow.

"I was asked to do some narration for a documentary about her," Carly said.

"Get out! Really? She disappeared, you know." He tried unsuccessfully to snap his fingers. "Just like that. No one knows where she went. Very mysterious. Very romantic."

"Romantic?"

"Sure," he said. "Maybe she skedaddled off to some South Sea paradise to be with her swarthy island warrior-lover."

She raised her eyebrows. "Or maybe she was running from a loan shark or the Mob."

"I prefer the island warrior-lover scenario," he chuckled. "So are you gonna do it?"

Carly paused, momentarily sidetracked by visions

of doing it with Evan. "Quinn wouldn't like it. There's not a lot of money in documentaries."

"Aw, don't listen to him."

"Ignore Quinn?" she said, scandalized by his suggestion. "Don't you think that's biting the hand that feeds me?"

"No, darlin'," he said with confidence. "I'm the hand that feeds him, so you listen to me. There's more to life than money."

"Like swarthy island warrior-lovers?"

"Absolutely."

At the end of the appointment they exchanged phone numbers and promised to get together again soon.

"Thanks for a wonderful evening, Glen. This was probably the best date I've had in a long time," she said as they waited for the valet to bring their cars around.

"Oh, Carly," he said sympathetically as only the nonsingle can. "You need a man in your life."

She thought about Evan. "I've got one but for all the wrong reasons."

The answering machine was bursting with voices when she arrived home. The first four messages were from Dana, all demanding a call back. The following two messages were from Quinn, with schedule updates. Her siblings, Julian and Stacey, both called. And, finally, there was Evan.

"We need to talk. Call me."

His was the only message she played more than once. But no matter how many times she listened to it, she couldn't get a feel for his mood. His delivery was matter-of-fact. She couldn't tell if he was angry or nervous or disgusted. Nothing.

She had made a personal vow to let Dana stew for a few days, but she didn't think that she herself could wait that long. Carly had to talk to her. After cleaning up, she climbed into the safety of her bed and dialed her friend.

Dana's machine answered the call.

"Dana pick up. It's—"

"So?" Dana said, expectantly, eagerly. "Did you?"

"Well, it's a long story," she said with a sigh. "What with the cashew and the kissing and Gumby . . ." Carly laid out the gruesome details of the previous night in a semichronological, semi-coherent fashion. She also brought Dana up to date on her career's downward spiral.

"I'm impressed. That's weirder than anything I've ever written for *Hog*. Too bad we've already done a hairball show."

"I think I'm hanging up now."

"No! You know I wouldn't write about something so personal."

Carly wasn't totally convinced, but she was desperate enough not to hang up. "Okay, but cross your heart and hope to gain twenty pounds you will not repeat this to anybody. Okay?"

"You drive a hard bargain, but okay."

"All right. Here's the other strange part of this story. He left one of the shoes."

"Huh? He left a shoe? His shoe?"

"No," Carly said, staring at the lone red shoe sitting on her nightstand. "My shoe. My lucky shoe. I just found it in my closet right now."

"Really?" she said thoughtfully. "Maybe it's a deposit. You know, like, fifty percent up front. A good-faith sort of gesture. I saw it in a movie once." Dana rattled on excitedly. "This Mafia guy does that with a hit man—"

"He gives him a shoe?"

"No. Money."

"Dana, I need help here," Carly said urgently. "He left me a phone message."

"Was he mad?"

"No, he wasn't mad, or sad, or glad. He wasn't anything. He might as well have been calling for a pizza."

"I can get pretty excited calling for a pizza," Dana mused. "You should call him."

"And?" Carly was hoping for a more fleshed-out plan of action. Between the two of them, Dana was the dreamer and schemer. Sometimes that was a good thing.

"Tell him you'll do his movie. Tell him that you're allergic to him personally. Who knows what his sperm would do to you. Tell him your doctor advises you to stay at least an arm's length away from him or you'll puff up big as a sumo wrestler and have to be rushed to the hospital to be deflated. My friend Jerry can write you a note."

"Jerry's a large-animal vet," Carly said dryly.

"I don't see why it wouldn't work."

Carly was saved from enumerating the many holes in Dana's plan by the doorbell.

She threw her robe over her cherry-print panties and matching tank top, shoved her feet in her slippers, and went to answer its call. It wasn't quite ten o'clock, too late for a sales call, but she wouldn't put it past the *LA Times*. Ever since she had dropped her subscription, they'd been hounding her like a jilted lover.

She had to get up on tiptoe to look through the peephole, something that bugged her every time she had to use it. The distorted figure standing on her doorstep was large and menacing; defiant stance, angry, jutting chin, unforgiving mouth. Definitely a serial killer candidate. He wore all black, no doubt to better blend into the shadows and camouflage any telltale blood stains. She opened the door.

Evan stood on her stoop looking irritated and intense. Scanning her up and down, his eyes narrowed and seemed lit from behind by an unholy light. He looked unusually tall as he towered over her. Unconsciously, she rose up on tiptoe again, trying to even things out. She hated him for looming. If she wanted to loom, she had to go to an elementary school.

"What?" she finally snapped, tired of his silent scrutiny.

"You didn't call me." He shook his head as though unreturned calls had been an impossibility until that moment.

"You haven't given me enough time to call you back."

"You've had all day. Besides, your phone's been busy for the last hour." He pushed past her and entered the house.

"Make yourself at home," she said, taking a deep breath before she turned around to follow him.

"You didn't call me," he repeated, his voice still ringing with disgust and disbelief.

Evan took a seat in the middle of the sofa. Carly remained standing, still doing her best to loom. If her attempt at physical intimidation was working, he hid it well.

Eventually she gave up looming and went back to just standing around impatiently. "I was busy."

He leaned back on the sofa tiredly and ran his hand over his face. "It was the least you could have done."

"Yeah, right," she said, folding her arms across her chest. "For what? For being strip-searched?"

His voice, along with his irritation level, deepened. "For staying here all night to make sure you didn't fall into a coma. People die all the time from mixing drugs and alcohol, Carly. Or is this something you do normally?"

"Of course not," she said icily, knowing it was useless to deny anything to Evan. His mind was made up. And what could she say? That she'd passed out only twice in her life and he just happened to be there for both incidents? She was an eyewitness and even she had trouble believing it.

"Thank you," Carly said tightly, "for making sure I didn't die a tabloid death and bring shame upon my family and friends."

"Grace must be your middle name."

"Sorry, but that's about all the tact I've got right now."

"Apology accepted," he said curtly. "Now, sit down."

She didn't budge.

"All right." He started to rise. "Then I'll stand up."

"Forget it." Carly settled into the rocker, tucking her robe in to cover her legs. Normally she wouldn't have been so modest, but wearing fuzzy slippers and a chenille robe while he was dressed in his all-black Antichrist outfit made her feel particularly vulnerable.

"Don't bother for my sake," he said, watching her tighten the belt on her robe. "I've seen you in less."

She made a face.

"You looked better in less."

She stuck her tongue out at him.

"Whenever you want."

Odin emerged from the kitchen, approached Evan, and began to investigate his shoe. Repelled, Evan pulled his foot away. The cat batted at a shoelace. Carly crooned her cat's name softly, using the silky indulgent whisper women use to draw and disarm animals and lovers. Odin immediately made a beeline for her and flung himself joyously onto her lap.

"Must be nice," Evan said with disgust as he stared at the ridiculously happy pile of fluff in her arms. The cat began to drool and Evan's frown deepened. "Look, we need to figure out what we're doing here."

Carly wasn't sure she was ready for this discussion. She wasn't sure she would ever be. "Do you want some coffee?"

"No, I'm fine."

"Well, I'm not and I want a cup of coffee." She got up and let Odin flow out of her arms like slow-moving lava.

Carly took her time with the preparations. While waiting for the water to boil, she hummed "Your Song," same as she always did when she felt at loose ends.

Her father, Beck Rudolph, loved music with a

youthful enthusiasm that never left him even when, one by one, his friends switched radio stations from contemporary to classic rock, then oldies. Beck's taste in music was eclectic; from Elvis Presley to Costello, Sarah Vaughan to McLachlan, Johnny Cash to Rotten.

One of his all-time favorites was Elton John. Among Elton's greatest hits, "Your Song" was special; it was Beck's cheer-up song for his little girl whenever school, life, or her mother were weighing too heavily on her tiny shoulders.

Carly was six when she realized that the lyrics about buying a big house where they both could live were not an actual declaration of intent. That was the year her parents divorced. The dissolution of Beck and Judith's marriage was like the breakup of the Soviet Union. What was once a loosely held arrangement of disparate parts suddenly and irrevocably split into warring factions. Her father and his music collection moved out, leaving Carly with nothing but her mother's bitter lamentations for a soundtrack.

For years afterward, "Your Song" became just an unhappy reminder of Beck's patriarchal shortcomings. Carly was in college when she finally popped out of the constrictions of juvenile egocentricism and realized that her father was never going to morph into Superdad and kick some serious ass. The fact that Beck often lost his way in the harsh wilderness between thought and deed was something he had to live with as much as she did. At that point, "Your Song" lost its bitterness and was her song once again, a souvenir of special moments between a father and a daughter.

While Carly hummed and made coffee, Evan sat quietly at the kitchen table, hardly moving, except for his eyes, which followed her every move. Grudgingly, she had to admire his patience—it was certainly a character trait she wished she had more of. Odin had taken a seat next to Evan and watched him as intently as Evan watched her, two black-haired, testosterone-powered males, one with upturned green eyes and one with hooded blue ones.

"You came to my house, Evan." She set the coffee press and two mugs on the table. "I didn't invite you. You can lead this conversation."

"Fair enough," he conceded. "I think we need to rethink our deal."

Carly fought back the urge to shoot back something deep and meaningful like, "No shit." But losing control of her mouth over coffee was what got her into the present predicament, so she held her tongue and just sipped quietly.

Evan cleared his throat. "I think it's safe to say that there would definitely be some pluses to getting naked." He looked at her like he was itemizing every one of those pluses in his head. His breathing got a little heavier, his nostrils flared, and his lips parted slightly.

Snapshots flashed quickly through Carly's mind like an erotic flip book. Plump breasts with rosy pink peaks resting in a pair of strong hands. A smoky whorl of dark hair that thinned to a slender trail down a muscled belly. Intertwined arms and legs. Yeah, there were definitely some pluses. She sighed softly and answered with a half-smile and a dreamy nod.

His eyes rested on her mouth before reluctantly

moving back to her eyes. "I think it's also safe to say that there would be some negatives."

This time the photos in her head were of the morning after. Yellow crime-scene tape strung across the front door. Scorched bedsheets and bullet holes in the walls. Mug shots of the both of them, bruised and disheveled. Her sigh was sad but wise.

"Therefore," he concluded, "I think we should go back to the original plan. You narrate my film."

"Or," she said hopefully, "you could just hand over my shoe."

"Not on your life." His response was immediate and nonnegotiable.

He who has the shoe makes the rules.

Carly rubbed her temples. "If we do this, we draw up a contract, signed, notarized, the whole nine yards."

"We can't just shake on it?" It was his turn to be hopeful.

Her response was just as quick and unrelenting. "This is business; we do it up right or not at all. Talk is cheap, Evan."

His face hardened. "Except when you do it."

"And don't you forget it." Ten years of big-city hard knocks and near misses had taught her that once money gets thrown in the mix, unless she was willing to give it away for free, it was best to smile politely and get a lawyer.

"All right," he said. "Let's deal."

Two hours later, the kitchen table was littered with scribbled sheets of lined yellow legal paper. The coffee press was empty, and both Carly and Evan were drained from hammering out their deal.

Carly's eyes ached and her head felt as heavy as a boulder as she looked over the final draft of the contract. In exchange for voicing his film and "investing" her talent checks back into the film, Carly would get a 5 percent stake in the documentary. It had been a fight to get any percentage at all. She would be credited in type as big as his at the end of the film but she would be allowed no creative input. He'd have her for one month. During that time, she would make herself available, within reason, to record whenever he needed.

The deal was pretty straightforward, but pounding it out hadn't been. They had both dug deep and fought hard.

She looked at him through bleary eyes, then put her head down on her arms. His elbows rested on the table with his head propped up between his palms.

"I'll have my guy write it up and we can both sign it early next week," she said, her voice muffled by the tabletop.

"Nuh-uh," he grabbed the paper and stood, slouching. "I'll have my guy write it up and we'll sign it on Monday."

She got up and matched his weary stance. "All right. Your guy will write it up, and me and my guy will look it over on Monday, and we'll sign it on Tuesday."

"Shit." He leaned into Carly's face. "I hope working with you isn't going to be like this the whole way." He moved in even closer. "We should have just gotten naked."

The tiredness left Carly's body as she breathed in his warm scent. If she'd been holding a light bulb, it would have lit up brightly enough for airplane navigation.

His lips touched down on hers in a perfect three-point landing. Carly felt the pleasurable impact of his mouth to the soles of her feet and all points in between. Evan untied her belt and slipped his large, warm hands under her robe. One hand caressed her breast through her tank top while the other slid underneath her panties to squeeze her bottom. He kissed her deeply, thoroughly with his lips and his tongue and his body. Carly knew the longer she kissed him, the harder it was going to be to stop, but she didn't stop. It felt too blindingly good to stop. Then Odin landed like a fuzzy meteor at her feet.

"Sorry, nakedness has been canceled," she said, catching her breath and pulling away. "It's the film or nothing."

"I thought you'd say that," he grumbled and straightened back up. He looked her up and down as he had done earlier in the evening. A slow sexy smile stretched along his lips, the same one she remembered from the night before. She felt like he was kissing her all over again.

"Nice cherries," he said, reaching out to run a fingertip down her breast and over one ripe nipple.

Carly pushed him out the door and slammed it behind him.

"Decomposition isn't such a bad thing. Without it, all the fallen leaves and grass clippings would pile up and everybody would be up to their ears in 'em!" In character as Ella Earthworm, Carly's voice was pitched up high as if she'd been sucking helium. She gesticulated with her hands for emphasis, but her head never turned or moved away from the microphone. "So you see, us earthworms play a real big role in helping to keep things tidy. And we're recycling, too!"

"That was terrific, Carly." From the control room, a woman with short curly hair gave her the thumbs-up. "Okay, last page."

The four other members of the *Compost Critters* cast paged forward in their scripts. Carly, who wasn't featured in the scene, took her headphones off and took a seat on a tall wooden stool behind her. Denny, an elf of a man, and Marina, a pretty Hispanic girl, assembled in front of their microphones.

"Simon Stinkbug at your service," Denny answered as his character, his voice as gravelly and crotchety as an old man's.

"Edgar here." Marina piped up in a mischievous boy's voice.

Carly watched as the other actors recorded their parts. *Compost Critters* was a fun cartoon with great characters. The writing was good, as were the other actors. Unfortunately, there was only one recording session left before they went on hiatus for a few months. There was always a chance the show wouldn't get renewed. No one would know until right before they started up again. *Critters* was a popular show and the chances of its getting canceled were pretty low, but given the changing tide of her career, Carly was taking nothing for granted.

Minutes later, the engineer was swapping microphones and adjusting stands as new actors filed in for the next session. Still brooding, Carly picked up a script for the final recording as she made her way to the parking lot.

"Carly! Wait!"

Carly saw the reflection of Marina sprinting after her in the Audi's window, her long curly hair springing as she ran.

"Jeez," Marina said, catching up with her. "What planet were you on? I've been calling you from the lobby."

"Sorry, *chica*. My *cabeza's* not on right these days."

"Me, my cousin, Gabby, and my mom are going to Ensenada for a girl weekend. You want to come? There's lots of room at the condo," Marina asked as she downed a bottle of water.

"Tell your mom thanks," Carly said gratefully. *Tia* Connie was nicer to her than her own mother. "But the last time I was in Baja, Dana almost burned down a restaurant with some flaming tropical drink. She had to beat back the fire with her blouse. The men gave her a round of applause."

"I remember that on *Hog Heaven*." Marina laughed as if she'd been there. "That was a good one. Did you really get kicked out of the motel for shorting out the electrical system?"

Plugging the blow-dryer, curling iron, electric toothbrush, coffeemaker, and night-light all into the same socket was possibly a mistake. Turning them all on at once certainly was.

"Hardly." Carly almost wished Dana's show would get canceled. It was ruining her reputation. "And you know, Marina, everything that happens on that show isn't real. Some of it Dana actually makes up. Don't forget, Charlie is not me."

"I know. But the characters are so much like you guys."

"Stand back, this could be dangerous." Carly began to imitate the ultra-soothing voice of a pre-recorded airport announcement as she unlocked her car door. "The white zone is for loading and unloading of passengers only."

She opened the door to the Audi as gently and warily as a member of the LAPD bomb squad. Hot air surged out like an angry genie from a big metal bottle.

Marina eyed the leather seats and shook her head. "Black interior? You are *loco.*"

"Car lust," Carly admitted sheepishly. "I wasn't thinking about the morning after."

"I hear ya," Marina said with a sympathetic smile. "Let me know if you change your mind."

Chapter Six

Carly arrived home as wilted as her take-out spinach salad. The backs of her thighs, thanks to the car seat, felt like seared steaks. Odin was splayed across the kitchen floor like a catskin rug and the interior of the house was as inviting as a fully stoked kiln. It was hot but it was home.

The answering machine had the usual odds and ends on it. Julian and Stacey had left messages. There was the regular schedule update from Quinn. Even Glen had called. Nothing from Evan, but she didn't really expect there to be. If he wanted to tell her anything, she assumed he would just throw a note attached to a brick through the window.

She was reaching for the phone when it rang. Heeding a sudden premonition, she let the answering machine pick up.

"Carly? Are you there? It's Mom." Judith had a beautiful voice. In fact, it was her transforming feature. She was a pretty woman already, but it was the dulcet tones emanating from her Lancôme lips that elevated her from mere eye candy to supreme object of desire. Needless to say, her inevitable whiplash conversion from warm and petable to cool and predatory was more than a bit unnerving for the uninitiated.

"Fine," Judith snapped after a long pause. "I'll have to assume you're not there. I need you to talk some sense into Julian and Stacey. Carly?" Another lengthy pause ensued. "This is important," she finally said before hanging up.

"Good to hear from you, too, Mom." Carly hit the delete button on the answering machine.

Dialing her sister's number by heart, Carly walked through the French doors to the backyard and settled onto the lounge chair. The sun was laying low in the sky, bathing everything in a buttery yellow glow. She had no intention of "talking sense" into her siblings, of being her mother's henchwoman. Carly was the quintessential doting older sister. For them she would fight dragons and spill blood, even when the dragon in question was her mother and the blood her own.

"Hello?" a soft voice answered after one ring.

"Hey, honeybunny," Carly said, smiling. "I heard Mom was on a rampage."

"Oh, Carly," Stacey gurgled with unabashed pleasure. "I'm so glad you called!"

"Carly." Julian's warm tenor voice broke in on another line.

Just like that, the residual tension from Judith's call slipped from Carly's shoulders and was replaced with a blankie of 100 percent genuine affection. She could have easily walked away from her mother, and had done so more than once, but she would always come back to try and make peace. Why? Because Judith, Stacey, and Julian were a package deal. Because while Judith would forever find Carly a loser, her brother and sister would just as staunchly forever declare her a winner. Was putting up with her mother's unrelenting criticism worth a few moments of uncensored, undiluted adoration? Hell, yes.

The battered wingback chair needed reupholstering. The leather was stained and bore pinpricks and claw marks. Several of the decorative brass nail heads were missing. Her father had called it his "thinking chair." Unable to bear the high cost of shipping, he'd given it to Carly for her office before taking his last job in Hawaii. It was a manly man's chair, perfect for smoking illegal Cuban cigars and drinking twenty-year-old scotch, or for a small woman and a large cat to sit comfortably while reviewing work schedules and reading scripts.

Carly suspiciously unsealed the manila envelope that held the season's last *Critters* show. For the second time that day she felt a sense of foreboding envelop her.

One shoe wasn't good enough. It was like caboodle without kit, fro without to, yon without hither. It was incomplete, irrelevant, and sadly, magically impotent without its other half. She knew this to be a fact.

Ella the Earthworm was no more.

The red wiggler had bitten the dust. In the season's very last episode of *Compost Critters*, Ella is mortally wounded when Farmer Ron turns the compost heap. It was a case of being in the wrong place at the wrong time. One twist of Farmer Ron's lethal pitchfork and it was pretty much over. Carly felt as if it had been she, rather than Ella, who had been stabbed and left twitching in the humus.

With a heavy heart, Carly hauled herself off to the kitchen. Some women shop when they're depressed, some eat or call their girlfriends. Carly did all those things, but when she was really down, she liked nothing better than to get up to her eyebrows in flour and bake—cookies, cakes, breads, anything with flour, sugar, and butter. The goods she baked weren't necessarily for her consumption. The therapy was in the making and the giving—the eating was incidental. It was her nonviolent way of dealing with a messed-up life.

The oven was fired up and it burned long into the night. The CD player was loaded up with blues and country, both genres satisfying her need to hear wrenching, tragic tales of love and grief. "Lover Man" followed "I'm So Lonesome I Could Cry." Billie Holiday competed with Hank Williams as to who had it bad and who had it worse. All the while, Carly made cookies; batch after batch of chocolate chip and oatmeal raisin came out of the oven. Bags of gingersnaps, snickerdoodles, and shortbread piled up on the counters and kitchen table.

The weekend passed in a haze of confectioners' sugar, lovers' laments, and thoughts of Evan. It occurred to her once or twice, between sifting flour and pressing fork marks into the tops of peanut butter cookies, that she was spending a lot of time thinking about a man she didn't even like and that maybe she would be better served thinking about a man she did like. Sadly she couldn't think of another man who could hold her attention like Evan. Love him or hate him, she couldn't ignore him.

* * *

The contract was sitting on the doorstep Monday morning. Scanning the document, Carly realized that there was absolutely no mention of the shoes anywhere. Belatedly she realized that there hadn't been any in the draft they had cobbled together, either. How had she forgotten that detail? But putting it down in black and white meant that Quinn and the legal department, the biggest informational leak at the agency, would see it. She was caught between saving face and saving ass. Carefully, she tucked the contract into her briefcase and loaded up the car with cookies.

"No. I don't like it at all," Quinn groused, sitting at his desk. He was holding a turkey and cheese sandwich on thick, homemade wheat bread. Perfect ruffles of lettuce peeked out between the bread and slabs of real turkey breast, a thin rind of skin the color of brown sugar still clinging to it. Carly saw Glen's handiwork all over Quinn's lunch.

"Why? What's wrong with it?" Carly picked at her take-out, factory-assembled Chinese chicken salad.

"Let's start with everything." He put the sandwich down and gestured at the document in front of him. "Have you read this?"

"I helped put it together."

"Carly, remember me?" He glared at her through horn-rimmed glasses. "I'm your agent. You don't negotiate deals. That's my job. Stick to the voiceovers and cookies."

"I know," she said, trying to placate him. "And I

would never, never dream of doing this kind of thing ever, ever, but it was sort of a favor." She was very glad at that moment that there was no mention of the shoes in the contract.

"Favor!" His voice went up a notch. "What did this guy do for you? Donate a kidney?" He went back to his sandwich.

"Look, it's not all bad. You still get your commission and I get a credit and a percentage of the film."

"You'd be better off getting paid. Unless you're Ken Burns or Michael Moore, no one makes money on documentaries. Look, if you wanted to get into narration, I could have found you some work. You just had to say something."

"There are a lot of intangibles that I would be getting out of it." *Like my shoes and my career.*

Quinn didn't look convinced. "This sounds like something Charlie would do."

She flexed her jaw muscles and decided to ask Dana to kill off her *Hog Heaven* alter ego as soon as possible.

"Actually," Quinn went on, "it sounds more like a Daphne scheme. Anyway I look at it, it's a dumb idea, but if you really need to do this, I'm not gonna tell you no."

"Thanks, Quinn." Carly sighed and sank into her seat with relief. She felt like she'd just gotten permission to go to her first unchaperoned dance.

"But don't think it ends here. I'm keeping my eye on you. First it was that pool thing, now this."

Carly's eyes popped out so far they almost landed in Quinn's lunch. "How do you know about the pool thing?"

He gave her a pitying look. "I'm your agent. It's

part of my job to know all. And don't worry, it's not part of my job to tell all."

Carly reeled her eyeballs back in. "I swear I won't let this film get in the way of my regular work." She hadn't told him about the *Critters* situation and that there might not be any regular work.

"Oh, I don't doubt that. You've been a pro since day one. That's not what I'm worried about."

"Why, Quinn," a beautiful smile blossomed across Carly's face. "I do believe you care."

"Only ten percent." He bit into a homemade chocolate cupcake. It had a thick lid of icing on top, and miniature chocolate chips sweetly spelled out the letter Q.

Most of Carly's youth had been lived teeter-tottering between a father who loved her uncon-ditionally but who was as unreliable as a weather forecast, and a mother whom she could never please but who dutifully, if not happily, fed and clothed her. One parent she couldn't depend on, one parent she couldn't make love her.

Her father was a freelance journalist whose spe-cialty was business news. He knew how to write about money, but as far as steering his own career or finances, he should have just called the Psychic Friends Network.

After the divorce, Judith, done with Goofus, started shopping for Gallant. She found him in sta-ble, hardworking, and humorless Walter Engstrom, CPA. For Carly it was like having a news anchorman for a stepfather. Julian came along a year into the marriage; two years after that it was Stacey.

Carly smiled as she navigated home through the crowded streets of Hollywood, remembering how cute her siblings were as kids. They were like little blond Hummel figurines. So perfect. In contrast, Carly always felt like the odd man out, the filler candy in the otherwise decent Halloween haul. Her mother didn't help, constantly pointing out her less than stellar chromosomal heritage. According to Judith, Carly was destined, like her feckless and irresponsible father, to fall gleefully, lemminglike over the cliff of failure.

Despite her mother's dire predictions, Carly pursued a career in voiceovers as relentlessly as Elmer Fudd hunted that wascally wabbit, though with much better results, and for the first time in her life she was in the right church, right pew. Now, no matter what, she wasn't ready to let it all go yet. She was going to do her damnedest to make sure she didn't lose everything along with her lucky shoes, even if it meant working with Evan for a month. So be it, she thought, girding her metaphorical loins as she turned the car down her street.

Carly spotted Evan's dark blue Toyota truck parked in front of her house before she saw him waiting by the front door. He didn't look happy, but then again, he never looked happy. She wondered if he looked that way all the time or just with her. It was probably just her. He was, most likely, all positive attitude and giddy good feelings whenever she wasn't around. Resigned to another disheartening tête-à-tête with Monsieur McLeish, she parked the car in the garage, hauled a bag of groceries out from the trunk, and made her way to the front door.

Evan was sprawled casually on the front steps, his

back against the porch post. In her mind's eye, Carly stripped away his jeans, T-shirt, and sneakers, placed him on a divan wearing nothing but a toga and laurel leaves, and surveyed the results. Her eyebrows shot up at the picture. *Who knew a man in a dress could look so fetching?*

"How long have you been waiting around?"

"I just got here," he said as he came to his feet and took the bag of groceries from her.

Carly fumbled with the door lock, unable to find the right key first for the door, then the deadbolt.

"You could have called," she grumbled.

"I was in the neighborhood." He watched her try yet another key in the second lock. "You sure you live here?"

"I don't usually come through this way. The deadbolt on this one is kind of sticky." Carly rattled the doorknob while turning the deadbolt key until it opened. "You see? I do live here."

"Your door's out of alignment. That's why the key's so hard to turn. You should get that fixed."

"I like to think of it as a feature," she said brightly. "Like an antitheft device."

Odin greeted them at the door and deftly led the way to the kitchen like a guide cat for the kibble impaired.

"What if someone was right behind you and you needed to get into the house really fast?"

Oh, boy. Time for the Worst-Case Scenario pop quiz.

"I figure I'll just scream really loud and run, quick like a bunny, to the back door. Or better yet, I'll just avoid the front door altogether. Now I've just saved myself a hundred bucks in door repairs.

I'm a genius!" She placed her briefcase on the counter and took the groceries from Evan.

He opened his mouth to say something, then closed it, shaking his head. She was obviously proving to be a failure in urban self-defense. This would probably go down on her permanent record.

"What's for dinner?" he asked, changing the subject.

"I don't know." She put milk, eggs, and cold cuts away. "Where are you taking me?"

"Paris," he said dryly.

"How grand. Too bad I've got an early session tomorrow. Some other time, maybe." She picked up her pet and let him peruse the cat food selection in the cupboard as she spoke to him in soft, sympathetic tones. "So what do you feel like, big guy?"

"Ribs, salad, and chocolate cake sound good."

Carly ignored Evan. "Don't mind him, baby. He's a gate-crasher."

Evan watched in fascination as Odin's doting owner lovingly prepared the cat's canned dinner. Carly emptied out the congealed hockey puck of processed meat product into a special bowl and zapped it for a few seconds in the microwave before placing his dinner on a Mickey Mouse place mat.

"What?" Evan asked with unconcealed disgust. "No candles? No mood music?"

Carly rinsed the empty can and set it aside for recycling. "Do you have a reason for being here?"

"I was hoping you'd have the contract ready and we could make out a schedule."

"Yes, I've got the contract, even though we're not supposed to get together on this until tomorrow, and even though you didn't call, which most polite people would do, but don't let that stop you from imposing your schedule on others whenever you want." She retrieved a large envelope and her PDA from her briefcase and took a seat at the kitchen table. "And yes, we can make a schedule."

"How about dinner?" he asked again.

"I told you, Paris was out."

"It's hard to schedule on an empty stomach." He patted his tummy woefully. At six feet, 180 pounds, starvation wasn't exactly dogging his heels.

"Sit." Carly pointed to a chair and pushed the envelope toward it. Then she went to the cupboard, where she was momentarily tempted to serve Evan something from Odin's stash. But that wouldn't be fair to the cat. She reached for a couple of cans of soup instead.

"You're gonna wash the can opener, right?" he asked when he saw her put the cans on the counter.

"I use a different one for the cat," she assured him.

"A better one, probably."

Just like at their first dinner, Evan refused to talk business while they ate their soup and sandwiches. It was probably for the best. Food and antagonism are just not a pleasant combination. Still, she hated to admit, eating quietly with Evan was not so bad. Carly was past the point where she was out every night or even most nights. Workdays were so full of driving around that the thought of hitting the town in the evening wasn't as appealing as it once had been. Watching Evan eat a ham sandwich and tomato soup was as pleasant as watching him sleep, she concluded. So long as they weren't talking, they seemed to get along just dandy.

"What did you major in in college?"

Carly suddenly felt like she was on a first date. "Naked men."

"Good at it?"

"Very."

"I imagine you were."

"I'm a semester short of a bachelor's in art history."

He looked up from his meal. "What happened? Finally realize that there are no six-figure jobs for art historians?"

"I didn't think I could compete with a swinger like Sister Wendy." She was already sorry she'd offered up that detail of her life to him. Her lack of a degree always bothered her, making her feel second-rate. It might have been better, had she never even gone to college. But to stop so close to the finish seemed to make it even more pathetic. Carly was pretty positive Evan had a master's or a doctorate. Whatever she had, he probably had two.

"Why didn't you finish?" he pressed.

"I got my big break, so I went for it."

"Art historian or actor? Interesting choices. So much in common."

"Dumb or dumber, according to my mother. She wanted me to be a CPA or a nurse. You know, something highly employable and recession proof."

He gazed around the cozy kitchen with its gourmet appliances and cookware. They weren't in pristine condition, showing that she obviously used them, but they were definitely not discount store specials; neither was the china they were eating on.

"You do all right," he concluded.

"When can I see a script?" she asked, turning the conversation away from herself.

"I've got one in the car." They'd finished eating, so it seemed he was now amenable to talking business.

"Is it the same one you used when you originally recorded with the other guy?"

"Essentially. I've made a few changes and re-edited part of the footage, but it's 90 percent the same."

"Can I hear what you did before?"

"No, I don't want you to be influenced by it."

"That bad, huh?" She didn't expect him to answer.

"That bad." He looked pained.

Evan gave her a copy of the script and they settled on a schedule starting the coming Wednesday night. In order to get Dex and a deal on the studio time, they would be working after hours, once a week, for the next four weeks. That suited Carly just fine since it wouldn't conflict with her normal work schedule. She hoped it would go a small way toward appeasing Quinn.

As she closed the door on his retreating figure, she wondered at the who, what, and why of Evan McLeish. He was like the Santa Anas, the "Devil Wind" that periodically scoured the LA skies clean as the day God made them, but also filled the air with static electricity that snapped and sparked and could whisper and whip the tiniest excuse for a fire into an unquenchable inferno. He was a merciless force of nature and she was but a lowly pebble in his path. The coming month, she was sure, would test not only her luck but also her strength, determination, and fortitude. If ever there were a time for her to get religion, take up a martial art, or buy a chastity belt, it would be now.

* * *

Quinn was on the phone reading the riot act to some poor actor who'd shown up late to a session. Carly placed a bag of cookies on his desk and sat down.

"I'm dead, Quinn," she said after he'd hung up.

"Huh?" He looked her over. "You've got lipstick on your teeth, but otherwise you look fine."

Carly scrubbed her teeth with a tissue. "They've written me out of *Compost Critters*."

He squinted at her suspiciously. "It's the last week of recording. How long have you known this?"

"Since last Friday."

"Friday!" he sputtered, aghast at the gaping hole in his intelligence network. Quinn began rummaging through the drawers of his desk for aspirin. It was one of the duties of his assistant to keep the bottle constantly topped off. "Why didn't you tell me then instead of wasting my time on some no-money documentary? I thought you were one of the better ones."

"It wouldn't have changed anything. I'm still doing the film and I'm still dead."

He shook two pills out and shot nasty looks at the empty glass on his desk. "Crap."

"That pretty much sums it up." Carly grabbed a new green bottle of Pellegrino out of a small fridge in the back of the office and poured Quinn some fizzy water.

"Okay, well," he said, after gulping down the aspirin, "I guess you should know Mr. Bert's giving up the glue sticks."

"Crap." She held out her hand. "How long have you known?"

He dropped one aspirin into her palm. "Since Monday."

"When we were wasting time on the no-money documentary? And I thought you were one of the better ones." She chased the painkiller down with mineral water straight from the bottle.

"Okay," he conceded, "we're even."

"I'm sorry, Quinn."

"For what? What did you do? That's showbiz, Carly. You're up. You're down. You're up again. Get used to it."

"Sounds like a bar fight," she said gloomily.

"No, that's life. Now get the hell out of here. You've got a session in Burbank in thirty minutes. Don't screw it up."

Early on in her career, someone explained the actor's life cycle.

Act one: Who's Carly Beck?

Act two: Get me Carly Beck!

Act three: Get me a young Carly Beck!

Epilogue: Who's Carly Beck?

Carly felt as if she'd barely gotten to act two and was headed straight to the epilogue. She wasn't even going to get to be a has-been. There would never be a *Behind the Cartoon* episode about her meteoric rise, inevitable fall, and improbable, but hard-won, comeback. She didn't have a single failed marriage or stint in rehab to look back on regretfully or fondly, whichever the case might be. Not one dry cleaner or restaurant in all of Los Angeles had a yellowing eight-by-ten of her on the wall.

Chapter Seven

The TimeCode studio parking lot was mostly empty when Carly arrived. The one nice thing about working after hours was lots of parking space. She chose a spot underneath a light and parked her car carefully. The Audi was over a year old, but she still treated it like it was brand new, fretting over every little scratch and ding, a problem she never had with her previous cars. They had all come pre-dinged and, therefore, were totally worry-free in that respect.

The lobby was as deserted as the parking lot. During normal working hours, the place was packed with people—coming, going, hanging out, hanging on. The room was wide and deep, bisected by a long counter separating the waiting room from the reception and scheduling area. A couple of large black leather sofas were grouped together in the corner, the end tables piled with copies of *The Hollywood Reporter*, *Variety*, and other trade magazines. One wall was set up with a mini coffee bar complete with espresso machine, flavored syrups, and to-go cups. Framed movie posters of the latest releases from the facility's clients covered the walls.

Behind the counter was a moon-pale blonde with

a wide mouth covered in black-cherry lipstick, and light eyes rimmed thickly with eyeliner and mascara. A purple tank top offered an unobstructed view of a serpent tattoo that wound its way down her arm from shoulder to wrist.

"Hi, Layla," Carly greeted the scheduler. "Is Dex here? I'm a little early."

"Yeah, studio A." The girl ran her hands through her razor-cut hair and smiled. "We were all watching the gay cruise episode of *Hog* in the conference room earlier. You guys didn't actually do that, did you?"

"No! Absolutely not!" It was all a horrible, horrible misunderstanding. A singles cruise to the Caribbean sounded like a great idea at the time. And so cheap. They should have realized there would be a catch. The memory of a boatload of drunken men in Speedos singing "Daaay-Oh, Daaa-aaa-aay-Oh! Come Mr. Tallyman, tally me banana!" was something that she tried very hard to forget.

"Yeah," Layla said. "That's what I thought. You and Dana aren't that stupid."

Daylight come and me wan' go home.

A trio of tired, disheveled men stumbled zombielike out of one of the studios and into the lobby. They stood, blinded by the sunset shining through the glass front doors, as if they were only just realizing how long they'd been away from the real world. Carly slipped past them and made her way to Dex's room.

The studio had a fair-sized control room and recording booth. An eight-foot-long mixing console sat directly in front of a viewing window. A couple of monitors were suspended over the left-hand side of the console. Racks of equipment stood at attention directly to the left and behind. A red lava lamp bubbled on the producer's desk attached to the right of the console.

Dex sat in the middle of his electronic nest watching a surf competition on one of the monitors. He was wearing his usual warm-weather uniform: T-shirt, shorts, and sport sandals.

"Cowabunga, dude," Carly said in perfect Bart Simpsonese. "How'd your day go?"

"Better now that you're here." Dex stood and gave her a hug.

"You're just looking for cookies," she said, dropping a bag in his hand before moving to the sofa that sat against the wall to the right of the console. Above it was mounted a nine-foot surfboard made of varnished blond wood with a red band painted around the middle. "This is new."

"You like it?" Dex joined her, staring up at the board lovingly. "It's a bing."

"Sure is," Carly agreed, unsure if *bing* was an adjective or a noun.

"I won it on eBay." He caressed the board's surface. "I'm having a couple of vintage Hawaiian shirts framed for the booth."

"Soon you could have a luau in here."

"Thinkin' about it." He scanned the studio, no doubt wondering where to put the tiki torches. "Would you come in a grass skirt if I asked?"

"Just don't ask me to hula." Carly turned to the job at hand. "Did you record the original v.o. for this?"

"Yeah. He was just okay." Dex made a seesawing motion with his hand. "Kinda boring. You're gonna be a real improvement."

"I don't know. I've never done any real narration before. I did an audio book once, but that was a long time ago, and it was a really cheapo production. I didn't even bother to get a copy."

"You'll be fine."

She hoped so. Even though narrating the film wasn't her idea, she still wanted to do a good job. She'd read the script and was impressed by the writing as well as the amount of research Evan had done. It was nice to be working on a good project, but it irked her that he was both full of himself and deserved to be.

The door opened and the object of her disaffection walked into the studio, just as handsome and intimidating as ever. Wasting no time, Evan nodded at Carly and Dex, barely acknowledging their status as Homo sapiens, and handed them each a script.

"Here's what I want to record tonight," he said. "It's basically the same script, Carly, that I gave you before, with a few changes. Ready, Dex?"

Evan took the helm at the producer's desk. Carly took the new script and made her way to the booth as Dex followed to adjust the microphone for her.

Last-minute changes and rewrites were a fact of life in the voiceover business. As a professional, Carly was expected to be able to read a script at the press of a record button. Usually only cartoons had the luxury of ensemble read-throughs prior to recording. Rehearsal time for commercial and narration sessions were limited to the few minutes in the waiting room before the session and a couple of dry runs in the booth before take one. She considered herself fortunate that Evan had given her as much time as he had to familiarize herself with the script.

Dex returned to his chair and hit the talkback button. "Carly, can you read a few lines for level?" He fiddled with a few knobs as she read.

"Angela Arlene Barlow was the only daughter and third of four children born to Ed and Carol Barlow. The Barlows were second-generation Ohio corn farmers who'd—"

"That's good," Dex said, cutting her off.

A microphone tweak and one test run later, they were ready to go. Video of the film played on a monitor in the booth so Carly could see what she was reading over. Evan gave her a target time to shoot for.

Dex hit the record button. "Arlene Barlow, take one."

The session went smoother than Carly had expected. She was nervous at first, since Evan hardly gave her any direction. His comments were few and far between but showed that he was paying attention. Eventually, she figured that she must be doing something right, if only because he wasn't telling her she was doing something wrong.

"Angela left home at the age of fifteen and transformed herself from farm girl to city girl. She dropped Angela, a name she'd always disliked, and started using her middle name, Arlene. . . ."

After forty-five minutes, she took a break to rest her voice and make herself a hot tea and coffee for everyone else.

"Here you go," she said as she balanced a tray of mugs on one hand. "Cream and sugar for Evan, black for Dex."

"Thanks," said Dex. "Hey, you're good at that."

"When I was waitressing, I could haul dinner for

four with no problem at all." She made a muscle with her right arm and grinned comically. "I had biceps like Popeye."

Dex gave her arm a squeeze and snorted at the result.

"Had, baby, had," she pointed out.

Evan looked up from his notes. "You were a waitress?" His tone said he was pretending to be surprised. In Los Angeles *waiter* was synonymous with *actor.*

"My name is Carly and I'll be your server for the evening," she said earnestly as she held the tray against her stomach and smiled a big cheerleader smile. "The special for tonight is macadamia nut–encrusted ahi tuna served with braised root vegetables. The soup this evening is fava bean."

"Fava bean?" Dex echoed.

"No one ever ordered it," Carly admitted. "I've sold women's lingerie, men's suits, and did billing for a chiropractor, too. I've even worn a wench costume at the Renaissance Faire three summers in a row."

"I'd like to see that," Dex teased.

Carly punched his shoulder playfully, then turned to Evan, who'd gone back to studying his notes. "I've got a couple of questions about the script."

"Fire away," he said grimly.

Carly was pretty sure he didn't mean it the way she wanted to take it. She got her script from the booth and spread it out on the desk in front of Evan. "I need some pronunciation help. There's a Russian, Antole something, and a couple of place names."

She pointed to the underlined words. Evan said them aloud and she repeated them until they rolled off her tongue naturally. She scribbled phonetic versions in the margins to jog her memory.

"Also, there's this." She paged forward and stopped at a circled paragraph with a large question mark next to it. "I'm not sure which Raymond it's referring to. It says, 'She and Raymond remained together for the better part of that summer,' but is it her brother Raymond or the other Raymond, the manager's brother? I'm a little confused about that."

"You'll be the only one," he said dismissively. "If you pay attention to the visuals you can't miss that it's her brother."

"Well, since I don't get to see the video until right before I read it," she said stiffly, "I wouldn't know that, would I?"

"So maybe you should save your questions for later." He closed her script and pushed it toward her. "That is, if they're still pertinent."

Carly sucked back a nasty comment and continued with her questions, refusing to be tossed aside so easily. "Okay, one question that I don't think the video is going to clear up is where you say that she was engaged twice but never married."

He sat back in his chair and crossed his arms over his chest. "And you would like to disagree with that?"

"Yes, I would. Arlene Barlow was married to Pete Silver."

"Really?" he said, stretching out the word sarcastically. "And this is common knowledge?"

"Sure." *Wasn't it?*

"And your reference on this would be . . . ?"

She stuck her chin out. "My dad."

He made a sound in the back of his throat. "I guess I'll have to cite that in the credits. Your loyalty is admirable, Carly, but I'm sorry to say that dads are not infallible sources of information."

"My father's a journalist, Evan. He doesn't just make things up. He finds them out."

"Well, why don't you give Daddy a ring and see where he got that little tidbit of information that doesn't seem to be available from any other source? In the meantime, I'd appreciate it if you'd just stick to doing what you do best, which is reading the goddamn copy the way it was goddamn written."

The room was suddenly cold enough to flash-freeze a side of beef.

"I'm going for a cigarette," Carly said, even though everyone knew she didn't smoke.

"What the hell was that about?" Carly heard Dex ask Evan as she walked out of the studio.

The air outside was chilly despite the day's broiling heat. Even though LA had more trees per square mile than almost any other metropolitan city in America, it was still a desert with easily twenty degree shifts in temperature from day to night. Carly got in her car and pulled on a sweater that she always kept in the backseat.

"Shit, shit, shit," she chanted, letting off steam a little at a time like a potty-mouthed teakettle. She blinked back tears and willed away her hurt, focusing instead on anger. Anger she could use; it was powerful, forceful, and propelling. Hurt was a self-indulgence she couldn't afford at the moment. She would not lose control and she absolutely could not cry. If she cried, she'd get stuffy and be unable to record. She'd be damned if she had to cut the session short and she'd be double damned if she'd cry over Evan.

"Shit!"

She turned the radio on and for five minutes forced herself to concentrate on a radio call-in program. The evening's topic was food items for sexual gratification. It didn't take long for the show to bring her back to reality. Somehow listening to people confess on the air that they'd had carnal knowledge of mashed potatoes and microwave-warmed cantaloupes seemed to put things in perspective for her. Things could be worse—she could be one of those pathetic callers who trolled for dates down the grocer's aisle.

Evan and Dex stopped talking the moment Carly reentered the room. She said nothing as she snatched her script off the producer's desk and marched into the recording booth. She organized the papers on the copy stand and put her headphones on.

"Where do you want to start?" Her voice was as cool and neutral as a glass of water.

"Top of eight." Evan met her cool and neutral and raised her a blank, steady stare.

She opened her script to the correct page. "Ready."

"Take forty-four," Dex said, looking uncomfortably at Evan.

Carly straightened her shoulders. "Raymond Barlow, older than Arlene by two years, had already made a name for himself as an undisciplined but gifted jazz pianist when Arlene finally caught up with him in Chicago. . . ."

The time went by quickly with the three of them working like a well-oiled, angry machine. Carly immersed herself in the project, focusing solely on the words and pictures. Before long, her personal problems receded as she was caught up in the unfolding story of Arlene Barlow's life. Watching the footage and reading the script were all that she let matter to her. She rarely looked through the viewing window, preferring to deal with Evan and Dex as disembodied voices.

She didn't linger after the session. Once Evan signaled the end of the recording, Carly gathered her things and called out a general good-bye as she raced out of the studio. It wasn't until she was home in bed that she took a good look at her bruises.

She was furious with Evan for being such an insufferable jackass and at herself for being so thin-skinned. Her mother had been an expert at slash-and-burn criticism. Carly should have seen it coming, should have known better, should have ducked.

Once, when driving to Vegas, her car had plowed straight through a cloud of happily cavorting butterflies. One minute the winged beauties were making their way across the open desert, instinctively heeding the migratory call of the wild, the next they were so much insect protoplasm splashed across a dirty windshield. She knew exactly how they felt.

Pulling the covers over her head, Carly finally let herself have a well-deserved cry. It wasn't going to fix anything, but that gut-cramping loser feeling was looming large and it scared the absolute bejesus out of her.

Dana's kitchen was a heavy-metal chic: all glove leather, black marble, and polished chrome. The industrial grade stove and refrigerator were big enough to cook and store a decent sized steer. A glowing red and white neon sign in the dining area proclaimed LET'S EAT in two-foot-high letters against walls artfully painted to resemble faded denim. A television suspended from a swivel mount in the ceiling played music videos with the sound down low. Half-empty paper cartons containing rice, orange chicken, broccoli beef, and vegetable egg rolls littered the stainless steel top of the dining table.

Dana sighed contentedly, pushed her plate away, and leaned back into the black leather upholstered dining chair. Daisy, who'd been snoozing on a doggie bed in the corner, walked up to her owner and pawed her legs.

"What do you think about me having my thighs sucked?" Dana asked as she hefted the dachshund on her lap.

"Depends on who's doing the sucking," Carly answered as she began to clean up the table. Leftovers in hand, she opened the massive Sub-Zero fridge and tucked them in next to a dozen others. She prepared two coffees and brought them to the table. "Open your fortune."

Dana cracked her cookie and read, "Things are looking up."

"In bed!" Carly added with a wink before opening hers. "Beautiful things await you."

"In bed!" they shouted together.

"Sure you don't want to change your mind about Evan?"

Carly's heart jumped up and down in her chest like a gameshow contestant. "No, better not."

"It won't come true unless you eat it all," Dana

said, crunching down on her cookie. "So what's up with the sibs?"

Carly brought her up-to-date on the news that, come the fall, Julian would start grad school at CalTech and Stacey would attend Occidental College.

"Oh, God!" Dana exclaimed. "I remember when they were snotty little mall rats."

"I better get my luck back soon. Grad school for rocket scientists isn't cheap. And Stacey wants to go into advertising design. She's going to need a better computer and more design software."

Judith, Carly's mother, had really hoped that husband number two would be everything number one was not and, on the surface, he was. Walter Engstrom was an unremarkable but decent husband and father until he unceremoniously died of a heart attack at his desk at nine-thirty on a Monday morning, after a cup of coffee and a phone call from his bookie. The late Mr. Engstrom, it turned out, bet on anything and everything. He bet that he would be able to pay back the money he borrowed on his life insurance before his family would need it. Like most of his bets, he was wrong.

"You know," Dana said, "you're not the only one looking after those kids. They've already got a mom. How about they stop relying on the Bank of Carly to fix everything? They're not babies anymore."

"I know, but they've been through so much. They lost everything after Walter died—their father, their house, their college funds. I want to do what I can for as long as I can."

"You know I don't mess around when it comes to money."

Carly nodded. Dana might dress like a Vegas showgirl sometimes, but when it came to finances, she was as flinty-eyed and shrewd with her money as any pinstriped banker.

"As they say on the airplane, put your oxygen mask on first. You've worked hard for what you've got. Don't jeopardize it because you've got to be everybody's hero. You're not going to help Julian and Stacey if you end up having to live with them when you get old and incontinent because you forgot to look after yourself."

Carly grimaced. "Thanks for the incontinent part. That was very helpful."

"How was the session with Evan?"

"Oh, you know." Carly shrugged halfheartedly. "Dex engineered, Evan directed, I read. Then Dex compiled takes while Evan and I fought and insulted one another."

"So," Dana concluded brightly, "it's working out, then."

158A was the deep pink color of candy hearts. If it were up to Carly, she would have named that particular shade of nail polish "Be Mine." She stretched her bare legs out on the big blue cushions of the lawn chair and waited for her toenails to dry. A dessert plate with a half-finished raisin scone sat atop the mostly unfinished Sunday crossword puzzle on the grass next to the chair. A faint whirring sound filled the air above her head. Glancing up, she watched as a miniature Goodyear blimp crested the roof of her house and began to float over her back-yard.

"Jensen, you geek!" she yelled into the air.

The UFO was basically a silver Mylar balloon with a tiny remote-controlled motor attached to it. It was the latest toy of her technotweak neighbor across the street. Jensen had been dive-bombing the local dogs with it, driving them crazy for the last couple of weeks. She squinted up at the balloon through her sunglasses and thought it looked different. She lost it in the sun a couple times as it circled her yard but was finally able to get a good look at it. There seemed to be something attached to the bottom of it.

A camera? Carly's eyes narrowed. Slowly and ostentatiously, without ruining her manicure, she began to lower the zipper of her top. The blimp streaked across the yard like a heat-seeking missile. When it was directly overhead, she raised her arm and defiantly flipped it off. Sunlight glinted off the glossy 158A-colored tip of her middle finger. The blimp quickly retreated back across the street. Carly uncapped the bottle of nail polish and went back to finishing her nails.

Arlene Barlow and Pete Silver. Carly knew she was right about the singer and the musician's being married. A small part of her wanted to shelve her doubts and let it be Evan's problem if he was wrong. But wouldn't it be wonderful to prove him wrong?

Carly did the mental calculation for the time difference between LA and Honolulu, where Beck covered Pacific Rim business news. He never did make it to becoming a major market journalist but he did find his niche and, for the first time in his life, both his work and financial situations were doing rather well. Carly picked up the cordless phone lying by her feet and hit the speed dial.

"Rudolph here." Beck's voice was early-morning scratchy.

Carly pitched her voice down and added a cigarette rasp. "Big Kahuna? You put an ad in the paper for a surf bunny?"

"Lady," he said, not caring to hide his irritation, "you've got the wrong number."

Carly laughed. "Don't hang up, Dad. It's me."

"Carly!" he scolded. "Don't do that."

"I wouldn't, but it gets you so mad. Sorry."

"You did have me fooled," he conceded with a laugh. "Guess what, baby? I'm doing a piece on a guy next week who owns a handful of fast food tofu joints. He's set to make a bundle. I'll let you know how it goes."

Beck was forever scoping out successful businessmen for his daughter. Although he had never remarried and loudly proclaimed that he had no intention of ever tying the knot around his neck again, it didn't stop him from foisting the idea on his only child whenever possible.

Ignoring her father's attempts at matchmaking, she changed the subject. "Dad, do you remember telling me that Arlene Barlow was married to Pete Silver?"

"Yeah. Why are you asking?"

"I'm doing some narration work on a documentary about her. Something different for my reel other than cartoons and commercials. I think it's going to be really nice when it's done." She purposely left out the part about her participation being less than voluntary. Beck was a pretty worldly man, but she still doubted that he'd be blasé about the circumstances that led up to her working on the project.

"Way to go, Carly! I'm proud of you for trying something different. I know that kind of thing doesn't pay as well but sometimes you gotta do something from the heart."

"Thanks," she said, pushing down her guilt. Despite its being an interesting project, she'd have to admit that she'd never have gotten involved if she hadn't been coerced.

"Arlene Barlow's a great subject, too. She was such a talented singer. I'd love to work on a project like that."

Carly started painting a topcoat on her toes. A lawn mower sputtered to life in the distance. "Well, you sort of can. I need some help fact-checking and since you're the master . . ."

"Whatever I can do."

"First, was she or wasn't she married to Pete Silver?"

"Yeah, I'm pretty sure she was." The sound of Arlene singing "Come Rain or Come Shine" started playing in the background behind Beck. "Listen to that . . . what a voice," he said, keyboard clicks interrupting the music. "Hmmm . . . This might take awhile. How soon do you need it?"

Carly conjured up the image of her dad in his brightly printed Hawaiian shirt, neon swim trunks, and garish running shoes, sitting in front of his old putty-colored PC. "Yesterday, but I'd settle for as soon as possible. Also, I wanted to know if you could give me a crash course in hunting people down. There are a few people who worked with Arlene who I think are still in town, but I don't know how to find them."

"Sure," he said. Beck walked her through how to locate people directly and indirectly using the Internet, public records, and other avenues. "That's just the basics. If you hit a wall, let me know and I'll see what I can do for you."

"Mahalo, Dad," Carly said, using the Hawaiian word for thank-you. "You're the best."

"Aloha," he signed off in his best Jack Lord *Hawaii Five-O* voice.

Chapter Eight

It wasn't until Monday night that Carly could really start putting her father's investigative training to work. Quinn had her running to auditions all day long. She ping-ponged back and forth the twenty-plus traffic-choked miles between Burbank and Santa Monica, with periodic stops in Hollywood, from nine in the morning until six in the evening. As usual, lunch had to be on the run, and call times were ridiculously close together or had holes between appointments too long to avoid boredom and too short to actually get anything done.

Doggedly, she worked through a list of people culled from the pile of paperwork she'd received from Evan the first time they'd had dinner. One by one she eliminated names, put some aside for further research, and pulled out a few that seemed like they might actually have potential.

It was past midnight and only one good lead had materialized, Jessie Klumph, a choreographer who had once been a roommate of Arlene Barlow's. Jessie's phone number was unlisted, but she taught swing dance classes once a week at a club in Hollywood. Carly would have been disappointed with her lone find except that her father had warned her not to expect too much. Even seasoned journalists often came up with the most tenuous of leads, he'd said, so don't expect instant gratification.

Carly stretched her arms over her head and arched her back. Before she shut down her computer she checked her e-mail, which she had neglected to do when she arrived home.

"Gah!" She choked when she saw that she was booked for an eight o'clock morning session. It was a digital patch to New York, where it would be a comfortable eleven o'clock for the listeners on that end. Carly berated herself for not checking her schedule earlier. She realized she hadn't checked her voice mail or answering machine either.

"Gah!" she repeated a few more times before she finally got to bed. The next day was going to be brutal—starting at eight o'clock with her first session, a smattering of auditions all over the city, a meeting with her accountant in the afternoon, and finally, capping it all off, at seven o'clock for two fun-filled hours of Evan.

The Audi TT Coupe was Carly's very first abso-brand-spanking-lutely-new car ever. She'd never really been a car person but years of making do with crummy econo-cars, where the safety equipment consisted of a cardboard sun visor with "Help—Call Police" printed on one side, where true acceleration only took place going downhill, and stopping on a dime meant running into a large stationary object, made her love her new car all the more. She went about the care and maintenance of the coupe with the slavering devotion of a lovestruck teenager. Publicly she referred to her car as the Audi. Privately she thought of him—of course it was male—as Silver. As in "Hi-Yo, Silver, away!"

Carly pushed the seat back and grimly ate her umpteenth Happy Meal of the month. She'd been trying unsuccessfully for weeks to get an Ella Earthworm toy. Today had been no different. Frowning at a smudge on the dashboard, she wiped it clean with her napkin. She had ten minutes before needing to head to her next audition.

The cell phone merrily rang out the theme from one of her cartoons. Carly hit the speaker button on the dashboard holder.

"Carly," the deep voice drawled, "you never write. You never call. You don't come around no more."

"Glen!"

"Well, I guess I haven't fallen totally out of your consciousness," he sniffed. "So Quinn said you're doing the Arlene Barlow documentary."

"Yeah," she said, turning the radio off. "He wasn't pleased."

"Don't worry," Glen assured her. "He'll get over it."

"I really hope so." She sipped her soda.

"You know, the more I think about it, the more I think this documentary is a good idea. Diversification. Like mixing annuals in with the perennials. Good coverage all year-round."

The analogy was lost on her. The landscaping at Casa de Carly consisted of grass and gardenia bushes. The gardener mowed the lawn once a week and trimmed the bushes once a year.

"Hey, what are you doing Saturday night?" she

asked, remembering his fondness for big band music, and then caught herself. "That is, if you're not busy with Quinn."

"He'll be up in San Francisco attending a bris. I can't handle those things," he confessed. "And I grew up in cow country."

"How'd you like to take a swing dance class with me?"

"Absolutely! I love dancing but Quinn always wants to lead."

"No problem here." Carly checked her watch. "Sorry to cut things short, but I've got to hit the road in a few minutes."

"Fine," he said. "Tell me where I need to go."

Dex was sitting in his usual chair in front of the digital editor, tapping away at the keyboard, and Evan was huddled over the producer's desk, poring over his notes, when Carly walked in. Aside from the fact that everyone was wearing different clothes, the scene was unchanged from the previous week.

"Hey, sunshine," Dex said to Carly as he pushed back his chair and rolled his shoulders trying to get the kinks out.

"Hard day slaving over a hot mixing board?" Carly walked over and started to give him a friendly shoulder rub.

"Aaahh," he moaned as she worked his trapezius muscles. "Pushing buttons is hard work."

"Poor baby." Carly gave his shoulders a final squeeze before settling into the couch. She had a few minutes before the official start of the session to grab a bite to eat. Dinner, courtesy of the studio pantry, consisted of a soft drink and a small bag of chocolate-covered pretzels.

"Talk to your dad lately?" Dex eased himself down next to Carly and helped himself to a pretzel.

"Yeah, actually. We talked this weekend."

The sofa was perpendicular to the console and producer's desk, affording Carly a nice profile view of Evan, the sexy lout, hard at work. He was ignoring them, typing furiously on his laptop.

"You going to visit him anytime soon?" Dex asked.

"Probably not till Christmas." Carly split the last pretzel with Dex. "Looking for an invite?"

"You know me." Dex smiled. "Always praying for surf."

Evan smacked the return button on the keyboard loudly.

Carly winced sympathetically on behalf of the innocent laptop. "You don't need me. Dad'll put you up anytime."

"It's more fun if you go, sunshine."

"Uh-huh, right," she said with a gentle shove. "You just want someone to handle the plane tickets and the rental car."

He tugged a lock of her hair in retaliation. "You couldn't get dressed without fashion advice from Dex's House of Style."

"'Wear the black bikini' is not helpful."

"I'm also in charge of carrying bags and applying suntan lotion." He grinned and flexed his fingers suggestively. "You take care of my butt, sunshine, I'll take care of yours."

Carly laughed and pinched his bare knee. "Dex, you are so full of—"

Suddenly Evan was looming over them. Irritation charged the air around him, making it shimmer and crackle. He dropped a set of scripts onto each of their laps. "Time to push some buttons," he said pointedly to Dex.

Unperturbed, Dex picked up the script and headed for his chair. Aside from being technically versed with the equipment, he also possessed an easygoing nature, which was often just as important to the job. Dex made a face at Carly behind Evan's back. She knew better than to giggle.

They started the session off re-recording some lines from the previous session that Evan was unhappy with. Then they moved on to the new material.

"Always playing by her own rules, Arlene Barlow was only seventeen when she got her first job singing in a Chicago nightclub. She used a fake ID and claimed she was twenty-one." Carly stepped back from the mic and waited for Evan.

"Good." Evan scribbled notes on his script. "Let's move on."

Carly was relieved. They were both still angry from the last session. She had no apology planned and knew better than to expect one from him. Her fervent hope was that they could manage to get through the next few weeks without doing physical damage to themselves or the studio, although she did fantasize about bonking him on the head with the surfboard once or twice.

Dex hit the record button and slated the next take.

"The Frim Fram Club was where Arlene met trombonist G. G. Taylor. Although Taylor—"

"Hang on," Evan's voice came through the speakers, interrupting the take.

Carly watched Evan and Dex through the viewing window that separated the booth from the control room. Evan was standing, peering over Dex's shoulder at the monitor. Dex's eyes were fixed on the screen while his fingers danced over the keyboard. Used to interruptions, Carly took her headphones off and started to pace.

Sandals, comfy, relaxing, and red, but not lucky, slapped softly against the floor. Maybe Dana would go with her to Italy to see the pope and have him bless something . . . and write it into her show. She pushed the thought away immediately.

"Come on in, Carly," Dex said over the speakers.

Evan wasn't in the control room when Carly emerged from the booth. "What's up?"

"It crashed," Dex explained calmly.

"Ouch. Did you lose much?"

"Just that last take. But I won't know until I restore the job." He rubbed the back of his neck. "I was worried this might happen. They installed a new software upgrade yesterday to fix some bugs, but that always means you get a new set of bugs."

"Where's Evan?" she asked. "Out kicking puppies and kittens?"

Dex chuckled. "Yeah, he was pretty ticked off. You know, he always seemed like an okay guy, but last week he was totally out of line. He had no right to talk to you that way."

"It's his film. . . ." she said lamely. "His baby."

"That doesn't give him the right to be a dick."

"No, but I said I'd do the film, so I'm just going to try and make the best of it."

"Hang in there."

"Thanks," she said, giving him a hug. "You, too."

"I don't think that's going to do anything to fix the hard drive," Evan said as he strode into the room.

Carly pulled away.

"No," Dex said sweetly, "but it makes me feel better."

The look on Evan's face said he wasn't interested in what made Dex feel better. "So what's the status?"

"I'm going to reboot and see what's left of the job."

"Shit." Evan looked like he wanted to throw something, preferably at someone.

"Happens," Dex said philosophically. "Give me fifteen minutes."

"Fine," Evan said, even though it clearly wasn't. "We'll pick up some dinner." He motioned to Carly to go with him.

"I think I'll stay here with Dex."

"No," he said, taking her arm and marching her out of the studio. "He doesn't need your kind of help."

Carly shook his hand off when they got to the lobby. "What the hell does that mean?"

"You know exactly what it means."

"No," she said combatively, "you'll have to tell me."

A young kid in baggy pants and a black T-shirt with the words HI, I'M IN THE WITNESS PROTECTION PROGRAM emblazoned across the chest stuck his head into the lobby and quickly ducked back out. Whatever was going on was probably not worth risking his minimum-wage job as a dub guy to find out.

"I leave the room for five minutes and you two

are already at it hot and heavy. I'd hate to walk into whatever you can accomplish in fifteen minutes."

"You're sick," she said, disgusted by what he was implying. "Only you would turn an innocent hug into foreplay."

"I call 'em as I see 'em. C'mon," he said, grabbing her arm again and heading for the front door. "I meant what I said about not leaving you here."

Evan drove to a nearby pizza place and ordered a large pizza with everything on it. Carly wanted to wait in the car, but even that seemed to be too far out of Evan's sight to make him happy.

While he leaned against the wall, she sat in a booth by the window waiting for their order. Ignoring him entirely, Carly watched the traffic chug sluggishly down Sunset Boulevard. At the bus bench across the street, a couple of teenage girls sat closely together, their hands moving animatedly as they spoke. A young man wearing headphones lolled on the other end of the bench, eyes closed, his head bobbing rhythmically. A Mercedes halted in front of the trio and disgorged a stout Hispanic woman, one of the legions of undocumented housekeepers and nannies who kept the city's households, old and young, clean, fed, and diapered.

On the drive back to the studio, Carly avoided Evan by checking her messages. There was nothing on her schedule for the next day, a situation that made her twitchy. Not even one lousy audition. It nagged at her, itching like a mosquito bite that wouldn't go away. Her career had two more weeks of pants-peeing free fall to get through before her shoes could parachute her to safety. That is, if her nerves didn't give out before then.

Dex was still hard at work when they arrived back with dinner. The three of them ate silently, Dex working at the keyboard, Evan back to his notes at the desk, and Carly on the sofa tapping information into her PDA. After another twenty minutes of trying to get the system back up, they called it a night and rescheduled the session for later in the week.

Evan twice in one week. Oh, joy.

"I'll walk you to your car." Evan got up to follow her out.

"Don't bother," she said, rushing out of the studio.

He caught up with her at the front door. "Stop being so damned difficult."

"Then stop being such an ass!" She hurried across the deserted parking lot toward her car, irritated with the ease with which he kept up with her. Evan's thoroughbred legs ate up the asphalt like Black Beauty on a deserted beach. In contrast, she felt like a coked-up My Little Pony, her feet clipping along at a two-to-one ratio to his. "I know you're not crazy about me, but don't take it out on Dex. Don't blame him if the system crashed. He's a good engineer."

"Not when you're around." He stood in front of her car door, blocking her way. "That system and Dex were working just fine all night before you showed up."

"Look, I'm only going to say this once. Dex and I are friends. Nothing more. And really, I don't know why you'd care."

"I care when it messes up my recording session." He folded his arms across his chest. "He's easier to replace than you are, so if I have to choose, I'll record somewhere else."

This was one more bend in the road she didn't need. Dex didn't deserve to take the hit because she and Evan didn't get along. "Don't do that, Evan. There are only two sessions left. Picking up with someone else would seriously screw up your schedule. Whatever you want, I'll do it. Just don't fire Dex."

She watched him as he mulled over his choices. His lips pressed together in a rigid line, which didn't give her much hope. A car drove by, music thumping into the night air. One of the passengers yelled something obscene out the window. Well versed in urban etiquette, Carly had long since learned to block out anything that came after the trigger words "Hey, baby." She hardly gave it a thought.

"Fucking assholes," Evan spat, staring angrily in the direction of the speeding car.

Surprised by his fierce reaction, her eyes darted to the street expecting to find nothing but scorched earth where the car had been. She wasn't sure if she should be flattered or frightened, pleased or piqued.

"All right, Carly," he said, turning his attention back to her. "But if things aren't better at the next record, then your boyfriend's outta here." He moved away from her car.

"He's not my boyfriend."

"Funny, that's not how he tells it."

Wearily, Carly climbed into her car, her mind unable to process another thought. She had reached her Evan aggravation threshold for the day; her brain could take no more.

Skipping the freeway for the scenic route, she drove Sunset Boulevard west. As the grime of Hollywood gave way to the glitz of West Hollywood, the streets got cleaner and prettier, as did the people themselves. Prostitutes and drug dealers included. At the start of the Sunset Strip, she made the right onto Laurel Canyon and began the climb up into the Hollywood Hills, past homes big and small, and all expensive, that lined the twisty, narrow road. Cresting at Mulholland, Carly coasted downhill toward Ventura Boulevard and the Valley, toward home.

If Hollywood is the entertainment capital of the world, then the San Fernando Valley, home of the porn industry, is its libidinous evil twin. Unlike the mainstream studios like Disney and Universal, which proclaim their presence on every vertical surface available, the purveyors of smut prefer their anonymity and go about their business behind unmarked, cinder-block walls. That pornographers should exist so peacefully and invisibly among the Valley's middle class is not so much a testament to the broadmindedness of its people as it underscores the fact that no one really gives a rodent's behind what their neighbors do, as long as they do it quietly.

Carly was a Val, born and raised. Her Westside friends felt that the edge of the known world ended just a few blocks north of Ventura Boulevard, Sunset's country cousin that ran parallel to it on the other side of the Santa Monica Mountains. To them, beyond that line of demarcation, in the map of their minds the words "Here Be Monsters" were scrawled in bold black ink. Carly laughed off the silly jokes and snide remarks like a shipwreck victim who'd lived to tell the tale. Nothing in the endless miles of tract homes, strip malls, industrial parks, and warehouse stores scared her. Except maybe parts of Pacoima.

Chapter Nine

Cinderella didn't have to buy shoes. Her fairy godmother just waved her wand, and a harp gliss later, *brrrrrrring*, there they were—gorgeous glass slippers that fit like they were cobbled by elves and guaranteed to match any outfit. One minute she's cleaning out the grease traps; a pair of shoes later, she's shaking her groove thing with the prince himself, wearing a nifty new outfit and holding the keys to a turbocharged pumpkin.

"I bet nobody ever told old Cindy they're just a pair of shoes," Carly grumbled as she marched across the TimeCode parking lot. She'd spent a good part of her morning and a sizable chunk of change at the Nordstrom shoe department. Hoping to re-create some bipedal magic, she'd returned to the same store and the same salesman who had sold her the original lucky shoes. She was putting it all down on black this time; high-heeled, pointy-toed, with an elaborate hand-beaded trim.

TimeCode was winding down for the day when Carly pushed through the front doors. She showed up a little early, hoping to have a few minutes alone with Dex before Evan and his badass, bad attitude self showed up. The kid who ran the espresso bar in the lounge was still there, so she snagged herself a ridiculously large cup of coffee before entering the studio.

Dex had his feet up on the console and was watching a pack of handsome young men on bicycles pump madly up a hill somewhere in France.

"Hey, sunshine." He muted the sound on the monitor and checked his watch. "You're early."

"I know." She took a seat at the producer's desk. "I wanted to talk to you before the session."

"Yeah?" He pulled his feet off the console and scooted his chair up to hers.

"Dex, did you tell Evan we were together?"

A little-boy grin flashed across his face. He'd hooked quite a few women with that grin. "He told you, huh?"

"Why did you do that?" she said in absolute disbelief.

He shrugged off his crime easily. "I thought it might help keep him from jumping all over you if he thought we had a thing."

"A thing," she said woodenly.

"Besides, I don't like the way he looks at you."

"Huh?"

"Like he wants to bend you over and—"

"Aaack!" Carly put her hands over her ears and began to belt out the national anthem as she watched his lips move. She did not want to discuss Evan and sex, even hypothetical sex, with Dex.

He waved a hand in front of her face.

She stopped singing and put her hands down.

"Anyway," he continued slyly, "you get the picture."

Mouth shut tight, she shook her head emphatically. "I understand you were just trying to look out for me, Dex. And it's really sweet of you to try, but I don't think this was the way to do it. I mean, maybe Evan thinking we've got, well, a thing makes him think we're ganging up on him. You know?"

"So what do you want me to do? Tell him we're not together?"

"Yes. No. I mean . . . Crap, I don't know." She paced around the room, her brain clicking through possible scenarios. Having Dex take his words back would only add to Evan's suspicions. But acting like they had a relationship wouldn't do, either. Ignoring it was hardly a solution, but it was all she had at the moment.

"It's too late to take anything back," she finally said. "I think maybe it's better if we just play it cool. From now on, we should be more businesslike around him. More professional. No more joking around. That seems to piss him off."

"Everything pisses him off," he pointed out.

She stopped in front of his chair. "Just trust me on this, okay, Dex? I think it'll make things go easier."

He stood up and caressed her cheek with his thumb. "Okay, sunshine. It's your call. I don't give a damn about Evan or this project anymore. The only reason I'm still doing it is for you."

Forget covering her ears, Carly wanted to drop down the nearest mine shaft and seal it up behind her. What next?

"Hello, lovebirds," Evan said with saccharine sweetness as he walked in. "No lap dancing until the session's over, okay?"

Dex dropped his hand away from Carly's face slowly and gave Evan a smug smile.

The video consisted of black and white stills of a young Arlene, her blond hair swept back, dressed to the nines. In photo after photo she was either singing in front of a band or on the arm of a stylishly dressed man. Carly's voice, layered with an instrumental track, played over the sequence.

"Arlene spent two years in Chicago going from club to club. She switched bands five times and boyfriends just as often. Despite her inability to stay committed to either bands or men, she never lacked for suitors."

The video paused.

"It's still rough right now, but that's pretty much the feel I want for all of it," Evan explained. "Do you know what I mean?"

She nodded. "Yeah, I do. Straight but with just a touch of bluesiness? Not too dry. Enough personality to make it go."

"Yes, that's it exactly. I want to redo a few lines, then we can go on to new stuff." He handed her a new set of scripts.

"All right." She entered the booth relieved that Evan had been nothing but business that night. Perhaps things might work after all. She was more than a little excited after viewing what they'd done so far. If the rest of the documentary were as good, she might consider more narration projects. Just not with Evan.

Narration was different from the frenetic dialogue work on cartoons and from the short, intense recording sprints of commercials. The pacing was more leisurely, allowing her the luxury of a slower buildup, a more thoughtful approach. This was marathon work that exercised different mental and physical muscles. Carly caught herself more than once really enjoying herself and wishing that the circumstances were different. If she had been a willing participant from the start, she wondered, would things with Evan have been better? Maybe even been good?

Nah! Who the hell was she kidding?

Working with Evan would never be a piece of cake. He was a regular little dictator. Nothing and no one was going to tell him what to do. Especially someone as artistically amoral as Carly Beck, huckster of tropical breeze–scented rug and room deodorizer. He'd rather eat dirt.

Despite the feeling that she was being escorted to the principal's office, she didn't argue when Evan insisted on walking her out to her car. She had been vacillating all week about telling him about Jessie Klumph. The rebellious part of her wanted to get the scoop and throw it in Evan's face. The part of her that actively monitored her retirement plan thought otherwise.

"I've found Jessie Klumph," she said without preamble when they'd reached her car.

"Bravo," he said tonelessly. "Who the hell is Jessie Klumph?"

"Jessie Klumph," she repeated, surprised that he didn't recognize the name immediately, "Arlene Barlow's old roommate when she was living in New York. The choreographer."

"Oh, her," he said unenthusiastically.

"She teaches a swing dance class in Hollywood,"

Carly said, proud of her find. "I'm going this Saturday night to talk to her. Maybe she might know something."

"Trying to prop up your Barlow-Silver marriage theory?"

"Sure, why not? Won't know if I don't ask, now will I?"

He shook his head. "Bad idea."

"Why?" she snapped. "Because it wasn't yours? Well, you can't stop me from going and you can't stop me from asking."

He shook his head, pressing his lips together in his trademark way. "I'm going with you," he finally said.

"I've already got a date," she shot back.

"Call it off."

"I can't do that."

"Are you researching or not?" He wrapped his hand around her wrist and pulled her close. "Work or play, Carly? Which is it?"

She snatched her arm away and stepped back. "What's with you? Just a minute ago you told me it was a dumb idea. First you make fun of my plan, now you tell me I'm not taking it seriously."

"It's my film." His voice took on a hard edge. "I've worked my ass off for two years on this project. Don't think I'm just going to let you blithely waltz in and screw things up. I don't trust you. Why the hell do you need a date anyway?"

She threw up her hands. "It's a dance class, you idiot! I'd bring Odin but he's got two more feet than I need."

"Fine. What time do I pick you up?"

* * *

It was martini and manicure night. Once a month, Carly and Dana met up at the Beauty Bar in Hollywood to dish or to drown their sorrows while inhaling alcohol and nail polish fumes. The bar was outfitted like a retro hair salon with vintage vinyl seats along one wall, each with its own clear plastic hair-dryer dome. The color scheme was sea-foam green and shell pink, the walls imbedded with silver glitter. In one corner were a couple of manicurist stations and a woman painting henna tattoos. A DJ spun dance tunes in the back and, of course, there was a bar that served up a dozen flavors of martinis.

Dana had a head start on her first martini and was getting a manicure when Carly arrived. Carly waved and headed for the bar.

"What'll it be?" The bartender wore a red and white football jersey with the number sixty-nine on it.

"Martini and a manicure, please. Make it a watermelon." Carly slid her money across the counter.

A few minutes later, Carly sat with Dana at the hair dryers while the bigger-than-life blonde waited for her nails to dry and Carly waited for her turn with a manicurist.

"So how goes the quest for shoes?"

Carly glanced down at her new shoes. So far, the beaded black heels had accompanied her to a couple of auditions and to a cartoon session where she had a recurring role as Princess Ninja Dragonfire, and nothing truly fortuitous had happened, but nothing really bad had happened either. Maybe that was good enough.

"Not so good. Still dreaming of Gumby."

"Fucking Gumby."

"No kidding. It's been a tough week." She sipped her drink and launched into the blow-by-blow description of the last two sessions with Evan plus the *Critters* and *Mr. Bert* bombshells.

"There'll be other shows."

"Let's hope so." Carly clinked her glass to Dana's. "So what do you make of the Dex situation?"

"Oh, Dex," Dana said, sipping her martini.

"What do you mean, 'Oh, Dex'?"

"Don't be dense, Carly. He's had a big-time stiffy for you for freaking ages."

She was incredulous. "You knew this and you didn't tell me?"

"Geez, Carly. You'd have to be Helen Keller not to notice."

"How long has he had this . . ." Carly paused and made a face.

"Stiffy? Oh, I don't know. Since you guys went to Hawaii."

"I thought he was going for the waves."

"I think he was hoping for a different kind of body surfing." Dana drained her glass and stood. "You want another round?"

"Sure," Carly said dejectedly. Fishing out the maraschino cherry from her glass, she held the vivid fruit aloft by its stem. "Do you think this counts as dinner?"

Dana thought about it for a moment. "You have to chew it, so yeah, I'd say it counts."

"Ask for two cherries then, please."

Carly picked out a new shade of polish while she waited for her friend to return. 158A was a sweet pink memory and Scarlet Fever had taken its place.

The manicurist was working on the final coat by the time Dana made it back from the bar.

"I need you to do me a favor," Carly said as she watched the henna lady paint an evil eye on the back of a woman's neck.

"Sure. What?"

"I need you to go on a date for me."

"How long do you think that lasts for?" Dana asked, also watching the tattoo artist.

"Don't know. A week, maybe?"

Dana sipped her drink. "Why can't you go on your own date?"

"Because I've got another date."

"And that's a problem?" she asked innocently.

"For me, yes," Carly sighed. "I was supposed to take this swing dance class tomorrow night to meet the teacher, Jessie Klumph, Arlene Barlow's old roommate, and I asked my friend Glen to go. When I told Evan, he insisted that I had to go with him because he doesn't trust me to talk to her on my own."

They watched a burly guy in chaps and a black mesh T-shirt get his nails painted a stunning shade of metallic blueberry.

"I doubt it's the teacher Evan doesn't trust you with," Dana said. "What's this Glen person look like?"

"Tall, gorgeous, built, brown hair, melting brown eyes." Carly thought about his landscaping business. "Outdoorsy."

"Hmmm." Dana was intrigued but not quite hooked. "Maybe."

An hour later, Carly and Dana were in a Yellow Cab slipping through the Cahuenga Pass, the notch in the Hollywood Hills between Hollywood and Burbank.

"Okay. I'll do it," Dana said suddenly, only slightly slurring her words.

"Do what?" Carly hadn't drunk nearly as much as Dana, so she had a hard time following the conversation.

Dana tried to roll her eyes but they were slightly out of sync. "Go on your date. Anything I should know about my date other than he's tall, dark, and handsome?"

"Yeah," Carly said, "he's gay."

Evan arrived just a few minutes before Glen and Dana. He looked almost relaxed in his khakis and crisp cotton shirt. His hair was still a little bit damp from a shower and Carly had to resist the urge to bury her nose in his open collar and take a deep hit of Evan heaven. Instead, she shoved an oatmeal cookie into his mouth. Excitement about meeting Jessie Klumph had her spending excess energy baking. To her relief, Evan just ate the cookie and headed for the refrigerator in search of cold milk.

Sitting at the table, in front of a plate of cookies and a glass of milk, Evan looked almost happy. Fresh-baked cookies, a potent peacemaking tool. Carly was convinced that even the most hardened barbarian would lay aside his cudgel and take a momentary break from pillaging and plundering to savor a just-from-the-oven cookie. Evan the Horrible, it seemed, was not immune.

The doorbell rang and Evan's grumpy face reasserted itself. Carly hoped she'd made enough cookies as she headed to the door to greet her friends.

"Evan," she said pleasantly, escorting her guests into the kitchen, "Dana and Glen are here. They're going to the class with us."

"Hi, Dana." He stood and hugged her. He offered his hand to Glen, who shook it warmly. "Nice to meet you."

"We should go," Carly said, popping cookies into Dana's and Glen's mouths like corks. "Don't want to be late."

Dana and Glen were driving in his Porsche Roadster, so Carly headed to her car, keys in hand. Evan followed, finishing his last cookie along the way. She unlocked the doors and took a minute to admire the Audi, giving the roof a little caress. Out of the corner of her eye, she caught Evan making a face.

"Just get in the car," she ordered. He had no idea how long it took her to save for that car and she wasn't about to tell him. Instead, she settled herself behind the wheel, put her seat belt on, and waited for him to do the same.

He didn't. He just sat in his seat for a moment with a quizzical look on his face and then, suddenly, he grinned.

"It smells like leather and . . ."

"Gardenias," she said, finishing his sentence. Carly often picked a blossom on the way out to the car, preferring the midnight scent of fresh gardenias over cardboard pine tree.

Leaning toward her, his face inches from her neck, he breathed her in.

"And sex."

She felt the heat of his words wash over her skin and nearly creamed her panties. Having hot, screaming, hip-grinding sex in her car had been a long-running and persistent fantasy since the day she drove the car out of the dealership parking lot. So far it was still only a dream.

"Ever have sex in here, Carly?" he said, pinning her with an I-got-what-you-need look.

That time she did cream her panties.

"Get out," she said, pointing to the door. She released her seat belt, letting it snap back with a *whoosh,* and stumbled out of the car while she still had all her clothes on. She hurried over to his truck and waited for him to follow.

Evan ambled up to her, still grinning, still teasing. "Okay, I'll drive."

It was going to be a long night.

"I take it that was your date," Evan said as he propelled his truck onto the Hollywood Freeway, merging at seventy miles an hour, snatching a space no bigger than a gasp between two SUVs. "You two could make a beautiful shampoo commercial together. Does Dex know about him?"

"Dex and I aren't together."

"Just in the biblical sense, then."

Carly wished mightily for the power to smite Evan at that moment. Plague and pestilence wouldn't be bad, either.

When they arrived, the club was already humming with people wearing everything from athletic gear and tank tops to vintage suits and dresses. At the front door they paid the class fees and had their hands stamped. Carly pushed their way toward the stage in hopes of getting a moment with Jessie before class, but the choreographer was busy talking to the DJ.

Jessie, who must have been in her seventies but looked younger, had carroty colored hair, lips, and nails. She wore wide-legged navy trousers and a brightly printed short sleeve blouse, tied at the waist. Chunky red and black Bakelite jewelry accented her wrists and earlobes.

"Welcome, everybody," Jessie said into the microphone, her voice cigarette-husky with a slight New York accent. She was joined onstage by a handsome young black man in a sharp blue suit. "I'm Jessie and this is Daryl. Are you ready to dance?"

The audience whooped and a few regulars called out greetings.

"All right, everyone grab a partner and fan out."

The moment Evan took her hand, Carly knew she was in trouble. They were going to spend the next hour in close contact, very close contact. Touching, bumping, sliding. This was going to be torture. Hellish, sweaty, rapturous torture.

They practiced the steps, Carly trying to stay as far away as possible, Evan closing the gap at every opportunity. He let his thighs and hips brush against hers with appalling frequency. His hands held her firmly, caressing her skin whenever possible. Carly could barely hear the music over the frantic howling of her own libido.

Evan's body bumped up against hers and she jumped back, almost pulling him off balance.

"I'm driving," he reminded her, reeling her back into his arms tightly.

"You're not driving," she huffed. "You're pushing your luck."

"No, babe," Evan said. He smiled like sin itself, came to an abrupt stop, and pulled her right up against him, his hand cupping her derriere, raising her slightly off her feet. "*This* is pushing my luck."

They were pressed together, nipples to kneecaps and everything in between. And there was definitely one big thing in between. Despite the fact that women her age never have heart attacks, she definitely felt one coming on. Holy moly, she hadn't been this excited the last time she'd had sex. For that matter, she'd never been this excited about sex, period.

The music stopped, but Evan still didn't let go. A drop of sweat rolled down his gorgeous neck and Carly had to clamp her jaw shut to keep her tongue from darting out to lick it off. Turning away from the temptation, she looked across the club and found Dana and Glen avidly watching them. They both had matching "Oh, aren't they cute?" expressions on their faces as if they were watching kittens cavorting in a pet shop window.

"Time to change partners," Carly said, breaking loose.

She walked drunkenly toward the bathroom, even though she'd drunk nothing but mineral water all night. What she really needed was to sit down and put her head between her knees, but she settled for patting her face with a moistened paper towel.

"Bet I could fry an egg on your forehead," Dana said to Carly's flushed reflection. She'd followed Carly into the bathroom. Dana licked her fingertip, placed it on the top of her friend's head, and imitated the sound of sizzling.

Carly left Dana grinning like a Halloween pumpkin and headed to the bar, where Glen was having
a drink with Evan. Without a word, she drank down
Glen's gin and tonic and pulled him onto the
dance floor as a new song started up. "All of Me"
was a plaintive ballad that let them talk without having to yell.

"So that's the guy you dumped me for, huh?"
Glen said, pretending to be hurt before giving her
a sly smile. "I can't say I blame you one bit. What is
that line? Mad, bad, and dangerous to know? I'd
have slept with him in a heartbeat."

"Glen!" Carly's voice rose high above the music.

Evan looked over Dana's shoulder and glowered
at them from across the dance floor. Glen chuckled
to himself.

"I guess Dana told you everything," Carly grumbled and tried to edge them away from Evan and
Dana. "Some friend."

"Don't be too hard on her. She only told me because she thought I knew. I told her I'd seen the
contract." A frantically exuberant couple, who
danced as if they were slipping on banana peels,
swept across the dance floor toward them. Glen
deftly maneuvered Carly out of the way. Then suddenly he whirled her around, snapped her against
him with a flourish, and dipped her backward before righting her to resume the normal dance
steps.

"Uh, Glen," she asked after catching her breath,
"what are you doing?"

"Just giving our bad boy something to think
about."

Carly thought of all the other times in her life

when she would have been over-the-moon ecstatic about being held by not one but two outrageously handsome men in the same night. Why now? Why did one have to be Evil Evan and the other Gay Glen?

"Don't antagonize him," Carly warned. "He's already mad at me half the time as it is. And he's not 'our' bad boy."

Glen did the spin, squeeze, and tilt move again. "Oh, but he wants to be."

Evan was not happy. Dana was yapping in his ear while he continued to keep a bead on Glen and Carly. The look on his face was probably one of the driving forces behind the five-day waiting period for gun ownership.

"C'mon, Glen," Carly pleaded as she eyed Evan nervously. "Stop kidding around. I mean it."

Glen released her from his intimate embrace. "Just taking the temperature. I say you should have a fling."

She snorted. "I prefer to fling with someone who likes me."

"Don't be too sure, Carly," he said. "I thought Quinn couldn't stand me, either, but he gave me a landscaping job even though he claimed he didn't like anything I did. One day we're reenacting the Civil War in the front yard over the agapanthus and gazanias, the next day I'm moving in."

"Unbelievable." She had trouble envisioning her agent arguing over anything as domestic as flower beds and steer manure. "But it's different with Evan. He really doesn't like me."

"Hmmm," Glen said, unconvinced. "I think you should have the wedding at our place. The rose arbor looks best in May. Do you think you could wait a year?"

Carly wondered if introducing Glen and Dana to each other was such a good idea. They both seemed to share the same blatant disregard for reality.

"There's jasmine climbing through the Cecile Brunner roses," he said, lost in his landscaping vision. "Very romantic . . ."

Chapter Ten

Carly managed to buttonhole the choreographer at the end of the lesson. With Evan following right behind, she finagled a few minutes of Jessie's time outside the club, explaining quickly that she wanted to talk to her about Arlene Barlow for a documentary.

"Honey, everybody wants to know about Arlene," Jessie said as she lit up a cigarette.

"You must admit it's intriguing, her vanishing into thin air," Carly said. "People just don't do that."

"Most people, yeah. But Arlene was different. You couldn't talk her out of a burning house. I'm sure she had her reasons."

"Any idea what those reasons were?" Carly could feel the heat of Evan's body enveloping her as he stood close behind.

Jessie blew out smoke and laughed. "It coulda been anything. That's just how she was."

Carly hid her disappointment. "What about her and Pete Silver? Can you tell me anything about their relationship?"

"Nope." Jessie twisted her foot up and put out her half-finished cigarette on the sole of her shoe without losing her balance. She flicked the crushed cigarette into the gutter. "Arlene and me, we kept different schedules. I mighta met him maybe once or twice. Wouldn't know him from Adam, really."

"Well, thank you." Carly shook the woman's hand. "I appreciate you answering my questions."

"Sure. You kids going back in? You could practice your moves." Her last comment was aimed over Carly's head at Evan.

"No, thank you," Carly said. "I think we'll head home."

Jessie gave Evan the once-over. "I don't blame you, sweetheart. I'm kinda partial to the strong, silent type myself." She adjusted her bracelets and headed back into the club.

"Well," Carly said, stepping away from Evan, "you weren't much help."

"You seemed to have all the bases covered." He took her arm, aiming for the parking lot.

"I want to say good-bye to Dana and Glen before we go."

He made a sour face at the mention of Glen's name. "Where'd you meet that guy?"

"At a spa."

"Figures. Which one of you was wearing the towel?"

Carly was still feeling a little deflated when Evan parked the truck in front of her house.

"What's that?" he said, looking at her left shoulder.

Carly slapped her hand over her upper arm. "Nothing."

He peeled her hand away and pushed the sleeve of her dress back. "Doesn't look like nothing."

"It's just a henna tattoo. Dana insisted I get it. It's not permanent."

"What's it say?" He leaned closer than necessary to see the writing. "'What if . . . ?' What's that supposed to mean?"

The words were written in fancy script with lots of baroque curlicues around it.

Carly brushed his hand away. "It's just a crazy idea Dana had. She said it was thought-provoking or something like that."

"You always do what Dana tells you to do?"

"Only when I'm drinking." She made a mental note to stick to a one-martini maximum next time she was out with her friend.

"It does make one think," he finally agreed. Evan skimmed the tips of his fingers across the words written on her skin as he read them out loud. "What if . . . ?"

She had to fight a shiver that was quickly rippling its way up her spine. He was using that voice again, the one that she imagined hypnotists used to mesmerize their subjects into taking their clothes off. It was a pretty compelling voice. She was probably wearing too many clothes as it was.

"What if . . . ?" he whispered as he moved his head closer to hers. "What if I kissed you, Carly Beck?"

She couldn't answer because he was kissing her, answering his own question. His mouth moved slowly and smoothly over hers, coaxing and teasing her lips until she opened for him, kissing him as deeply as he was kissing her.

"Good question," she said, breaking contact.

He pulled her close for another kiss. A memory flashed brightly in her head of herself as a child on the backyard swing, pushing herself higher and higher, exhilarated and scared spitless, until she was practically parallel with the ground. Carly wrapped her arms around Evan tightly, hanging on as she did then, wondering how high she could go. All the way around? What if . . . ?

"I'll have to think about it," she said, pulling back, disengaging herself from his embrace.

"I've changed soaps," he said in that persuasive voice of his. "Ivory, just like you said."

She filed that fact away for consideration. Then decided a change of subject was in order. "Sorry the Jessie Klumph thing turned out to be a waste of time."

He wasn't perturbed. "I expected that going in."

"Thanks for the vote of confidence," she said, miffed.

"No, I talked to her on the phone ages ago."

"What?" she yelped, staring at him in astonishment. "Why didn't you say so? Why did you let me go to all this trouble?"

"I thought you might as well play detective and get it out of your system."

"Get it out of my system?! Why, you patronizing piece of—"

"Don't," he said coldly, cutting her off. "I've been making documentaries for years. It's what I do. I don't expect to suddenly get behind the microphone and make my living doing voiceovers just because I watched you do it once. Don't you think you're being a little patronizing yourself, thinking, in two days you can dig up what I've been looking for for two years?"

"Maybe I was being naive and probably a lot optimistic." Carly ground her words out through her teeth. "But that was it. You didn't have to go out of your way to rub my nose in it. I don't know why you get such a kick out of pointing out my mistakes, Evan. Get yourself a new hobby!"

She stormed out of the truck and slammed the door. When she got to the back door, she slammed that, too. Humiliated, angry, and tired, Carly headed for the shower. She shampooed, soaped, and scrubbed her tensions away, but despite vigorous attempts at washing, the tattoo stayed. Eyeing it dejectedly in the mirror, she considered having "What if . . . ?" replaced with "Fuhgedaboudit!"

The next morning Carly awoke feeling nervous and twitchy. At breakfast she studied the cat, but Odin was his usual laid-back self. He wasn't going apeshit the way he was supposed to prior to a natural disaster, so she figured that an earthquake wasn't pending. By late afternoon, when nothing had happened, she chalked it up to post-Evan weirdness.

It wasn't quite a natural disaster—there was no loss of life or limb, FEMA wasn't coming to assess the situation, and the Red Cross was not going to be setting up an aid station. Certainly not the worst thing that could happen. It was just another symptom of the disintegration of her happy life.

Silver, her precious Audi, was no longer a virgin. The ignominious event happened in the Hollywood post office parking lot, which to Carly made it a federal offense. After standing in line for forty-five minutes and buying enough stamps to make sure she wouldn't need to go back for at least a year, Carly walked out to the parking lot to find that Silver's cherry had been popped.

Right across the passenger door was a deep dent as long as Carly's arm. The assailant left streaks of green paint in and around the dent. Furiously, Carly scanned the lot for any suspicious green cars. The only one was an immaculate vintage BMW. Not the culprit, but she gave it a dirty look anyway for being offensively green and unscathed.

Still reeling from the crime on the drive home, Carly almost ran over her kooky neighbor, Jensen, who was out walking his dog, Megabyte, in the middle of the street. There were very few streetlights on her block and, absurdly, he was dressed in black to match his black dog. He was also wearing night-vision glasses. Blinded by the headlights he froze in his tracks while his dog (certainly the more savvy of the pair) tried to pull him to safety.

"Jensen, you moron!" Carly yelled and honked the horn as she swerved around him.

Happy for any kind of female recognition, Jensen merely waved. Embarrassed, the rottweiler headed for home.

Carly parked in her driveway and rested her chin on the steering wheel. Like many times before in her life, she could hear the universe snickering.

"Aloha." It was midnight in LA, eight o'clock Hawaii time, when Beck called. "How's my teeny wahine?"

"I'm baking." Carly popped a muffin tray in the oven and set the timer.

"Uh-oh. You want to talk about it?" He sounded concerned. Baking itself wasn't bad; baking at midnight was something else.

"Not really," she said. "It's no big deal, just a little car trouble. I'm glad you called. How was the tofu man?"

"Short, fat, and smoked cigars constantly."

"And you wanted me to date him," she said accusingly.

"I'll do better next time," he chuckled. "How'd the Jessie Klumph interview go?"

"She was interesting but it was basically a bust."

"Behold the world of journalism," he said dramatically. "It's not easy, but you do meet a lot of incredible, unusual people."

"That's for sure." She thought about Evan. He was an incredible jerk and unusually difficult.

"So what's the director like? Good to work with?"

"Yes and no," she said, hesitating. "He's really talented, but he's also a total perfectionist, a real control freak. I'd say we get along like oil and water, but we're more like bleach and ammonia. Mix us together in a room and someone's gonna die."

"Just make sure that someone's not you," Beck warned.

"Don't worry, Dad. I've got my gas mask on. And it's turning out to be an interesting project in any case. I just wish that I could prove that Arlene married Pete."

"Well, maybe you'll do better with this lead. I finally tracked down my notes on the music royalty

article I did and came up with a phone number for
Raymond Barlow, Arlene's brother."

"Dad, that's fantastic! Where is he?"

"Barlow's living out his geezerhood in Twentynine Palms. You know, north of Palm Springs. He's
been living there for the last ten years under the
name James Raymond."

"Dad, you're beyond fantastic."

"Anything for my girl," he said.

No one was home at the Raymond Barlow residence, not even an answering machine. Carly had
been trying all morning. She had the number pro-
grammed on the speed dial and automatically hit it
whenever she had a free moment. While killing
time shopping for cat food at Petco between auditions, she tried again.

"Hello?" an elderly voice croaked. He sounded
about the right age to be Raymond.

Standing in the cat toy aisle holding a bag of cat-
nip, she started her campaign. "Yes, hello. My name
is Carly Beck and—"

"Young lady, if you're trying to sell me something, I'm not buying," he said sternly. Then he
continued in a lighter tone. "But if you're still game
to talk to me, I'm willing to listen."

"No, no! I don't want to sell you anything." A
woman with an asthmatic bulldog came up next to
her while carrying on a high-pitched animated conversation with her pet.

"You sure?" he asked suspiciously.

"Absolutely." Carly wheeled her squeaky cart over
to the next aisle and wondered how good his hear-

ing was. "I'm looking for Raymond Barlow. Would that be you?"

"I could be him."

A heavyset man with a beer gut and a big green parrot on his shoulder lumbered her way.

"Well, as I said, my name is Carly Beck." The parrot gave an incredibly loud and lifelike imitation of a belch, then lifted its tail and pooped.

"What's that?"

"Carly Beck," she repeated. "I'm working on a documentary on the life of Arlene Barlow, the singer. I'm trying to track down people who knew her and would be available for an interview." Carly made her way to the small-animal section of the store.

"So you're making a film, eh?" he said cautiously.

"I'm one of the participants, yes," Carly said, side-stepping the issue. "I'm doing the narration, among other things. Evan McLeish is heading the project."

A pair of kids ran past her, shrieking like Halloween ghouls, as one terrorized the other with a squirming handful of garter snake. Carly shuddered and aimed for the fish tanks.

"Quite a few people have already given interviews," she said, hoping to assuage his fears as fish tanks bubbled around her. "G. G. Taylor, Cecil Monroy, Royce Blankenship . . . Jessie Klumph."

"Never heard of her," he said flatly.

"She was an old roommate of Ms. Barlow's."

"Don't say?" he said, clearly not impressed. "But you got G. G. and Cecil, that's impressive," he conceded.

"Clinton Pace, too," she crowed, stealing undeserved credit.

"Heh!" His laugh crackled like cellophane. "I take it you want an interview with Raymond Barlow?"

"It would be nice," she said timidly. This was probably not how they solicited for interviews at CNN.

"I'm going to have to think about it."

"I understand." Obscene snuffling and demonic snorting mixed with happy squeals indicated the woman and her bulldog were back.

"Exactly what kind of movies do you make?" he asked suddenly.

"Documentaries," she assured him, fleeing the disharmonic duo. "Only documentaries. Let me give you my number, Mr. Barlow."

She left the pet store elated but anxious. By Raymond Barlow's reaction, she figured that Evan hadn't spoken with him previously. After her Jessie Klumph fiasco, Carly wanted to make certain that she had a sure thing before going to Evan. Now that she'd sort of passed herself off as his representative, the idea was starting to look less brilliant. More of a blunder, actually.

Firsthand experience had taught her that Evan wasn't interested in her help. Any attempt at assistance on her part was perceived as meddling of the Scooby-Doo variety.

With a heavy sense of doom that had recently become her constant companion, she exited the final audition of the day and handed her ticket stub to the valet.

"What's that?" he said, pointing down.

Carly had parrot poop on her shoe. She stared in

disgust at the huge birdie bombshell on the toe of her brown linen flats.

"Wite-out?"

"Yeah, right," he laughed, as he went to retrieve her car. A few minutes later he pulled it up. "That was already here when you drove up," the guy said, pointing to the new dent.

"I know," she said sadly, patting the car's fender. "I know."

"I'm every woman . . . it's all in meeeeeeee!"

Singing softly under her breath, Carly tried to shore up her sagging spirits as she drove to the studio. Although no amount of positive thinking and feel-good songs was going to have as much power to change her circumstances as her lucky shoes, she was ready to try anything.

"I'm walking on sunshine! Woo hoo!"

Unfortunately, no matter how she started it, the words of every song seemed to inevitably turn into "I'm a loser baby, so why don't you kill me?"

She wondered if, in some way, the bad fortune that was hers could somehow rub off on those close to her. Maybe Evan's blackmail scheme would come back to haunt him by torpedoing the film he was endeavoring to make better. It was a thought that brought her little satisfaction. While the idea of a woeful and miserable Evan was quite heartwarming, a ruined film was not.

Carly waited until the session was over and Evan was walking her to her car before she brought up the subject of Raymond. The recording had gone smoothly, no machine breakdowns, no overt shows of affection from Dex, and only minimal sniping between her and Evan. It gave her hope that perhaps Evan would be in such high spirits that he might not take the news too badly. He might even be pleased.

"You did what?" He made a growling noise in the back of his throat. The disgruntled-dog-on-the-other-side-of-the-chain-link-fence sort of growl. Only there was no fence.

Carly stepped out of arm's reach. "I found Raymond Barlow. I spoke to him this afternoon."

"You *spoke* to him." His voice low and menacing. It made his previous growl sound like a mere yip of annoyance.

"I had to make sure I had the right number," she said weakly.

"I can't believe you!" he yelled. "You had absolutely no right to call him."

Carly stepped back. They were within a few feet of his Toyota. Her car was about fifteen feet away—she could probably make a run for it, if she had to. "W-what did you expect me to do? After you rubbed Jessie Klumph in my face, you can hardly expect me to come running to you with every little thing just so you could do it again."

"All I wanted you to do was narrate my film," he said, menace filling his voice. "Then you wanted to help me write it. Now you want to produce it, too. I just wanted to make a simple documentary and now I'm partnered with Ella Freaking Earthworm!" He stepped closer. "I'm starting to think bringing you on was one of the dumbest ideas I've ever had."

"Fine then," she said tartly, stepping back. "Hand over my shoe and we can call it quits."

"You'd like that, wouldn't you?" He took another step forward, sandwiching her against his truck. "No way, lady. You started this, you're going to finish it. Give me the number."

"No." She clutched the briefcase to her chest like a shield.

He leaned harder, pinning her in place with his body. "No?"

She shook her head, nervous but determined. "Not until you move back and apologize for being so nasty to me."

Incredulously, he stared down at her, his eyes sharp, angry shards of blue ice. "You interfere with my film, stick your nose into my business, and you want *me* to apologize?"

Holding her ground, nails gouging crescents into her briefcase, she swallowed. "I-I deserve an apology. That contract doesn't give you the right to insult me. You might not like me, but at least you don't have to—"

"Be so mean?" he said, mocking her in a petulant voice.

"It's hurtful," she said softly, ignoring his sarcasm.

"All right, fine," he relented, his face inches from hers. "I'm sorry I was mean." He held her head steady with both hands and kissed her.

Carly's brain was slower on the uptake than her body, which threw itself into the kiss with unabashed eagerness. It took a few moments for the gray matter to reassume command and convince her lips to pull away and gather up some indignation.

"What do you think you're doing?" she sputtered.

"Apologizing," he said. "I wanted to show I was sincere."

"That wasn't from your heart!"

"The hell it wasn't." He kissed her once again, hard and fast, blindsiding her brain again and flooding her senses with undiluted pleasure. "Now are you going to give me the number?"

Carly gave him a shove that accomplished nothing. "Let go of me first."

He scrutinized her face. "Okay," he said and stepped back.

It was then, as the ground rushed up to greet her, that Carly realized her knees had gone weak. She managed to catch herself on the truck, and using it to lean against, slowly slid her body up to its original locked, upright position.

He grinned. "You said 'let go.'"

"I know what I said!" She found her father's e-mail, threw it at him, and walked to her car with as much dignity as she could muster. "You're a creep, Evan McLeish! A low-down creep."

"Hey," he called after her. "That contract doesn't give you the right to insult me."

Friday's schedule was a bleak, empty page, without so much as a library book due to relieve the monotony, so Carly spent the day shopping for a Father's Day gift. She left her phone on but refused to answer unless it was Quinn. She was not feeling particularly sociable since she was still kicking herself for her inept handling of the Raymond Barlow imbroglio.

It galled her that, without her and her dad, Evan

would never have gotten the chance to talk to Raymond, and now she wasn't even going to be a part of the interview if Evan could help it. She was persona non grata into the next century.

Carly had no doubt that Evan would get his interview. The notes and references in the folder he'd given her showed how successful he could be at getting people to participate in his film, although it was doubtful that he resorted to the strong-arm tactics that he'd used with her. One thing was for certain, Evan didn't need a good luck charm to get what he wanted. Smart, tenacious, talented, and handsome, he didn't need luck. The only thing he didn't have was money.

Settling herself in the old leather thinking chair, she ran down the list of calls to return. Evan had left the most messages, but she put him last on the list anyway. Unfortunately, returning calls didn't take nearly as long as she expected or wanted, and before long she found herself dialing Evan's number.

"Where the hell have you been?" he snapped. "I've been trying to reach you all day."

Carly pulled the phone away from her ear, wincing. "Maybe I should call back later."

"No, no, don't hang up," he said quickly, trying to control his temper. "What are you doing tomorrow?"

"Where have I been? What am I doing tomorrow? You're worse than Quinn. You should be an agent."

"Just answer the question," he said tightly.

"I was going to get my car smogged."

"Do it Sunday. Tomorrow you're going with me to Twentynine Palms to interview Raymond Barlow."

"I am?" she squealed. Odin came running in

from the kitchen to see what all the commotion was about—maybe she'd found a bag of mice krispies stashed behind the seat cushion. Carly picked him up and danced around the room. "Oh my God, this is fabulous!"

"Settle down," Evan said in ominous tones. "Raymond seems to think that you're a key member of this project for some reason."

"Really?" she said innocently and crossed her fingers.

"Yes, really," he said snidely. "He insists that you have to be there for the interview."

Yes! Carly danced around a little more with Odin, rocking him back and forth in her arms. The cat endured, stoically paying the price for unconditional love and never-ending bowls of kibble.

"Don't think that because he thinks you're important that I think you're important."

"I know," she said, her enthusiasm undimmed. "You hate me."

Chapter Eleven

The morning emerged hard-edged and brittle. It was only eight and already hot enough to blister paint. The sun was laser-bright, knifing through the slits in the bedroom blinds, landing in brilliant, glittering pieces on the glossy hardwood floor. Most of the city's population would head west that day, straight into the Pacific. Carly and Evan were going east to the desert.

Carly slathered sunscreen on her bare arms and legs. On a day like this one, anyone, not just vampires, was liable to go up in flames. Makeup was a minimum of lipstick and mascara; anything else would melt off in the heat. She wore sandals and a short-sleeve dress that covered the fading remains of her tattoo. Next time, not that there would be a next time, but just in case, she'd get the tattoo on her butt.

She went to the kitchen and set her tote bag by the back door. Perhaps, she thought hopefully, he's feeling more mellow today. The obnoxious blare of a car horn outside her house said differently. He was early. Quickly, Carly grabbed her tote and flew out the door before Evan could feel the need to hit the horn again and offend her neighbors.

She sprinted down her driveway and scrambled into the passenger seat of his Toyota. He hadn't even bothered to pull the truck to the curb; he just sat there idling in the middle of the street, quite prepared to take off without her if she wasn't out fast enough.

"Hi," she said cheerfully. Come heat or Gila monsters, she would try to be agreeable even if Evan refused to be. She was excited about this interview. The thought that they might be able to find out exactly what happened to Arlene Barlow caught her imagination, lifting her spirits high. She wanted to know.

Evan grunted a greeting as he looked her up and down. She waited for the inevitable smart remark, but instead he drove along in silence. Once on the freeway, Carly offered Evan a homemade muffin as a peace offering. He took it with a spare nod of what she presumed was thanks. That was a good sign. Anything short of brandishing a weapon was cause for celebration.

They zigzagged away from Los Angeles, east on the 134 freeway to the southbound 5, and east again on the 10, through Pomona, San Bernardino, and on toward the desert. The temperature rose steadily as a procession of garish billboards promised model homes, strip clubs, and car dealerships up ahead.

Over an hour had passed when they reached the sprawling outlet mall at Cabazon. It showed up like a mirage in the empty desert, followed by Hadley's, famous for its gritty but pleasant date shakes, then Casino Morongo with its towering hotel. Finally there were the dinosaurs, two of 'em, rising several stories above the landscape. A gargantuan apatosaurus and a tyrannosaurus rex stood side by side, teeth bared, staring menacingly at the endless stream of cars that whooshed by.

"Ever visit the dinosaurs?" Carly asked as they approached the Flintstonesque tableau. She imagined Fred sliding down the T. rex's back after a hard day at the quarry.

"Nope." Evan didn't even give the overgrown lizards a glance.

"One of them has a gift shop in the tummy." She was tired of the silent treatment.

He had no response.

"They used to let you go up in the Tyrannosaurus's head," she continued hopefully. "But they don't anymore."

Dead air. He was obviously not as tired of the silent treatment as Carly was. She turned her attention to the windmill farms in the San Gorgonio Pass outside of Palm Springs. The rows of white towers, giant sentinels, arms spinning madly, pulled electricity from the hot, dry air.

The desert reclaimed the land as they merged onto Highway 62 and started their climb toward the High Desert. Twentynine Palms awaited them, shimmering in the heat, temporary headquarters of countless Marines and permanent home of endless stands of alien-looking Joshua trees, their bushy arms raised beseechingly toward the heavens.

Carly pulled out a new tin of Altoids from her bag and offered one to Evan. "Curiously strong mint?"

He rolled his eyes tiredly but did take one. Mentally she chalked up another mark under the "good signs" heading. They motored along silently as the scent of peppermint filled the cab.

"Here," Evan said, grudgingly breaking his self-imposed code of silence. He retrieved a sheaf of notes and directions from the door pocket and pushed them toward Carly. "Help me find the place. It's in the middle of nowhere."

Staring out at the lunar landscape of scrubland and boulders, she wanted to say, And this isn't? Instead, she took the roll of navigator, calling out directions and pointing out potholes.

"This is it," she declared as the truck shuddered down yet another rutted dirt road. "His house should be at the end here."

Beige dust billowed out from behind the truck in enormous clouds. She tried to hand Evan back the directions, but he waved them away, too intent on driving. She tucked the papers into her tote bag, very glad they hadn't taken her car.

"Two nuns were bicycling back to the abbey," she said, staring in the visor mirror as she reapplied her lipstick—no small feat as the truck bounced and swayed. "The first nun says she knows a shortcut and turns down a narrow street. The second nun follows, and after a few minutes she says excitedly, 'I've never come this way before!' The first nun replies, 'It's the cobblestones.'"

She turned to Evan and gave him a dazzling smile.

He braked suddenly and Carly was thrown forward in her seat.

"We're here," he said without a hint of amusement.

Carly's head thudded back against the headrest as she wondered what he had against nuns.

* * *

Raymond's home was a dilapidated white trailer, its once-green trim bleached by the unceasing efforts of the blazing California sun. An aluminum awning extended the roofline, creating a carport and patio area. The parking spot was vacant at the moment. Half-buried tires painted white, like giant powdered donuts, trimmed the foundation of the structure. Three wooden steps covered with green plastic outdoor carpeting led up to the front door. Old keys made up a wind chime that hung just in front of the kitchen window.

The hot, parched air was overwhelming after the air-conditioned coolness of the truck, drawing moisture from their lips and sweat from their bodies.

"Let me do the talking," Evan warned as they approached the door. He wore a cream-colored, short-sleeved shirt and cargo shorts. His low-top hiking boots left complicated shoe prints in the dust. "Don't make this more difficult than it already is."

"Got it," she said, honoring her vow to be agreeable. She couldn't help but grin in the face of Evan's grumpiness. The thought that Raymond Barlow might have a clue about Arlene had her almost skipping with excitement.

"Morning." A spry old man with crinkled white hair and a furrowed brown face stepped out of the trailer and down the carpeted steps. He wore a thin yellow golf shirt and dark green golf shorts. "You must be Carly and the film fellow."

Carly smiled and nodded like a bobblehead doll.

Evan held out his hand. "I'm Evan McLeish— we spoke earlier. I want to thank you for doing this interview."

Raymond shook his hand with a firmness that belied his age. "It's my pleasure. Not like I've got a lot going on out here." He made his way to Carly and took her outstretched hand. "Hello, my dear. Cat got your tongue?"

"Oh, no," Carly responded quickly. "I mean, it's nice to meet you, Mr. Barlow. And thank you again for the interview."

"Pish." He waved them toward an outdoor seating arrangement under the awning: a glider, a folding chair, and a cooler that doubled as a table. "Call me Raymond. I'd invite you in but the air conditioning's broke. My son-in-law's gone into town to fetch me a new one. It's hotter than Hades in there. You, my dear, can sit on the glider with me, and you, young fella, can take the chair. Help yourself to a drink from the cooler. I'll have a beer. Hold this thing steady for me, sweetheart."

Carly held the glider still while the old man lowered himself into it. She accepted a soda from Evan and sat next to Raymond.

"Well, now," Raymond said, looking back and forth between Carly and Evan, "how do you two want to do this?"

Evan shot Carly a glance and took over. "I know you wanted to keep this fairly low-key, so I've just brought my camera and a microphone. If you're happy out here, that's fine with me."

"Sounds good to me."

"I'll get set up. It'll only take me a minute."

"Can I help?" Carly asked.

"No," Evan said dismissively. "I'm used to doing this on my own."

She sighed quietly, point taken.

"You just sit right here with me," Raymond assured her. "It's not every day I get to visit with a beautiful girl. Nothing but dust and cactus out here."

"Do you like the desert?" she asked politely.

"It's cheap," he said, sipping his beer. "No crime."

Evan returned carrying a couple of aluminum cases full of gear. He carefully mounted his digital camera on a tripod and set up reflectors around Raymond. The DAT recorder went on top of the cooler. He approached Raymond with a small lava-lier microphone in his hands. "I'm going to clip this on you."

Raymond sat up straight in the glider. "Go right ahead."

Evan attached the mic to Raymond's shirt, then put the headphones on and adjusted the recorder as Raymond talked.

"You two do a lot of these documentaries?"

Carly caught the irritated twitch of Evan's mouth. "No, we don't. Evan makes documentaries and I usually do voiceovers for commercials and car-toons."

"Don't watch cartoons and I usually skip through the commercials. You ever do any singing?"

Evan positioned the folding chair behind the camera, shot some test footage, and tweaked the setup again.

"I can carry a tune, but it's nothing to get excited about."

Raymond wasn't put off. "I play piano sometimes in Palm Springs. Could use me a pretty singer once in a while. You don't need to do much. 'Sides, I can do all the fancy stuff." He pretended to play an imaginary keyboard.

"I'll think about it," she said honestly. After all, a job offer was a job offer. It was nice to be wanted.

"Okay," Evan said from behind the camera. "I'm ready."

"Nice setup you got," Raymond said, staring down at the mic clipped to his shirt and then at the camera. "Everything's so little now. The mics we used were huge. Probably antiques now."

"They still use them," Evan said. "A lot of people prefer the sound you get with those old microphones."

"Don't say?"

"Are you ready?"

"Born ready," the old man answered emphatically.

Evan had Raymond sign a release form before he started recording. "Can you tell me about Arlene's childhood in Ohio?"

Raymond smiled, his teeth shining whitely against his tan skin. "She didn't like the farm much. No, sir. Our father grew corn. Acres and acres of corn just like the neighboring farmers. Arlene couldn't stand corn—refused to eat it after she left home. I miss it, myself. Hard to get good fresh corn nowadays. Just canned or frozen."

The interview continued for over an hour. Raymond didn't have a lot of facts to add to what they already knew, but his firsthand account was important in itself, adding depth and shading to otherwise sketchy areas of Arlene's life. Evan was a skillful interviewer, guiding the process without injecting himself or his personality into it. Carly watched, impressed by Evan's direction and entertained by Raymond's stories and anecdotes even if a lot of them had to do with corn.

"Tell me about the last time you saw or heard from Arlene."

Raymond shifted in his seat, causing the glider to sway a bit. Carly placed her foot firmly on the ground to still the movement. "She'd just got back from Paris. We went out and had a nice steak dinner, baked potato, corn. She'd gone to see Pete, Pete Silver, who was living out there at the time. Arlene was gonna stay for the summer, but she wasn't even gone a month. No surprise there. Those two were always fighting."

Evan took notes discreetly while manning the equipment. "What was your reaction when you realized that she'd disappeared?"

Raymond shrugged. "When Arlene had a mind to do something, she just did it, you know? She wasn't gonna ask permission."

"Any ideas where she might have gone?"

He chuckled. "Could be livin' down the way for all I know."

Evan asked a few more questions before calling an end to the interview and thanking Raymond for his participation.

"Oh, anytime," Raymond said warmly. "I'm not going anywhere."

Evan unclipped Raymond's mic and started breaking down the equipment. "I'll let you know when we have the screening."

"Appreciate it." The old musician turned to Carly and took her hand. "Now, Carly, you gonna sing for me?"

"Oh, Raymond, I'm flattered, honest, but I'm really not a singer. I'm sure you could do so much better."

"Okay, then how about getting married?"

Carly laughed. "Does that line really work?"

He smiled impishly. "Well, I've been married four times."

"Well, good luck on five," she said, giving him a peck on the cheek.

The atmosphere in the truck as they retraced the route back to the highway was much lighter than the drive in. Evan was still not interested in socializing, but he was no longer being icy. He was just being quiet. Carly's head was too full of Raymond's stories to be much interested in talking either.

They were halfway into their descent from the High Desert when Evan suddenly turned onto Indian Avenue toward Palm Springs. He didn't offer an explanation, so Carly was forced to ask for one.

"Where are we going?"

"I need to make a quick stop."

"All right." Carly's stomach growled as she rummaged in her tote bag. She was starving. There was nothing edible left in her bag but a bottled water, a tin of Altoids, and a petrified pack of sugarless gum. Supermodel food but hardly real-life fare.

"Are you hungry?" she asked hopefully, muffling another stomach growl with her bag.

"We can get something after this next stop."

"Great," she sighed with relief. The Altoids tin promised ten calories per three mints. She popped three in her mouth and instantly cleared her sinuses with a blast of peppermint.

Indian Avenue merged with the 111 Highway and became the main road that ran through Palm

Springs. Carly stared longingly at the restaurants and cafes as they drove through town. Water misters hung over the outdoor tables, sending clouds of vapor down to cool and replump the dehydrated diners.

Evan veered off the highway and headed for the outlying part of town where motels and vacation condos gave way to grand single-family residences. They pulled up in front of a lushly landscaped, two-story Spanish-style house with a Mercedes in the driveway. Evan reached behind the seat for a small package. "This should only take a minute."

Carly was curious but knew better than to ask questions. After all, she expected to be lying dead in the desert turning into beef jerky by now.

Ignoring the meandering brick walkway, Evan marched straight across the verdant expanse of grass. The front door was already opening by the time he reached the steps. An older woman dressed in Palm Springs chic—sandals and a linen tunic—stepped out on the stoop. She had Evan's eyes and nose. After a kiss and hug, Evan handed her the package. She gestured toward the interior of the house but he shook his head. She glanced toward the truck and smiled. It took her less than a minute to reach the vehicle.

"Hello, I'm Sara McLeish, Evan's mother," she said through the closed window.

Carly, unable to roll down the electric windows, opened the door and stepped out of the truck. She shook the woman's hand.

"I'm Carly Beck, a friend of Evan's." It was stretching the definition of the word, but "mortal enemy" seemed a bit too precise.

"Carly, would you like to come in and have some lunch?" Sara asked as Evan loomed up behind her. "I was just putting something together for Evan's dad and myself. There's more than enough for four."

Carly's stomach growled on cue.

"I'll take that as a 'yes,'" she said, taking Carly's arm.

"Thanks, Mom, but we've really got to go," Evan said kindly. The face that he gave Carly, over his mother's shoulder, was not nearly as kind. "We'll pick up something on the way."

"But why when I've already got lunch ready? Evan, Carly's starving and I imagine you are, too. So I don't want to hear it."

Carly followed Evan and his mother meekly, caught between a rock and a soft place.

The interior of the home was as tastefully and expensively appointed as the outside. Instead of a Mercedes, a grand piano was parked in the living room, the top covered in silver-framed black and white photographs. Everything was done in shades of white, cream, and beige. The carpet was a tone-on-tone Persian wool, the sofa, a taupe cotton-velvet sectional. Classical music played unobtrusively in the background.

Carly squirmed uncomfortably, feeling garish in her bright yellow dress and orange striped tote bag. Her outfit that was so upbeat and sunny when she left home now made her feel tourist tacky. Evan, however, didn't seem overly worried about tracking dirt into the house from his hiking boots.

"Sit," Sara said, ushering them into the dining room and gesturing to two seats at a long damask covered dining table. "I'll just get some extra place settings."

"Can I help?" Carly asked, eager to avoid Evan's company.

"No, you two relax. I'll be done in a minute." Sara walked out of the room. "Bill! Guess who's here?!"

"I didn't plan on staying," Evan grumbled after his mother left the room.

"What was I supposed to do?" Carly asked.

"Stay in the car."

Sara set the table for four with fine china and stemware. In the middle of the table she placed a pitcher of iced tea and platters filled with small assorted sandwiches and pasta salad. She took a seat across from her guests, leaving the head of the table for the as-yet-unaccounted-for Mr. McLeish. "Go ahead and start. Dad will be here in a minute."

With a look of relief, Evan served Carly first, then himself before filling their glasses with iced tea.

"I'm so glad you stopped by," Sara said happily as she filled Bill's plate with food. "I didn't think you would be able to make it for Father's Day tomorrow. It's just such a nice surprise to have us all together."

"I've been really tied up trying to finish the Arlene Barlow documentary," Evan explained. "I don't mean to ignore you, Mom."

"I know, honey." Sara mixed sugar into Bill's tea. "That's what I tell Bill, but sometimes he doesn't hear me."

Carly ate her lunch quietly and watched the interaction between mother and son. She was starting to wonder if Bill McLeish was invisible. She stole a peek at his plate to see if the food was slowly disappearing.

"Carly, are you doing anything for Father's Day?" Sara asked.

She swallowed a mouthful of pasta salad. "I'd like to, but my father lives in Hawaii, so it's a little difficult."

"That's a shame he's so far away." Sara sighed and looked at Evan. "Honey, don't eat so fast. You'll upset your stomach."

Carly stared at the empty chair and then at Evan, who'd been tearing into his meal like it was his last. She had a feeling that his mother's warning was a little late.

Sara toyed with a spiral of pasta. She, like Bill, had hardly touched her food. "Your dad's got a conference in London at the end of the summer. We'll be renting a flat for a few weeks. It's a big place. Maybe you could join us."

"Some other time, Mom," Evan said softly.

"You could both come," Sara said eagerly, including Carly. "We're out a lot. You'll hardly even notice we're there."

Carly almost choked on her sandwich. She looked to Evan for some guidance. He was gulping down tea and staring at the Invisible Man's empty seat. Exactly how out was Bill? X's over the eyes kind of out? Permanently horizontal kind of out?

"Thanks for the lunch, Mom," Evan said, placing his napkin on the table. "But we really have to go. We're running late."

Carly followed his lead even though she was still hungry.

"Evan!" a voice boomed from the doorway. "It's about time you came around." Bill McLeish took his place at the head of the table and made strong eye contact with all the attendants CEO-style. He had Evan's tall build and dark hair. He wore shorts, a rugby shirt, and a Rolex wrist weight.

"We've got to go, Dad," Evan said firmly.

"No you don't," Bill said, diving into his food. "Now, who's this you've got with you?"

"Carly Beck, meet Bill McLeish," Evan said flatly.

"Well, Carly," Bill said, sizing her up. "What do you do?"

"Advertising," Evan cut in before Carly could answer.

"Good business." Bill nodded his approval before turning to Evan. "Ever thought about product placement? I just read about it in the *Wall Street Journal.* Advertising in movies. You get one of your stars to hold up a Coke at some point and, boom, you get a hefty fee from Coca-Cola. I bet you could make a bundle."

"No doubt," Evan said sarcastically. He took Carly's arm and helped her up. "Thanks for the lunch, Mom."

"Yes," Carly chimed in, "thank you."

"You're very welcome." Sara rose to walk them out.

"Bye, Dad," Evan said.

"Did your mom mention London?" Bill asked, ignoring Evan's farewell. "You two could keep your mom company while I make the rounds. I bet I could rustle up some product placements for your movie while I'm there."

"Bye, Dad," Evan repeated, more firmly this time.

"My assistant, Katie, will give you a call this week." Oblivious, or perhaps indifferent to his son's lack of interest, Bill went back to his lunch. Evan walked Carly out of the house with his mother trailing behind.

"See you later, Mom," Evan said.

"Good-bye, honey." Sara hugged Evan and favored him with the sort of adoring smile that mothers reserve for their sons. "Thank you for coming to see your father; he really appreciates it."

Evan looked at her wearily for a moment, kissed her cheek, and walked around to the driver's side of the truck.

"It was nice meeting you, Mrs. McLeish," Carly said.

"Please, call me Sara," his mother said. She ignored Carly's outstretched hand, giving her a hug instead, and whispered in her ear. "Don't worry, Carly, he's not always this bad."

As they drove off, Carly wondered which McLeish she was talking about.

Chapter Twelve

The traffic thickened as the desert slipped away and the cities grew closer together. Evan hop-scotched his way through traffic, skillfully cheating death at seventy miles an hour. Carly, inured to near-collisions and almost-accidents, stretched her legs and toed off her sandals. They had a hundred miles of asphalt between them and home. It was going to be awhile.

"No more jokes?"

His voice surprised her. She figured he'd had enough of her for one day.

"That was it." She shrugged. "Pretty much my whole stand-up routine."

"It was pretty funny."

"Yeah?" she asked with a sidelong glance.

"Yeah." The corner of his mouth rose ever so slightly. "I've heard worse."

She laughed. "You're as bad as my agent. On a good day he tells me I didn't suck."

"Well, today, Carly," he said, gracing her with a blinding smile, "you didn't suck."

"Yeah?" she asked, stunned.

"Yeah."

She basked in his approval, wrapping it around

herself like a mink coat. *Ummmmm,* she wanted to hum out loud but didn't lest he somehow get the idea that she cared.

"So what's the deal with the shoes?" he asked, interrupting her basking time.

"I'm sorry," she said, looking down at her bare feet. "Does it bother you that I took my shoes off?"

"No," he said. "You've got cute feet. Really cute feet. I mean the other shoes."

She squirmed, unable to savor the second compliment because she was too busy worrying about what to say. Evan changed lanes to pass a poultry truck leaving a blizzard of feathers in its wake.

"What's the story?" he asked again when she didn't answer. "I'm assuming there's a story."

Carly tucked her feet back into her sandals. "It's nothing."

"Uh-huh. You're doing a month's worth of work because you bought the matching purse and didn't want to break up the set."

"They just have a lot of sentimental value, that's all."

"Why?"

Carly knew her explanation wasn't going to raise herself in his eyes. On the mammalian scale of evolution, she figured he put her somewhere in the petting zoo category between lop-eared bunnies and pygmy goats. She also knew that he would keep at her all the way back to LA if she didn't tell him.

"They're my lucky shoes," she finally said.

He took his eyes off the road to stare at her, his eyes sweeping over her from head to toe. "Lucky? As in CFM pumps?"

"No!" she cut him off irritably. "Lucky as in general all-around luck. Good fortune. Good karma."

"Karma you make yourself," he corrected.

"Oh, pardon me," Carly said sarcastically. "How stupid of me to forget! I'm paid to read the words, not understand them."

She crossed her arms and stared angrily out the window knowing that getting emotional was not helping her cause. If anything, it would only underscore his conviction that she was a few pecans short of a pie.

"Lucky," he spat out scornfully. "You call being overscale lucky? People pay you double the going rate because you're so damned lucky, not because you're worth it, not because you're good at what you do. Just because you're lucky. Right."

How could he ever know what it was like to be her? Evan was a somebody, a winner; everything about him was suffused with the golden light of achievement. Success had never been a given for Carly. She used to joke that whenever she bought a lottery ticket, the odds went up for everybody else.

"Someone like you wouldn't get it," she said quietly. "When you were a kid, I bet no one ever complained that you were on their team. Uh-oh, here comes Evan, hope we don't get stuck with him. What a boat anchor."

He shrugged, not disclaiming the obvious.

"I was the biggest goof as a kid. I was never popular, dressed like a goon, had weird taste in music, and said dumb things. I lost stuff constantly and showed up on the wrong day for everything. I had bad hair, glasses, and braces, so I used to hide on picture day and hope they'd forget about me. Later on I dumped the glasses and braces and crappy hairstylist, but I was still just as pathetic at everything else."

He shook his head, perhaps in disbelief, more likely pity.

"Bet you weren't someone's what-the-fuck alternate for the prom, or college, or anything else for that matter," she continued bitterly. "I can't see your mom giving you books like *Social Skills for Dummies.*"

He was incredulous. "You're kidding me, right?"

"Welcome to my world, Evan McLeish," she said airily and then dropped her voice in a rough imitation of an overblown movie trailer announcer. "Coming to a theater near you! *La Vida Nada,* starring Carly Beck, based on a boring but true story. Rated NC-17 for full frontal stupidity and graphic displays of loserdom."

"You're hardly a loser, Carly," he said, looking her straight in the eye before turning back to the road. "Those shoes don't mean shit. Your life is what you make it. Lucky charms have no effect, good or bad, on your life."

She shook her head stubbornly. "You have absolutely no idea how awful my life used to be. The fact is, ever since I got those shoes, life has been good. There's no way in hell I'm messing with that."

"The shoes are nothing."

"They're everything."

He was giving her the Area 51 Roswell look and his voice returned to its normal smart-aleck tone. "Lucky for me, though."

She went back to staring out the window, sorry she'd spilled her guts. Whatever tiny bits of respect Carly had earned that day had been completely obliterated by her confession. She'd slipped below petting zoo and was now being classified with bacteria and other non-brained organisms.

The final recording session would be the coming Friday. After that, her obligation to Evan would be fulfilled, and she'd get her shoes and her luck back. So long as her life returned to the way it was before, she could endure a little humiliation, a little bruised pride for the sake of a better future.

She woke up to a kiss, just like Sleeping Beauty. However, Evan was hardly Prince Charming.

"I thought that might bring you around," he said.

Carly pushed him away and looked out the window. They were parked in front of her house.

"You know," he continued, "a lot of men might get put off by the way you're always falling asleep."

She gathered her things together and muttered, "But not you."

"Not me," he grinned. "So what is it today, Carly? Shooting stars? Lightning bolts? Duckies?"

She stared at him for a second before she realized what he was talking about. What the hell did he do? Inventory her entire underwear drawer while she was passed out? Maybe Dana was right and he did have some kind of fetish.

"Go to hell," she said without much conviction.

He gave her a knowing grin. "Must be little devils then."

The Pasadena City College Flea Market was already crammed with shoppers by the time Carly and Dana arrived. Their first stop was a food booth manned by some nursing students who were investing in their careers by selling fat-, salt-, sugar-, and nitrate-laden goodies, thereby creating a need for future services.

"Coffee? Doughnuts? Hot dogs?" A fresh-faced Florence Nightingale waved a platter of treats under Dana's nose. Dana swayed with the movement of the plate.

Carly pushed her sleepwalking friend aside. "Pay no attention to the dead woman. We'll take two coffees, two doughnuts—one chocolate, one powdered sugar—and make the coffees large."

"Don't forget Daisy," Dana said dully. She shook the leash in her hand, making her tags rattle. The dog looked up eagerly.

"And a bag of potato chips," Carly added. She paid for the food and prepared their coffees, liberally dosing both cups with sugar and cream. Carly handed Dana a coffee. "Drink."

She took a big gulp of coffee and sighed.

Carly pushed the chocolate doughnut at her. "Eat."

Dana bit into the doughnut, chased it down with more coffee, and sighed again.

They started to walk down the aisles with the dachshund leading the way, scurrying from one booth to the next as if she were actually shopping for something.

"Arf." Daisy stopped in front of a bunch of large tin signs propped up against the side of a battered station wagon.

Carly perused some salt and pepper shakers on an old card table. Rows of elephants, penguins, and other ceramic animals marched, Noah's ark fashion, two by two across the tabletop.

"Do I need this?" Dana held up a large dented MEN AT WORK street maintenance sign. Daisy wagged her tail enthusiastically.

Carly barely gave it a glance. "No."

"The style maven has spoken," Dana said to Daisy as she put the sign back. "How was the desert?"

Daisy headed for the next booth, both women in tow.

"The interview went really well. Raymond Barlow is a neat old guy. Yes, Arlene and Pete Silver were lovers, but that's about it. He doesn't know where she went but he figures she had her reasons. Seems Arlene was always a free spirit. At the end of the interview, he asked me to marry him."

"Raymond or Evan?"

Carly wrinkled her nose. "Raymond, of course."

Dana stopped at a rack of vintage accessories and pulled out a black tooled-leather belt with an elaborate silver and mother-of-pearl buckle. She tried it on for size. "What do you think?"

Carly nodded. "Evan was a total grump the whole time."

Dana bought the belt from a woman in a lime green sundress.

"We stopped by his parents' house on the way back from the interview," Carly said as they resumed walking. "They live in this huge house in Palm Springs. His dad's some kind of mogul. The kind of person my dad is always doing interviews with. We had lunch there, but it was like he was at a business meeting or something. I'm pretty sure Evan and his dad don't get along. His mom seems really nice, but I feel sorry for her, having to keep the peace between Godzilla and son of Godzilla."

"I never thought of Godzilla as being married," Dana mused.

"Well, how do you think they got Junior?" Carly pointed out.

"Probably wiped out a small Japanese village just gettin' it on. Speaking of which, you and Evan do the deed yet?"

A man digging through a pile of magazines cocked his head up.

Carly grabbed Dana and propelled her down the aisle. "Of course not! We've got an agreement, remember?"

"I know, will work for shoes. But he seems interested and you seem interested, so why not?"

"I'm not interested," Carly said stiffly.

Dana's eyes twinkled. "What was that?"

"I said, I'm not in the tiniest bit interested."

"Oh, Daisy." Dana picked up the wiener dog and they both faced Carly. "Lookie, Auntie Carly has the hots for Evan."

Carly squinted hard at two pairs of inquisitive eyes.

Dana put Daisy down and began to sing. "Carly and Evan sitting in a tree. K-I-S-S-I-N-G. First comes love . . ."

Carly grabbed the dog's leash. "Come on, Daisy. Let's go."

"You've got it bad, Tinkerbell." Dana laughed as she caught up with them. "Oh, I can't stand it. It's just so cute."

"It's not cute. It's a part of my bad luck streak is what it is. My career is in the toilet, my car's been mauled, and I'm attracted to a man who hates my guts. So frigging typical."

"Evan might hate your guts, but he likes the rest of you just fine. I thought he was gonna rip out Glen's liver the other night. He was pumping me for information the whole time you two were dancing."

"What did you tell him?"

"I told him you preferred tall, blue-eyed brunettes."

"Nice going."

"So what are you gonna do?"

"Nothing," she said, grimacing at a shoebox full of vintage valentines. "I'm going to do nothing. Bad luck may be following me around, but that doesn't mean I've got to flag it down."

Odin was out. The moment Carly unlocked the back door, she was hit by a peculiar emptiness, a feeling of nothing where something should have been. Of course, the fact that he wasn't instantly attached to her ankles, crooning his love, was a dead giveaway. Odin was on permanent house arrest. Outside was a no-cat's land of rabid dogs, speeding cars, and bloodthirsty coyotes.

Fighting panic, Carly tossed her backpack and take-out dinner on the counter and did a quick house check. It didn't take her long to confirm that her little Viking had set sail for the New World, leaving port through the open bathroom window. Cursing her carelessness and the fading daylight, Carly grabbed a flashlight as she ran out the door.

"Odin!" she called into the crawl space under her

house. The flashlight beam landed on nothing but dirt and spiderwebs. She shook a can of treats, the rattling of edible nuggets between the metal bottom and plastic lid being a feline siren song. Carly waited for his answering call but got nothing.

Working methodically, Carly covered both sides of her street and then started moving out, block by block, in ever-widening circles. She peered under every car and into every hidey-hole. Every car washer, gardener, and dog walker was thoroughly questioned and reluctantly released. The sun had set and the night air was turning chilly. It was disemboweled-cattle and crop circle time. Vampire prime time.

"Odin?" She checked under an old Explorer a few streets over from her house, the sound of her own tremulous voice stoking her fears. The fading flashlight flickered and reflected weakly against two glowing eyes. Where the hell was Jensen and his damned night-vision glasses when she needed them? Carly dropped to her knees and angled her head under the truck.

"Odin, baby? Is that you?"

It was a cat, definitely, and it was the right size, but the waning flashlight barely illuminated the animal huddled against the far wheel. The only way to get to him would be to crawl.

"Mrrrew . . ."

"Odin!" Relief passed over her momentarily before worry reasserted itself. "Mommy's here. Hang on, baby."

She put the can of treats aside, got down on her belly and began to wiggle toward her cat. A lump the size of her fist was wedged in her throat; her stomach was permanently set on the spin cycle. Grit and gravel sanded her clothes and the palms of her hands as she inched forward. Odin was hunkered down, his body still. Really still.

"What the hell are you doing now?" a familiar voice rumbled.

Startled, Carly whacked her head on the car's undercarriage.

"Evan, help me! Odin's under here and I think he's hurt." Carly twisted around to look behind her. The streetlight illuminated the scenery but left Evan in shadow. But, just like she'd know her cat's meow, she'd recognize that voice anywhere.

"Can you reach him?" he asked.

"Yes, I think so. I hope so. Oh, God . . ." The flashlight's dim beam gave everything a frightening and gruesome cast. The closer she got, the worse Odin looked. He'd obviously been in some sort of fight. His face was a mess and one of his eyes was partially shut. "I need something to wrap him in."

A hooded sweatshirt was tossed in her direction. Carly proceeded cautiously, placing the hood over Odin, making sure to cover his head. He cried piteously but didn't put up a struggle. Gently, Carly rolled him up like a kitty eggroll. Trying not to jostle him too much, she partly carried and dragged the heavy bundle of black cat, apologizing the whole way.

"Here." Evan's capable arms came from behind her when she'd shimmied most of the way out. "Hand him to me."

Carly contorted herself sideways and extended her arms, passing the cat to Evan. Her whole body was shaking when she finally stood up. Under the sickening sulfurous light of the street lamp she could see stains on her hands. Blood.

"We have to go to the hospital. He's hurt. We have to go now!" Carly intended to say. Instead, her words tumbled out in a jumbled, burbling, incoherent rush. Realizing she wasn't making sense, Carly attempted to get her point across by waving her arms and gesturing wildly.

If Evan was even the tiniest bit tempted to say "Sounds like . . ." he didn't do it. Instead, he placed Odin back in her arms and herded her toward the truck.

"It's okay, Carly. My car's right here. Just tell me where to go," Evan said calmly as she gasped and sobbed and gibbered. "Uh, well, maybe you could just point."

She sat miserably in the cold, pale green waiting room, nervously playing with the sleeve of Evan's stained sweatshirt. Her clothes were filthy from her belly crawl under the car. The asphalt had scraped her palms and elbows raw. Same for her shoes. There was some sort of car gunk in her hair.

"Here," Evan said, extending a cup of coffee. "Drink this."

She took the paper cup from his hands, the smell of hot coffee temporarily masking the odor of disinfectant and wet dog.

Evan took the plastic seat next to her and sipped his coffee silently. Carly looked at him over the rim of her cup. He looked great, a little grim, but the look was starting to grow on her. They'd hardly spoken all evening except to answer questions from the vet. Odin, to Carly's relief, wasn't hurt too badly. Mostly minor cuts and scratches despite all the blood.

"What were you doing driving down the street?" she finally asked. Evan hadn't mentioned her earlier psychotic behavior and for that she was truly grateful.

"I was on the way to your house to pick up my notes. I forgot to get them back from you yesterday."

"You could have called."

"I was in the neighborhood."

"I'm glad." For once she was happy about his impromptu visiting habits.

They had just finished their coffees when the veterinarian came into the waiting area to give a status report on Odin. "He's beat-up but doing fine. I'm going to keep him at least for tonight. It's important that we keep his wounds clean and keep an eye out for infection. He's a big cat and he's very healthy, so that counts in his favor."

Carly nodded, hardly breathing. She squeezed Evan's hand hard enough to start turning his fingertips red. He was nice enough not to pull away.

"Can we see him?" Evan asked.

"Absolutely. I think he'll be glad to see you, too."

One entire wall of the recovery room was triple stacked with stainless steel cages. They were half full of listless and hurt cats of all makes and models. There was a separate room for the dogs next door. It was eerily silent except for the dirgelike hum of a small refrigerator in the corner.

Odin meowed a tired greeting when Carly appeared in front of his cage. The vet tech opened the front grill so that Carly could pet him. Antibiotic ointment was smeared over most of his face, his right eye was swollen, little islands of bare gray skin dotted his body where they had shaved away the hair to tend to his wounds. An IV dripped medication into him and a plastic collar that resembled a small lamp shade was clipped around his neck to prevent him from licking his wounds.

"Oh, look at you!" Carly tried and failed to find an unwounded spot where she could pet him. The best she could do was to pat his front paw and give it a little kiss.

Odin began to purr. Carly began to cry.

The cat gave another weak meow.

"He said," Evan interpreted, "you should see the other guy."

"Men," Carly scoffed through her tears. "All that macho crapola got you into this mess. Let's hope it'll help you out of it."

Chapter Thirteen

"I'll get your notes," Carly said as they entered the kitchen. Exhaustion bowed her shoulders and worry dragged at the corners of her mouth.

"Dinner?" Evan pointed to the foil tin on the counter.

"Yeah," she said, digging in her tote bag. "I picked up some Mexican on the way home. It's yours if you want it."

Evan had already opened the container and was slipping the contents onto a plate. He nuked the burrito and brought it to the table along with utensils and another plate.

"You should have some of this," he said.

Carly shook her head as she dropped into the chair next to him. She placed his notes on the table. "I'm not hungry."

"You need to eat. You've had a rough night." He divided the burrito and placed half on the other plate. He'd found a jar of salsa in the cupboard and poured about half on his dinner. Evan and Dex, Carly had found out, both liked their food on the incendiary side, perversely attracted to menu items highlighted with little flames. He held the jar of salsa over her plate but put it down when she shook her head.

Carly didn't want to eat, but she also didn't want to fight with him. It struck her that they hadn't argued over anything the whole evening. A record so far. She was pleased with the cease-fire and was in no hurry to resume lobbing bombs. Carly liked this kinder, gentler Evan more than she cared to admit. Maybe his mom was right.

Evan was done with his food in the time it took Carly to eat a few token bites. She pushed her plate over to him and he finished it off along with more salsa.

"Why don't you get cleaned up?" he said, rising out of his chair. "I'll deal with this stuff."

Carly hesitated. A shower sounded great, but she hated to end the evening so abruptly. Being with Evan took her mind off thinking about her pet in the hospital.

Evan started collecting the dishes. "I'll make coffee."

She hoped he'd still be there after her shower. "There's beans in the freezer. Decaf please."

A short while later, a freshly bathed, shampooed, and lotioned Carly emerged from the bedroom. She wore a pair of red boxers with cupids on them, a red tank top, and her white chenille robe. On her feet were her comfy leopard slippers.

Evan had made himself at home on her couch. Two mugs of coffee sat on the table in front of him. He was reading a *National Geographic* magazine with a shark on the cover.

"You don't have to wear the robe on my account," he said, putting the magazine down.

"I'm cold," she lied. Carly settled herself next to him and reached for a mug.

"Is that your family?" Evan pointed at the photos on the fireplace mantel. The picture in the center featured a group shot taken at Julian's graduation.

"Yep, la familia Engstrom. That's my brainy little brother, Julian, in the wrinkly cap and gown. This fall he's going to grad school at Caltech to be with his own kind. Next is my mom, Judith, and my little sister, Stacey, on the right. She's a super-talented artist. That's her work hanging above the mantel."

The large framed drawing was a series of charcoal sketches, studies of a nude woman, standing, sitting, reclining. The lines were strong and sure, capturing the emotional as well as the physical likeness of the woman. The face was represented by only a few lines and often she was turned away.

"It's you," Evan said without hesitation.

"No, it's not," she answered quickly, but her cheeks, red as raspberries, gave her away.

"Is too."

"Is not!"

"Carly," he said, all too knowingly. "I don't need to see your face to recognize the rest of you. Like I said, you don't have to wear a robe on my account."

"Well," she said, caught speechless. No one had ever noticed the likeness before.

"Don't worry," he said, smoothing out the worry lines on her forehead with his thumb. "No one else would know."

"You knew."

"I've got a very good memory. You don't suppose your sister has any more of these drawings she'd be interested in selling?" He let that idea linger in the air for a bit before he let her off the hook and changed the subject. "I wouldn't exactly call your brother and sister little."

In the photograph both her brother and sister were a head taller than Carly.

"No," she agreed, glad for the lane change. "But they'll always be little to me."

"You don't much look like them, either."

"They look like my stepdad. I look like my dad." She pointed to a photo of a good-looking gray-haired man. He was standing at a train station somewhere in Japan, grinning and holding up a sheet of paper that said HAPPY BIRTHDAY, CARLY! I LOVE YOU, DAD in bold black marker. "That's Beck."

"You call him by his last name?"

"No, it's his first name." Carly placed her half-empty cup on the table and tucked her legs underneath her. "I changed my name from Rudolph to Beck when I started acting. My stage name."

"Rudolph too boring?"

Carly searched for a trace of malice in his words and found none. "When I joined the union, I wanted to be Carlotta Rudolph, my real name, but there was already a Charlotte Rudolph, which was too close for comfort, so I went with Carly Beck."

"I've always been Evan McLeish." He placed his cup next to hers and leaned back on the sofa.

"I couldn't imagine you any other way."

It was late. Carly hadn't checked the time, but she was sure it was close to midnight. By all white knight standards, Evan had discharged his duty in a fine and chivalrous manner and could feel free to take his leave.

"I want to thank you for everything you did

tonight." Carly's words broke the silence that had surrounded them for the past few minutes. "I know you think he's just a cat. But Odin means a lot to me. We've been together for a while now. This is number three."

"Years?"

"Lives," she answered solemnly. "Six to go unless he's had some near-death experiences I don't know about."

"Carly, Carly," he said, shaking his head. "Soon you'll be buying a rabbit's foot for your cat. How about a lucky collar?"

"Anyway," she said, ignoring his jibe, "thank you so very, very, very much, Evan. I really appreciate it."

"I've had pets." He said it like he was confessing a petty crime.

"Yeah?" She tried to picture him as a boy with a dog. A collie, maybe. Or a German shepherd. Yes, definitely a shepherd.

"A turtle or two."

The image of a young Evan bounding through fields with his trusty canine at his heels changed into a kid hanging over a terrarium housing a small green reptile. Somehow the vision lacked romance.

"And a husky once," he continued.

Carly pictured an intense, dark-haired lad mushing his stalwart team of dogs through the frozen Alaskan wilderness to bring much-needed medicine to a far-flung outpost. Better.

"What was his name?" she asked, still caught up in the Jack London ideal of a courageous boy and his loyal dog.

"Her," Evan corrected. "Snowball."

Snowball? "That doesn't sound very heroic."

He shrugged. "Her mom was Snowflake, so the breeder named her Snowball. Not my choice, but my mom liked it."

"Breeder, huh? Odin was a stray. He's the first pet I've ever had." She sighed softly. "It's weird not having him here. He's always here. Walking around. Shedding." Her chin started to wobble dangerously and the room began to blur.

"Hey," he said softly, reaching out to brush away her tears. "He's not going anywhere. He's got six left, remember?"

"I was so stupid," she said, bemoaning her thoughtlessness. "If I hadn't left the window open, he wouldn't have gotten out. Now he's all alone at the hospital."

He drew her close and she went willingly into his arms. "He'll be fine," he whispered, his voice low and soothing, his lips brushing the top of her ear. God, she loved his voice.

Suddenly, she pulled away, her eyes wide with anxiety. "Evan, what if it's me? Geez, can't you see it? He would be the first black cat whose owner brought him bad luck."

"Carly," he warned, "you're losin' it, babe. Listen to me. This has nothing to do with your shoes. Okay? Not a thing." He pulled her back into his arms.

"Then I'm just a terrible kitty mom."

"You're a great kitty mom," he assured her, kissing her forehead. "The best."

"I should have brought him his pillow and a toy," she blubbered. "What if he gets scared?"

"You sound like my mom the first time I went to summer camp." He kissed the tip of her nose. "She showed up the first night to make sure everything was okay. Talk about losing face."

Carly buried her nose into the collar of his shirt. He smelled nicely of Evan and warm cotton. "How old were you?"

"Eight."

She smiled into his shirt. "Ruined your rep with the girls, I'll bet."

"Don't you know it." He said as his warm hands rubbed her back slowly, tenderly soothing away the ugliness of the day.

It was at that moment Carly realized, using the cold, analytical part of her brain that never seemed to assert itself until it was too late, that it was too late. If ever she should have run away screaming, it wasn't when he had her spread-eagled, half-naked, with his hand on her breast and his tongue in her mouth. Oh, no. That kind of trouble was small change compared to the mess she was presently headed for. Having him cuddle her and tell her everything was going to be okay was decidedly more dangerous. Throw in a devastating smile, buns you could bounce bullets off of, mix in a little hero action, and Carly was ready to follow around at his heels like Snowball the husky. Inexorably the balance was tipping in Evan's favor bit by bit, kiss by kiss.

Carly finger-combed her wet hair, threw on a T-shirt and shorts, and followed the irresistible scent trail of French roast from the bedroom to the kitchen.

Evan was sitting at the table drinking coffee like the lord of the manor. He was so handsome she had to grip the floor with her toes to keep from flying across the room. Yesterday's Sunday paper lay scattered in front of him, the crossword puzzle already completed.

Carly had fallen asleep in his arms but woke up in bed hugging a pillow. A sorry substitute by any standard. She was surprised to find him still there but not wholly disappointed by that fact. When she'd gone to take her shower that morning, she'd noticed that Evan had already helped himself to the guest towels and toothbrush. Carly tried not to get misty over the sight of his blue toothbrush snuggled in the glass next to her pink one but didn't succeed entirely. Getting mushy about a toothbrush was a bad sign. Soon she might want to start pairing his socks and folding his T-shirts. The thought was downright chilling.

"Pancakes," Evan muttered minutes later, frowning at the two pieces of whole wheat toast in front of him as if Carly had just served him dried pig ears on a plate.

"What?" Carly looked up from refilling their mugs.

"Dex got pancakes," he grumbled.

"Yes?" she asked, hoping for clarification.

"When Dex was here," he nodded his head toward the bedroom, to indicate where "here" was, "*he* got pancakes."

Carly let out an exasperated grunt. "I made Dex pancakes for putting together my demo reel. Not for . . ." She waved indignantly in the direction of the bedroom.

"What *did* he get for . . ." He raised his eyebrows suggestively.

"Nothing!" she insisted, wanting to still his lecherous brows and all that they implied.

Evan prodded the cooling toast with his finger, then made a face. "I thought you liked him."

"Of course I like him. He's my friend. But I don't," she waved at the bedroom again, "with him."

His frown receded a bit. "So you never . . ." Eyebrow wiggle.

"No! We never . . ." Wave, wave.

"Not once?" Just one skeptical brow this time.

"Never," she assured him, hand on her heart.

He grinned smugly, once again convinced of his proper place as the ruler of the universe. "Dex got pancakes."

"Fine," Carly said, disgusted at how quickly she raised the white flag of surrender. She put on her best 1950s housewife voice. "Evan, darling, how would you like some pancakes?"

"I'd love some pancakes." He pushed away the noxious plate of toast and reached for the book review section of the newspaper. "Don't forget the butter and maple syrup."

Chapter Fourteen

"Who's this?" Evan said belligerently into the phone.

Carly had just stepped back in from switching on the lawn sprinklers. She went down the list of people he could be insulting in her head and motioned Evan to give her the phone.

"Hey, you called here," he said, ignoring her. Someone barked a loud reply. "Okay, hang on."

Evan handed her the phone without apology. "It's your dad."

Carly grabbed the phone and walked toward the sink, away from the table and Evan. "Hi, Dad."

"Who's that asshole?" Beck asked sharply. "And what the hell is he doing answering your phone on a Monday morning?"

Busted. She was way past the age of consent and virgin was a store where she bought her CDs, but guilt was sitting on her conscience, wringing its hands anyway. "Uh . . ."

"Never mind," Beck said, his voice gruff but gentle. "It's none of my business. But once a dad, always a dad, and . . . Hey, wait a minute! That's him, isn't it? That filmmaker guy."

"Yeah," she conceded. The last thing she wanted

was to be having this conversation in front of Evan. Despite his momentary foray into nice-guy territory the previous night, she still wouldn't put it past him to pick up the phone and start describing her naked from memory.

"Listen, I'm doing an interview with a Swedish prince who's a banking whiz. How do you feel about dating royalty?"

"I prefer my dates entourage- and bodyguard-free." Out of the corner of her eye, she could see Evan browbeating the newspaper. "What's up, Dad?"

"The surf but not the stock market," he quipped. "Thanks for the CDs. You're too good to me, baby."

"Happy Father's Day, Dad."

Evan turned the pages of the newspaper noisily, giving his opinion of that particular holiday. Even when he wasn't talking he was making judgment calls.

"You make me proud to be one, Carly," Beck glowed. "But enough about me. I've got a hot lead for you. I've found Pedro DaSilva, better known as Pete Silver, aka Mr. Arlene Barlow."

"No way!" Carly slapped her coffee mug down on the counter, sending a tiny tidal wave over the rim and down the side. "You've found Arlene Barlow's husband?!"

Within seconds, Evan had crossed the room and was standing right next to her. He craned his head toward hers to bring his ear closer to the phone. She inched along the counter. He followed closely behind.

"Yep," Beck answered proudly. "Even from

smack-dab in the middle of the Pacific, no one is safe from my inquiries."

"Where is he? Is she with him? She's still alive, right?"

Evan hunched closer. Carly turned her back to him, twisting to get away. Evan anticipated her dodges like a six-foot sheepdog, hemming her in. She poked an elbow to prod him away. Undaunted, he pushed it aside and pressed against her back, trapping her against the counter.

"He's living near Ensenada, Mexico," Beck said. "Probably in one of those retirement communities full of old gringos living on Social Security."

"Have you talked to him?" Carly felt the weight of Evan's body pressed against her backside and the heat of his breath along her cheek. She was starting to pant and hoped her father couldn't read her mind.

"No," Beck said. "That's your gig. Got a pen?"

"A pen," she repeated, hoping Evan would leave her side and get one, hoping he wouldn't. Evan's hand reached past her for a paper towel and deposited it along with a pen from who knows where on the counter in front of her. "Okay, Dad. I'm ready."

Beck gave her the information, which Carly dutifully wrote down, glad she'd spent the money for the sturdy premium towels.

"Good luck, baby," her father said. "And, well, do me a favor and just don't jump into anything."

Maybe he could read her mind.

"I won't. Thanks, Daddy. Love you."

"Love you back," he said and hung up.

Carly's heart was pounding as she turned the

phone off. *I can't believe Dad found Pete Silver! I can't believe Evan McLeish has me up against the kitchen counter! Holy*— Evan spun her around and planted his mouth on hers before she could finish the thought. French-roast French kisses, an undeniable taste treat. Coffee with a different kind of kick. Carly dropped the phone and slid her arms around his neck. Evan gathered her up against him and placed his hands on her bottom. With an easy motion, he lifted her smoothly onto the counter and stood between her knees.

"Evan?" she asked tentatively, pulling away from the kiss. She wasn't entirely sure what she was asking. Maybe he could figure it out for her.

His hands slipped under her T-shirt as his lips moved down her neck. Talking did not seem to be on his mind at that moment. The only thing that seemed to interest him was his mouth on her skin and his hands on her breasts.

Carly felt her priorities shifting in the same direction. She dug her hands into his shoulders and pulled him closer, arching herself into him. Her nipples were as perky, shameless, and eager for attention as backstage groupies. She had just started to wrap her legs around his hips when the phone rang.

"Oh!" she cried sharply as the phone rang again. He stilled. "Oh?"

"Odin!" She pushed him away, slid off the counter, and scooped up the phone. "Hello?"

"Carly? It's Betsy from Dr. Mark's office."

"Betsy, thanks for calling. How's Odin?"

Evan pocketed the paper towel and went back to the newspaper.

"Just fine. The doctor says he should make a full recovery."

"Thank God," she said, relief flooding through her. Maybe she wasn't a jinx after all. "Can I take him home?"

"Not till tomorrow. But feel free to visit anytime today."

Evan drove Carly and an armload of cat toys to the pet hospital. Odin looked much better, not quite ready to run down and dispatch a gazelle with a single well-placed bite, but he could probably do some damage to a box of Cat Chow. Cat and owner had a very emotional reunion that seemed to cheer them both up immensely. She left him with so many toys in his cage that all it needed to take its place in an arcade was a joystick in front and a claw hanging in the center.

"I'm going to try and get ahold of Silver today and see if I can set up an interview," Evan said, driving back to Carly's.

"Will you keep me posted?" she asked hopefully.

"Yeah, sure." Evan kneaded the back of his neck and rolled the kinks out of his shoulders.

"I want to come along," she said, more forcefully than she meant to. She paused and added a soft "Please?"

Evan kept his eyes on the road and said nothing.

"I know it's your film," Carly assured him. "I promise, cross my heart and everything, I won't get in the way. Honest."

"He hasn't agreed to be interviewed yet."

"But if he does . . ." Carly pleaded. She understood now why Evan had been so mad when she hadn't shared the information on Raymond. She'd tried to lock him out of something he had a right to be part of. Now she was hoping he wouldn't do the same to her. "I know I was out of line on the Raymond Barlow thing. What I did was wrong and I'm sorry."

Evan parked the car in her driveway and turned to look at her. His butane blue eyes surveyed her face.

"Please don't leave me out of this." Of all the times in her life, just this once she didn't want to be found lacking. She not only wanted but absolutely needed to be a part of Silver's interview.

He sighed. Evan never sighed. He harrumphed or snorted or grumbled. He didn't sigh. This time he sighed.

"Maybe," he said, holding his hand up to stop her from interrupting. "But only if he agrees—some people won't talk to more than one person. If he says no, then it's no. And I'm not going to arrange things around your schedule. Once he agrees, I'm in the car headed south before he changes his mind. I can't sit around waiting for you to get out from making a soup commercial."

"Absolutely," she agreed readily. "Whatever it takes, I'll find a way. I promise."

He nodded, whether in acceptance or resignation, Carly didn't know. For the second time that day, he kissed her, fiercely at first, then softly, seductively, sinfully stretching out each kiss like a warm piece of taffy until it finally broke before he started the next one. For a few glorious minutes all the world's problems stood aside and waited. With a deep exhalation, they finally parted.

Carly stared at him as she tried to sort through a tumble of opposing emotions that threatened to clog and overload her brain.

"Don't think so hard about it," he told her as he watched the blizzard of thoughts whirling in her eyes. "It's nothing."

"Nothing, right," she repeated morosely. "I'll talk to you later."

Pete Silver wasn't interested. Carly had waited all day and most of the night for Evan's call. She knew that a refusal was a distinct possibility but it did little to temper her disappointment. Evan talked to Pete for an hour and couldn't persuade the aging musician to be interviewed. Later in the day, when Evan tried again, the answer was still no. Silver was amenable, however, to looking at a partial rough cut of what had already been done. Evan sent an overnight package and told Carly not to worry.

"But what if he says no again?" she asked anxiously.

"Then I'll keep trying till he does. Believe me, I'm not giving up that easily."

"But—"

"Go to sleep, Carly. I'll call you tomorrow."

She went to bed feeling anxious and alone. No Odin on her too-big bed, no Evan on her too-small couch. She tossed and turned for an hour before she finally fell asleep—straight into the arms of Gumby. And his pony pal, Pokey, too.

* * *

The cutting edge, people in Los Angeles love to be on it. Carly, cell phone pressed to her ear, stared out her kitchen window at the automatic lawn mower meandering over her neighbor's grass like an overgrown pill bug. Jensen, the unrepentant gearhead, sat on his front step sucking on a 32-ounce cherry Slurpee as he proudly watched over his latest robotic acquisition. The cutting edge was cutting the lawn.

"How's Hell Kitty doing?" Evan's tired voice asked.

"Better. We're thinking about a second honeymoon." Carly picked up a purring Odin on the way to the living room and settled into the couch. "Evan, I want to thank you again for helping me the other night. Odin means the world to me and I don't think I could have gotten through without you. Thanks."

"It's nothing."

Nothing. That one word summed up everything about their relationship. Once she would have been glad to hear it. Now she wasn't so sure. "Have you heard from Pete? Did he get the tape?"

"Yeah, he got the tape, but he's not sure how he feels, which is better than yesterday. I really need him to come through on this. At least he's not saying no anymore, he's saying maybe."

Carly was trying to convince Evan of the same thing. She had to smile at the irony of it all.

"Carly?" His voice took on a serious edge.

The hairs on her neck rose. Cringing, she tilted her head back and waited for the inevitable anvil or baby grand piano to drop through the ceiling. "Yes?"

"There might be a change in plans."

"Okay . . ." she said hesitantly while she checked the floor for signs of a hidden trapdoor.

"If I can get Pete Silver to say yes tomorrow, I'd like to postpone Friday's session until next week. I'll need the extra time to re-edit and rewrite."

Well, hell. Carly took a deep breath. She needed her shoes. She needed this film. She wanted both. "If I say yes, can I have my shoe back before I finish?"

"No, I can't do that."

"Why?" she demanded. "I promise I'll finish. I'll see it through, Evan. And not just because of the contract but because it's important to me."

"I can't," he finally said after a protracted silence.

"Because you don't trust me?" That hurt. Couldn't he see that she wasn't a quitter? She'd given her word.

"Because I can't afford to trust you," Evan said flat out. "I don't have a choice, Carly. I won't take any more chances. I need to make sure this gets done. It's not about you."

"No," she shot back angrily. "It's about you. You always want to do everything by yourself. You don't want anybody's help unless you ask for it. And you're not going to ask, are you?"

He didn't confirm or deny anything. Instead he said, "I'll make you a deal."

"I don't want to make a deal!" Odin jumped out of her arms, alarmed by her tone of voice. "You're not being fair, Evan. I've done everything I've said I would and I'll do more if you need it. I don't want to do another deal. Why can't you just ask me?"

"Listen to me," he insisted. "If Pete Silver says yes

and you'll postpone the session, I'll take you with me. I promise."

"And give me my shoes."

"No," he said, firmly rejecting her offer. "I'll take you with me. That's the best I can do."

"Will do," she said pointedly.

"Yes," he agreed. "The best I will do."

"Damn it and damn you," she hissed, frustrated by his blind determination to do everything his way, not to give in even the tiniest bit where she was concerned. "All right. It's a deal."

Dana stopped by Saturday night to pick up Odin. Carly was leaving at six the next morning and no way was Dana going to be coherent at that indecent hour. The only people she expected to see that early in the morning were naked, male, and left-over from the night before.

"Thanks for taking care of Odin while I'm away," Carly said, handing over the cat carrier. "It's only for tonight and tomorrow. But, you know, he's not used to sleeping alone."

"I only wish I could say the same," Dana said. She loaded the carrier and a bag full of enough food and supplies for a month into the back of her car. "Speaking of sleeping alone . . ."

Carly rolled her eyes wearily. "Don't start."

"You know, for a guy you're not sleeping with, he spends a lot of time sleeping at your house. Twice already."

"Just take care of the cat, all right?" Carly stuck a finger through the grill of the carrier and scratched Odin's chin.

"Don't worry about it. I know the drill." Dana started the car and rolled away before stopping abruptly and reversing back. She rolled the window down and waved a paper bag at Carly.

Carly took the package and peered inside. It was full of condoms and energy bars.

"Bon voyage!" Dana yelled out the window as she zoomed away.

There are two roads to get to Ensenada, the proverbial high road and the inevitable low road. They travel one above the other, two paths cut into the mountains that follow along the coastline. Separate but hardly equal. The high road is a toll road, well maintained with painted lines, guardrails, and everything. The low road is the public highway and lacks much of what the toll road has, mostly asphalt. It is not for the risk-averse.

Carly looked out the car window at the blue Pacific crashing and thrashing over the rugged coastline below. Los Angeles was three hours, one checkpoint, and one border crossing behind them. The contrast between the U.S. side of the border and the Mexican side was as startling as the difference between the toll road and the public road. There was a rigid uniformity and orderliness about the U.S. side, a monotonous sameness to the streets and cars and stores that comforted as well as dulled the senses. Once over the border, nothing was the same. A very personal and often artistic sensibility pervaded everything on the Mexican side that was both exhilarating and nerve-racking, freeing and frightening.

"Do you think Arlene was running away from

something or to something?" Carly asked, attempting the first real conversation of the day. She'd slept through the U.S. portion of their trip, waking up right before the border in San Ysidro. Driving in Tijuana was always a challenge, so Carly had remained quiet while Evan fenced and parried with the other vehicles for his share of the road.

He didn't answer her question for a long time, long enough to make Carly nervous.

"I'm not supposed to have an opinion," he finally said, gravely. "It could cloud the way I go about getting information, possibly color my choices of people I decide to interview, how I interview them, what I dig into, or avoid. I'm supposed to be documenting what happened, not justifying a theory."

Obviously she'd asked a dumb question. Carly looked at the steep drop to her right and wondered if she should hurl herself dramatically through the open window or just tumble out quietly.

"But," he continued, his voice taking on a lighter tone, "that's the official answer. The real answer is that I think she was running away. Although if I find out otherwise, it's not going to kill me. It's just how it was."

Carly pulled away from the door and sank back into her seat. "Why do you think she was running away?"

He slowed down the truck to avoid some debris in the road. "It just makes sense, given what I know so far. She was unhappy that last year; Raymond said so, everybody said so. Her affair with Pete Silver didn't pan out. Maybe they got married in France when she was visiting him last and it still didn't save their relationship. I think she was running away, just like when she left the farm as a girl."

Carly disagreed. "I think she was running to something."

"Yeah?" He actually sounded mildly interested.

"Well," she said, grinning, pleased that he wanted to know what she was thinking, "not being the filmmaker, I don't have to worry about yielding to temptation. I can yield all I like."

A smile lifted the corner of his well-formed lips. She was having serious trouble with that particular temptation.

"My totally out-there, not-based-on-much, gut reaction is that Arlene was running to something," she said. "She was unhappy, like you said, but I doubt she was running away from it. I think she was looking for happiness, just like the first time, when she left home. I don't really believe that she hated the farm so much as she really wanted to go to the city."

He made an encouraging rolling motion with his hand.

"Music was why she left home," Carly went on. "No one ever said she hated her family. She just wanted a more exciting life. She went to the city for the music. Maybe that's why she left again."

"Well, if everything works out," Evan said, "in a few hours we might actually find out what really happened."

"I can't wait." She smiled broadly, barely able to contain her excitement. For the first time since she lost her shoes she was well and truly happy. Then he smiled back. The impact hit her with the same force as the water pummeling the rocks below, and once again she was swept away.

It was around eleven o'clock when they finally rolled into Ensenada. Already the port city was bustling with weekend visitors taking in the sights, among which was the really hard-to-miss Mexican flag that dominates the harbor. The largest flag in Mexico, unfurled, was of *muy grande* proportions, as big as two football fields and weighing in at over five hundred pounds.

It had been awhile since Carly had been to Marina's family's condo, but she was able to find it without too much trouble. It was just south of the city, across the highway from a rocky beach. The white modern-style complex had thirty units, most of them owned by retirees or used as vacation rentals. Evan pulled the Toyota up to the Cortez condo, an end unit close to the highway. They had only a few minutes to drop off their things if they wanted to eat before their appointment with Pete Silver.

Carly checked the answering machine while Evan unloaded their bags in the foyer.

"Enjoy the condo, Carly." Connie's melodically accented voice floated out of the speaker. "Loved last week's *Hog* where you and Dana got caught counting cards in Vegas and had to make a run for it. *Ai*, that was funny! Don't worry about the laundry; someone comes by to clean on Thursdays. Have a good time, *mi hija*."

"Did you really do that?" Evan asked.

"Do what?" she asked casually as she hit the reset button.

"The Vegas thing."

"No, of course not. Dana always takes creative license."

"Really," he said skeptically.

"She was the one counting cards," Carly said defensively. "I only drove the getaway car."

"Only."

"Everything we do doesn't end up on her show. Just some of the interesting bits."

"Am I going to find myself in one of these episodes?" he asked, suddenly suspicious.

"You planning on doing anything interesting?" she asked, feeling bold.

"You offering to drive the getaway car?"

The room was getting hot.

He indulged in another of those "nothing" kisses. She was going to have to tell him to stop doing that. It made her forget things. Important things, like the fact that he didn't like her and he thought she was a nut, and that she didn't like him and she thought he was a jerk.

"We'll finish this later," he said confidently and headed out the door.

With no time to waste, they headed into town again to grab a quick lunch of fish tacos. The sidewalks were flooded with tourists from the cruise ships, many heading straight for Hussongs Cantina. Over a hundred years old and founded by a German immigrant, Hussongs was the birthplace of the margarita and, therefore, also the site of many a night of drunken debauchery. It was an enduring rite of passage for young Southern Californians to play the Ugly Americano—drive south of the border, drink too much, and throw up. *Vini, vidi, vomitus,* as it were.

"Ever go to Hussongs?" Carly asked as they passed the bar.

"Not any time that I want to remember," he replied ruefully.

"Yeah," she sighed, "I know what you mean."

Pete Silver's place was about twenty minutes southwest of the city. The road that led there needed repaving badly. As the truck reeled and bucked over the potholes, Carly was reminded of the bumpy road to Raymond's trailer. A smile tugged at her mouth.

"Don't tell me," Evan said, catching her grin out of the corner of his eye. "You've never come this way before."

She sat back in her seat. "After an all-night orgy in Valhalla, a sated god turned to his female companion and said proudly, 'I'm Thor.' The goddess answered, 'Tho am I, but it was worth it.'"

To her surprise, he threw his head back and laughed, straight from his belly. She drank it up, all the while kicking herself for melting like candy on a hot dashboard.

Pete Silver's house was a small white adobe structure surrounded by an orchard that sat on a rise facing the ocean. The land around it was scrubby and rocky, but the trees were laden with oranges, lemons, limes, figs, and apricots. In the distance, the hills were combed with grapevines marching in parallel lines long into the distance.

"I know," Carly assured Evan, as he parked the truck in the drive below the house. They would have to climb up a series of stone steps cut into the hillside to get to the property. "I'll only speak when spoken to and I'll do my very best not to get in the way. Scout's honor."

He looked at her for a moment, his easy manner gone, face unreadable, eyes nothing but a steady ocean blue, and nodded. Evan stepped out of the vehicle and pulled his setup out of the back of the truck.

Chapter Fifteen

The house was larger than it appeared from the street below, as much of it either couldn't be seen from the road or was blocked from view by the trees. A huge picture window to the right of the front door faced the sea. The risers of the cement front steps, as well as the frame around the front door, were faced in blue and yellow Mexican tile. Evan used the wrought iron knocker on the heavy front door to announce their arrival.

Impulsively, Carly stood on tiptoe and kissed his cheek.

He raised an eyebrow quizzically.

"For luck," she whispered and squeezed his hand. To her surprise he squeezed back, only dropping her hand when he heard the door unlock.

A tiny woman with iron-gray hair, braided and coiled around the top of her head, and skin as wrinkled and brown as a walnut shell opened the door. She wore a bright blue peasant dress with multi-colored flowers embroidered across the bodice and along the hem. She gazed up at Evan with quick, wrenlike black eyes.

"*Buenos días,* Señora," Evan said in broken Spanish. "*Es la casa de Pedro DaSilva?*"

"Pietro," the woman said in an accent that bespoke the hills of Tuscany, not Mexico.

She motioned for them to follow her, leading them from the foyer and through an archway into a huge living room, the Lucite heels of her gold sandals clicking on the tile floor as she walked. A large stone fireplace topped with a carved oak mantel sat opposite the window that looked out over the ocean. Two long, dark leather sofas dominated the middle of the room, separated by a tile-topped coffee table. Seated in a large leather wing chair facing the door was Pete Silver.

Carly had seen only a few pictures of him, but she recognized him instantly. He was a striking man with soulful brown eyes, high cheekbones, and a regal mouth. His hair, parted on one side, thick and white as cotton, contrasted dramatically with his coffee-colored skin. He wore black trousers and a white-on-white embroidered *Guayabera*, the formal short-sleeved shirt of the tropics.

"You didn't waste any time," he said, rising from his chair and extending his hand to Evan.

"I didn't want you to change your mind," Evan said, shaking his hand warmly. "This is Carly Beck, she'll be doing the narration for the film."

"A pleasure," Pete said, taking her hand in both of his.

"Thank you for allowing me to be here," Carly said. "It's very gracious of you."

"*De nada,*" he said and turned to the old woman. "In case she didn't introduce herself, this is my cousin, Marcella Orsini."

Carly and Evan exchanged multilingual greetings with her.

"Espresso?" she asked and left without waiting for an answer.

"Sit, please," Pete motioned toward the couches. Evan and Carly sat on the one to his left, facing the fireplace. "You have to be patient with Marcella. She doesn't speak English. Since you make movies, she assumes you're famous. She's very starstruck. Except by me. If I were Ricky Martin, however . . ."

"Pedro DaSilva, Pete Silver, Pietro," Evan said, "which do you prefer?"

"When in Rome . . ." He smiled and shrugged. "My father was from Italy, my mother Mexican. My American friends call me Pete."

Evan had the recorder up and running and the mic stand adjusted by the time Marcella arrived with coffees and biscotti. She set the tray down on the table and eyed the equipment warily before taking a seat opposite Carly and Evan.

Pete had watched Evan set up the equipment with interest and asked him a lot of questions about it.

"Everything is so small now," he marveled.

"That's what Raymond said," Carly spoke before thinking. So much for innocent bystander. Evan, headphones on, busy adjusting levels, didn't seem to notice or care.

"Raymond," Pete said thoughtfully. "Raymond Barlow?"

She gave a quick nod.

"How is Ray?"

Carly looked at Evan, who was sorting through a binder full of notes before answering. "Fine. He lives in Palm Springs."

"He always liked the desert. Did he ask you to marry him?"

"Yes." She chuckled. "As a matter of fact, he did."

Pete let out a small laugh that was more air than sound. He said something in Italian to Marcella, who answered with a quick smile and a staccato burst of laughter.

Minutes later, Evan started the interview.

"Tell me about this house. Did you grow up here?"

Pete shook his head. "I bought this property so Arlene could see the ocean. I planted the fruit trees for her, too."

He reminisced about the first time they met.

"She thought I had a funny accent," he said. "I thought she was the most beautiful woman I'd ever seen in my life. I told her that in Italian and Spanish."

About their relationship.

"We made each other crazy. We fought a lot, about everything sometimes, about nothing sometimes. I always yelled in Spanish. I didn't want to hurt her feelings. She was terrible with languages. I always told her I loved her, though, in English so she'd know."

About why she left.

"I begged her to marry me and come back to Mexico with me so we could take over the vineyards. My father was ill, you see, and I didn't want to go on playing clubs anymore, and I didn't want to keep chasing her anymore." He paused and sighed. "She was afraid. She didn't want to live on a farm again. I had asked her many times to marry me, but I told her I wouldn't ask again. She said no. She went back to the States, I went back to Mexico."

Pete stopped and sipped from a glass of scotch that Marcella had brought him not long after the interview began. He swirled the liquor around in the glass and watched the ice cubes spin, lost in thought. No one interrupted his reverie. Marcella was leaning back on the sofa with her eyes closed, maybe awake, maybe dreaming of Ricky Martin. Carly watched the readout on the DAT machine tick off the time in tenths of a second. Evan sat motionless, with all the patience of a man in a duck blind waiting for his quarry. After a while, Pete drained his glass and placed it on the coffee table.

"It took her almost a year to find me. I could have made it easy, but I knew that she had to do it on her own." He tapped two fingers against his temple. "Hardheaded, that one."

"You were sure she would find you," Evan said.

"Oh yes," Pete said with a knowing laugh. "I started building this house when I heard she was looking for me."

"It took her awhile. She didn't speak Spanish, but it didn't matter. Arlene was a very beautiful woman; all men speak the language of beautiful women. I was putting in the tile by the front door when she finally arrived. They were green and she wanted blue. I told her that only my wife could change the tiles on my house. Arlene had made up her mind. She wanted blue."

Pete and Arlene were married the following Sunday in the middle of the DaSilva vineyards. She couldn't really talk to anyone, so she sang for them instead. For the first dance, the mariachi band played a rousing rendition of her theme song, "Fly Me to the Moon." Arlene Barlow spent the rest of her life with Pete Silver and never looked back.

"Arlene died two years ago," Pete said, his voice

shaky with emotion. He swallowed and looked pained.

Carly looked away, afraid she'd start to cry if she didn't.

"She'd been sick for a while," Pete finally said, his voice strong but with a slight tremor. "It was the cigarettes. She couldn't give them up. She just got weaker and weaker."

He stopped again and looked out at the ocean.

"She went to the hospital, but there was nothing to be done. She wanted to come home, so I took her home. It was spring. She liked spring."

Pete put his hand up, signaling the end of the interview. Then he unclipped the microphone and walked out of the room.

"She wasn't running away from something or even to something," Carly said thoughtfully as Evan drove the truck away from the house. "She was running to someone."

"Seems that way."

"Are you disappointed?" she asked.

"No," he said honestly. "It's how it happened—there's no good or bad about it. Like I said earlier, I can't get too wrapped up in how it ends. The end isn't the story, just part of it. How it starts, how you get there, they're important, too."

"I know, I know," she said impatiently. "You've got to be objective about the whole thing. Me? I'm glad she found him. I love that she was finally happy, finally found what and who she was looking for."

He kissed her quickly at a stop sign before shooting through the intersection. "It doesn't mean I'm not glad to find out she was happy."

The streets of town were still busy with people when they got back from Pete's house. In the cantinas, patrons ordered rounds of drinks like the Federales might storm in at any moment waving their stinkin' badges. In some bars, drinks were an experience more than a libation. Large, heavily muscled bartenders were only too happy to pour a drink down the gullet of a partygoer and then grab him in a headlock and shake vigorously—a human martini as presented by the World Wrestling Federation.

Still too early to eat dinner, Carly and Evan took in the sights on the Avenida Lopez Mateos, the city's main drag. Street vendors hawked shaved ice or churros, pastries sprinkled with cinnamon sugar, from carts. Iguanas and burros were rented out by their owners as props for photo opportunities. Men carrying weak car batteries offered to shock people for a fee. For some, being a tourist allowed them to see new sights, dip into a different culture, experience the world anew. For others, it was the opportunity to grab both posts of a car battery and risk electrocution.

Evan scanned the clots of people suspiciously, holding Carly's hand as they walked. The crowds thickened and grew rowdier, bodies jostled each other accidentally and on purpose. Pickpockets and prostitutes worked the packed streets. Evan pulled Carly closer, winding his arm around her, his face directing a challenge at anyone staring too hard, looking too long. He watched over Carly as if she were a diamond in the showcase at Tiffany's.

He was protective and possessive all at once. She was intrigued and wary.

Evan stared at her with unapologetic desire while she drank her margarita in the small seafood restaurant where they eventually ended up. The room was dimly lit by wrought iron candelabras hanging over each table. Semicircular red vinyl booths hugged the perimeter of the room. Purple plastic grape clusters hung from wooden trellises stretched across the ceiling. A crudely painted copy of Botticelli's *The Birth of Venus* adorned one whole wall of the restaurant.

"Why do you keep looking at me?" she finally asked, twirling a tiny paper umbrella between her fingers.

"Why do you think?" He was using his "you're getting very sleepy" hypnotist voice again.

"Don't flirt with me," she said, nervously squirming in the booth. Familiar with his bait-and-switch brand of sexuality, she shied away from another embarrassing showdown.

"Why not?" He scooted closer to her until they were sitting snugly thigh-to-thigh. Carly moved away slightly. Evan chuckled silently but didn't follow.

The waiter presented their dinners with a flourish, lobster enchiladas for two. Evan took him up on a drink refill but Carly declined. She already felt a little too excited and out of control. Maybe it was the alcohol. Maybe it was the Pavlovian effect of too many hedonistic nights in Margaritaville; cross border, lose mind.

"And stop answering everything I say with a question," she continued irritably.

The waiter brought Evan's drink and he clinked the rim of his glass to hers.

"I want you," he declared and took a gulp.

Carly quickly downed the rest of her drink. Maybe she should have ordered that refill.

They ate their meal in a heavy, heady silence, broken only by food and drink inquiries from the waiter.

The creamy, sweet caramel taste of warm flan exploded on Carly's tongue at the same instant she felt Evan's hand slide underneath her skirt. She squeaked in surprise and her eyes grew huge. Anybody watching would have thought it was a hell of a dessert. She swallowed and opened her mouth to protest. He took it as a personal invitation to kiss her, so he obliged, turning her bones to honey in seconds. Flan on its own had just been ruined for her. Without a kiss chaser, it would never quite satisfy in the way that it once had.

She put her spoon down.

"Are you going to finish that?" he asked.

No, sweetheart, she thought, finally settling back to Earth, the question is, are *you* going to finish *that*? She waved the dessert away.

He picked up her spoon with his left hand and started eating. His right hand stayed right where it was, nestled warmly between her thighs. Very impressive. Carly could think of a lot of uses for an ambidextrous man. Evan licked his spoon clean. She had positive thoughts about that as well.

"Why do you keep looking at me?" he said, smiling lasciviously.

"Why do you think?"

The waiter brought the check, deposited it judi-

ciously between the two diners, and slipped away.
Both their hands reached for the bill at the same
time.

"I'll get it."

"I'll get it."

"Mine." Carly moved the tray her way. His right
hand slipped down toward her knees. She stopped
and raised an eyebrow inquisitively.

"Mine." Evan's left hand pulled the tray in his direction; his right hand moved higher up her leg.

Carly rarely heeded her mother's advice, but this
time she really had to agree that arguing over the
check was poor form. So déclassé.

"Yours." She slid the tray closer toward him. She
savored the hot skin-on-skin slide of his hand as it
slipped between her thighs. Nudging the tray with
the tips of her fingers, she controlled the movement of his hand until it was pressed against the
spot where all was right with the world.

"I'm glad that you see things my way." His face
was impassive but his hand was not.

Carly watched in wonder as Evan signed the
credit card receipt using his left hand, without
breaking a sweat. The same could not be said of
her. She was wet.

Really wet.

They walked out of the restaurant but broke into
a run when they reached the parking lot, heading
straight for the car.

"Evan," Carly said suddenly, grabbing his shirtsleeve, "we valet parked."

"Shit! Go to the car," he said, running back to the
curious valet. Evan offered the man a huge tip to
just hand over the keys. A minute later he was bar-

reling the truck down the *avenida* like he was practicing for the Baja 500 off-road race.

Safety adherents always stress the importance of putting both hands on the wheel, ten o'clock and two o'clock hand positions. Carly felt just plain ten o'clock was more than adequate, thank you very much. Evan caught the look on her face, moved his hand expertly between her thighs, and smiled a thoroughly masculine smile. As the truck rattled over a pothole in the street, she was very close to making her nun joke a reality.

They raced to the front door and tumbled into the darkened foyer. Evan locked the door behind them, picked her up, and walked into the first bedroom he could find.

"Evan," she asked as he stood her on her feet in front of the bed. "What about the contract?" A small matter, but . . .

"Not valid outside the U.S. and its protectorates," he said quickly between high-voltage kisses.

Carly reached for his belt. She wasn't a lawyer, so she'd just have to trust him.

Feverishly, they stripped each other with greedy hands, eagerly tugging and pushing at reticent pieces of clothing. Hot, crackling kisses rained down on hypersensitive skin as layers were peeled away. Evan stopped only to turn on the bedside light and pull a condom out of his wallet.

"Wait," she panted, reaching out to fold his hand over the packet. Maneuvering him toward the bed, she placed the tips of her fingers on his chest and pushed him down onto the mattress.

He had a dancer's body, tall and lithe with long, well-delineated muscles. Her hand skimmed appreciatively down the side of his neck and across his chest. The sprinkling of dark hair on his chest stood out against his fair skin. Starting at the top, she worked her way down his body, filling her senses with him—breathing him, tasting him, touching him. The sweet and the salty, the smooth and the rough, the soft and the deliciously hard. She bypassed his solid erection on the way down, saving it for the trip back.

"How the hell did you keep all of this in your pants?" She wrapped her hands around him eagerly and grinned.

"Look closely," he said, moving himself up and down within her grasp. "You can probably count the number of teeth on my pants zipper."

Carly ran the tip of her tongue wickedly along the underside of his thick penis. "Hmmmm, I believe you're right."

His laugh was cut short by a groan of pleasure when her soft lips slipped over the firm tip of his erection. She began to explore him intimately with her mouth. So far, there was nothing about Evan's body with which she could find the least bit of fault. He was absolutely perfect. She worked him with her tongue until she could just taste the silky raw edge of his desire.

"Oh God, Carly," he moaned, his hips rising from the mattress. He flipped her over easily, sheathed himself, and started to push into her. Slowly, inexorably, he slid into the hot, plush spot between her legs. "I'm so hard for you, I feel like I'm going to explode. Don't move. Don't even breathe."

She moaned and tried hard not to heed her body's call to rock against him as he filled her.

He slipped his hand underneath her head, holding it in place, and stared hard into her face. "Do you want me, Carly?" he demanded.

The sensation of every inch of him surrounded by every inch of her was overwhelmingly, unbelievably, mind-numbingly better than she thought it could be. And she'd given it a lot of thought.

"Do you?" he asked again, his voice low and urgent.

"I want you."

His mouth closed over hers and kissed her passionately, fiercely until she felt light-headed and wild. Evan kissed his way down to her breasts and began to suck and nibble and lick and rub, working her toward her climax. She locked her legs around him and held on tight, trembling and quaking as he started to thrust inside her.

"More?" he asked, flexing his hips quickly.

"More," she urged desperately. "A lot more."

With a deep groan, he began to slam into her, the muscles bunching and releasing under his sweat-slicked skin. The bed shook in its frame and the headboard slapped against the wall in a quickening rhythm. Carly felt an operatic scream coming on.

"Brace yourself, pretty girl," he warned, driving harder and deeper.

Wait, she tried to say, wanting just a little bit more. But her body, patience expired, let go, and, like tethered mountain climbers, Carly and Evan tumbled headlong, one after the other, yodeling a little, over the edge.

The rush was incredible, as if her entire body had

contracted into itself and then exploded with a nuclear fury laying waste to mind, body, and soul in the span of a handful of heartbeats. This was no ordinary orgasm. Evan was no ordinary man. Carly wasn't ready yet to acknowledge his supernatural powers, but if he could make her come like that, say, more than twice in her life, she'd have no problem awarding him superhero status. Hell, she'd start a religion.

"Am I too heavy?" Evan asked after a little while. Even demigods had to get their strength back.

"A little."

He slid most of his torso from her to the mattress and shifted his weight to his side. "Better?"

"Mmmm." She nodded weakly.

"This is a twin bed," Evan noted with concern, twisting his head around to survey the situation. His feet hung over the bottom edge. Carly's arms were outstretched, leaving her hands hanging over the sides.

"I didn't choose it," she said.

"It was handy." He disengaged from Carly with great reluctance and kissed her gently before leaving the bed. "I'll be right back, pretty girl."

A few minutes later he swept her up in his arms and headed upstairs in search of a bigger bed. The first room had pink rosebud wallpaper and a full-sized canopy bed covered in white eyelet ruffles.

"Better," Carly said from the vantage point of his arms.

He made a face. "Too fluffy."

She pointed toward the door. "Lead on, Goldilocks."

The next room had a queen bed and walls covered with angry rock stars and busty pinups.

"I could do this," said Evan.

"I don't need an audience," Carly said.

The master bedroom had a king bed and a balcony that faced the ocean.

"Just right," they agreed as they sank into the mattress.

"Stay one more day," he whispered into her ear as he spooned her tightly against him. Evan nuzzled her hair, took a deep breath, and exhaled slowly. "I love the way you smell."

The contract, her shoes, and Quinn be damned. She wanted one more day. She'd have hours on the ride home to call herself twelve kinds of stupid.

"Yes," she said and felt him start to relax. Moments later he was asleep and Carly was marveling at how good it felt to be lying next to Evan—almost as good as underneath him.

Chapter Sixteen

Carly awoke to a warm purr and a kiss behind the ear. Not Odin and not bad. Sharp teeth bit softly into her shoulder, followed by a soothing kiss. Really not bad. She opened her eyes and looked through the sliding glass door at the inky night sky studded with stars. The door was cracked, and the sound and smell of the surf rushed up the beach, into the bedroom, and back out again. Carly returned the purr, pressing her back against the warmth of Evan's chest and stomach.

"Awake?" he whispered, his breath warming her ear and cheek. His hand slid across her ribs and cupped her breast, fingers gently teasing her nipple to a hard, tight, happy peak.

She answered by wiggling her bottom against his hips. He was most definitely awake, up, and ready to go.

He explored her, much as she had him hours earlier. His mouth and hands mapped the terrain of her body, charted peaks and valleys, lingered at the various points of interest. She thought she'd already discovered every thrill in Carlyland, but Evan's mouth was deftly steering the little man in the rowboat ride toward some class five rapids she ⌐ never seen before, never even imagined existed.

"Evan," she said, pulling away. She was holding out for the Matterhorn.

He pulled her back, softly bit her inner thigh, and then kissed it. "I'm out of condoms, pretty girl."

What?!

She was simultaneously pleased and annoyed that he wasn't arrogant enough to come armed with a spring break–sized box of condoms. Carly relaxed as she felt his tongue start to work its magic again; she supposed there was nothing left to do but to let him make it up to her. She didn't want to be rude.

"Hold on," she cried suddenly, pushing away. "There's a paper bag in my backpack in the living room. Get it!"

Evan shot out of bed and down the stairs. He was back in seconds, switching on the bedside lamp, and yanking the zipper on the backpack open. He mumbled something as he grabbed a foil packet out of the paper bag and rolled on a condom. It was purple. Carly didn't care; she pulled him down on top of her and threw a leg over his hip.

He slid inside her, his erection hard and heavy, sending a shock wave of concentrated pleasure through her body. She thought what he had been doing before was incredible. This was better. Carly dug her nails into his back just because it felt so good and because it made him throw his head back and moan.

"Oh yes, oh yes . . ." she chanted and squeezed and released her muscles in response to his thrusts, building her orgasm.

Evan growled her name like a warning. "You make me insane."

"Good." She hated to think she was losing her mind all by herself.

He made some more growling noises and began to slam into her with authority, making the stars spin in place. She held her ground, just barely clinging to her climax. It was a race, a sexual game of chicken, to see who would be the first to crack. Technically, Carly lost it first, but Evan trailed behind by only a hundredth of a second.

Carly's prize was the mother of all orgasms. A through-the-roof mental and physical extravaganza that eclipsed everything that had come before. She'd been done and undone by a master, but Carly wasn't about to share that little secret.

"That was the best orgasm of my entire life!" she gasped, proving that mind and body had gone their separate ways and had yet to reconnect.

"You're very welcome," Evan said magnanimously before he collapsed on top of her.

"Oooof!"

"Sorry, babe, I didn't mean to squish you," he apologized a moment later. Evan gently rolled over, taking her with him. "I think I blacked out there for a sec."

"You have quite an emergency kit here, pretty girl," Evan noted with amusement, sitting up on the bed as he checked out the holiday assortment of hermetically sealed condoms and energy bars. He made a face and tossed a bar back into the sack. "Blech, I hate coconut."

"Who says I packed with you in mind?" she huffed.

He started tossing condoms into the air. "Just who did you pack for, Carly? The Army, Navy, Air Force, and Marines?"

She threw a packet at him.

He stopped to examine a glow-in-the-dark condom. "You're even prepared for a Boy Scout or two."

"I didn't pack it," she said, trying and failing to snatch the bag away. "It's Dana's idea of a gag."

Evan found the coconut energy bar again and threw it over his shoulder to the far side of the room. He discovered another unusual condom, inspected it, then tucked it under the pillow. "Remind me to thank her when we get back."

Carly swept the bed clean of its latex litter with her arm. "Feel free to take back what's left and thank her yourself."

He chuckled and pulled her into his arms. "Who says there'll be any left?"

"Men!" she said, struggling against and then snuggling into him. "Did she pack a gun, by any chance?"

"Nope," he said, turning off the light. "You'll have to wait till we get back to shoot me."

"Yes," she sighed. "But I have a better chance of getting away with it here."

Her first call, while Evan showered, was to Dana at work.

"Welcome to the Planet of the Apes. Head keeper speaking," Dana said dryly. "What's up, Tinkerbell? You need me to make bail or something?"

"Remember that bag of stuff you gave me?"

"The goodie bag?" Dana asked gleefully.

"It's down a few goodies."

"Got it. Odin's doing great. Just let me know when you're coming home."

"Thanks."

The call to her agent was less positive.

"What the hell are you still doing in Mexico?" Quinn yelled into the phone.

"Things are going really well with Pete," she said, which was true. "So I wanted to stay another day." Which had nothing to do with Pete but which was also true.

"Fine," he sniffed. "I'll cancel your auditions. It's only your career."

"Quinn . . ."

"Don't drink the water. And don't drink the tequila, either."

After lunch, Evan made a phone call of his own to Pete Silver letting him know that they'd be in town for another day.

Carly listened absentmindedly while she busied herself clearing up the dishes. As she expected, there were a couple of frozen tamales in the freezer that she and Evan had for lunch. For breakfast, they had coffee and energy bars in bed.

Evan was still on the phone when Carly headed upstairs to the master bedroom balcony. She pulled a plastic cover off a green and white striped lounge chair and curled up to look at the ocean shimmering in the distance. Only the highway and a wide, rocky beach separated the condo from the water.

She grinned at the memory of sleeping spooned up with Evan all night long. Both times after they'd made love, Evan had tucked her body into his with the same single-mindedness with which he did everything. Once he had her snuggled up against him just so, a seamless joining from ankle to shoulder, his nose buried in her hair, he let out a sigh of pure contentment and melted into sleep. Big bad Evan was a cuddler.

Carly had finally done the deed, several times in fact, enough to have satisfied her curiosity and sated her physical needs. And yet she wasn't quite ready to give it up.

Just a little bit more.

"Hey, pretty girl, you got sunscreen on?" Evan walked out onto the balcony and ran his finger down the bridge of her nose.

She smiled at the endearment and shook her head sheepishly.

Evan sat down next to her. "He wants us to come back."

"Really?" She suddenly felt better about lying to Quinn.

"He's got a bunch of photographs he's willing to lend me plus some old reel-to-reels of her singing."

"That's wonderful!"

"Pretty amazing," he said as he pulled her toward him for a languid kiss. Carly let the beguiling feel of his mouth on hers wash over her. She wrapped her arms around his shoulders and pulled him down onto the chaise. Kissing Evan in the warm sunlight was worth risking a sunburn for.

"Ever have sex on one of these things before?" he asked.

"No," but it had suddenly hit the top of her "to do" list.

"Me neither." He unbuttoned her blouse and laid down a trail of kisses from her mouth to her breasts.

Carly was willing to gamble on third-degree burns to find out what it was like.

"Well," he said, abruptly sitting up and refastening her shirt, "we'll have to save it for tonight because I told him we'd be right over."

She smacked his hands away. "I've changed my mind."

He stood and pulled her up with him, pressing her body tightly against his. "Don't worry. I can always change it back."

He was insufferable, but after her blurted confession the night before, she knew there was no denying it. She should have moved into damage-control mode that morning before embarking on the third go-round. Only the lure of going three for three, getting the Triple Crown of Orgasms, was just too hard to resist. And, in the end, well, it was worth it.

Marcella greeted them like old friends, muttering effusively in Italian and giving them each a warm kiss on the cheek, starting and ending with Evan. Carly plastered an innocent smile on her face and pinched his tush when Marcella went back for seconds. Evan pinched hers in retaliation when they followed the old lady inside. Bypassing the living room, Marcella walked them down a hallway, through a huge dining room with a long rough-hewn table, and outside to a flagstone courtyard. There, she motioned them to take a seat at a wrought iron patio set and mentioned something about espresso before she left. They sat down at the table and waited for their host to appear.

The courtyard opened up to a small, tired lawn; beyond that lay the fruit orchard, partially visible from the drive below. A fat calico cat emerged between a pomegranate tree and an orange tree and sniffed the air a few times. Marcella reappeared with a tray of coffee and set it down on the glass-topped table. She clucked irritably, tossed a comment in Italian to Evan who, for lack of an answer, just smiled. She patted his cheek fondly before heading back into the house.

A bee circled their table on a reconnaissance flight, surveying the spread a few times before heading back to the fruit trees. Carly idly watched the cat patrol the orchard.

"What are you thinking?" Evan asked softly.

"I'm wondering if it was worth it," she said after a while.

"What was?" He reached out and tucked a lock of hair behind her ear.

"Love," she said, placing her elbows on the table and cradling her chin in her hands. "Arlene must have loved Pete a hell of a lot."

"Or he loved her a hell of a lot," he offered.

"I've never loved anybody that much." She thought about her parents, who certainly hadn't loved each other that much.

"I hope I never do."

She looked at him. "Never love anyone that much?"

"Yeah," he said wholeheartedly. "It would get in the way of everything."

It wasn't news. Carly never figured him as a happily ever-after sort of guy. She doubted that it was in the cards for her either. Not because she didn't want it but because, unlike everything else in her life, the shoes didn't seem to have the power to change her destiny in that way.

"I didn't expect you so soon." Pete's voice came from behind them. He was dressed much the same as the day before, only this time his *Guayabera* was pale blue with dark blue embroidery. He waved them down as they started to stand, and took a seat opposite Carly. He looked at Evan. "You didn't want to give me time to change my mind, eh?"

"Don't want to miss out on a great opportunity," Evan agreed.

Pete nodded and aimed his next question at Carly. "How are you today?"

"Good," she said, thinking about all the good things that had gone on the night before and again the next morning.

He raised his eyebrows, eyes twinkling. "Just good?"

She felt a flush creep up her neck. Next to her, Evan looked, smelled, and acted like a well-fed lion. Carly was saved from having to answer since Marcella chose that moment to come back from the house. As usual, the diminutive woman was already, maybe still, talking.

"It was Marcella who convinced me to lend you the photographs and tapes," Pete admitted as his cousin sat down and began serving coffee. "Even now, I'm not sure. There will be a lot of people calling when this comes out. But you will make your film no matter what I do, and I think it will be a good one. So I might as well make it better."

"I'll send you a copy before it's finalized," Evan assured him. "I want to know what you think. I can't promise I'll change anything, but that doesn't mean I won't, either."

Pete held Evan's eyes for a moment, then Carly's. He smiled an enigmatic smile. "Yes, I think it will be very good."

Back at the condo, Evan was kissing Carly with one eye looking through the partially closed blinds at the truck, jam-packed with boxes, parked in front of the kitchen window. Pete had offered up a mother lode of photographs and old reel-to-reel tapes. It had been a hard exercise in brute strength and spatial manipulation to fit everything in, but Evan had been determined and was, as usual, successful.

"We can't stay the night," he said. "There's no garage and I can't leave those tapes in the car. We should head back."

Despite an early morning tumble, Carly's body was already making preparations for meltdown. "You've got a car alarm."

His hands slipped under her blouse. "Not much good if they're already down the street by the time I'm out the door."

"Oh," she said as she got up on tiptoe, wrapped her leg around his, and pressed herself up against him.

"Don't do that," he said but didn't pull away.

"What?" she said and rubbed against him again. "This?"

"Yes."

"Or this?" She reached between their bodies and stroked his erection through the denim of his jeans.

"Yes," he said, catching his breath.

"Then I guess you don't want me to do this, either." With a quick movement, she had his jeans unbuttoned and halfway down his thighs along with his underwear. She dropped to her knees and placed both hands around his rigid penis, looking up at him expectantly.

Evan glanced out the window quickly before looking back down at the sexy brunette. Wicked thoughts flashed behind her eyes.

"No," he said without much conviction as she started to stroke him. "You probably better not do that, either."

Desperately dividing his attention, Evan let his gaze sweep frantically back and forth between her hands and the car. Sweat popped out on his brow as he steadied his body against the sink. He swore inventively, alternately reveling in and cursing his predicament. He was caught at a fork in the road. To fork or not to fork, that was the question.

She ran her tongue, hot and liquid, up his thigh.

He froze, unable to peel his eyes away from the sight of her as she took him in her mouth. "Oh, God, yes . . ."

Minutes later Carly was flat on her back on the kitchen table. Evan stood between her thighs rolling on a condom while still desperately trying to keep one eye on the truck.

"Jesus, Mary, and Joseph," he said reverently, stealing a glance down at himself just barely inside her. He took two deep breaths before he plunged into her as deeply as he could.

"You're not Catholic," she said breathlessly, scrabbling to hold on to the table and her orgasm. "You're not even religious."

"And all the saints in heaven," Evan moaned, his hips pistoning back and forth. He seemed very close to being born again.

Seconds later, Carly was shouting amen and hallelujah along with him.

"You're right," she said brightly, untangling her legs from around his waist and letting them dangle over the edge of the table. Her face was glowing and her breathing was still fast and quick. "We shouldn't leave the tapes unattended."

He made a grumbling noise in the back of his throat and placed his hands around her neck. The moment of retribution was at hand.

"You make me crazy," he said, then he moved his hands to cradle her head and kissed his frustrations away.

The sun was setting on the Pacific Ocean as they left Ensenada. The western sky was a dozen shades of blue and pink, chased by a blanket of dark purple coming from the east.

Carly thought about the first time she'd laid eyes on Evan, about how caught she was by him, about whether she would have ended up in his arms, shoes or no shoes. She looked at his hands on the steering wheel. He had beautiful hands that did beautiful things. No, she concluded, it never would have happened because as much as she really liked the look of him, she would never have gotten past his antagonism. But that was then. If it weren't for the shoes, she never would have spent enough time with him to get to where she was now, somewhere between having the best time of her life and making the biggest mistake of her life.

"That night . . . at my house," she said, searching for something to call it, "when you brought the roses. Would you have really gone through with it?"

"Sure," he said easily, not looking at her.

"Oh." Disappointment colored her voice.

"Would you?"

Touché. In his eyes, he might have been a jerk taking advantage of her, but she must have looked like a reality-challenged nut bag chasing a pair of shoes like the Holy Grail.

"I never would have done anything," he continued, "that you didn't want to do. Not for a second."

"What if I was just going along with it?"

"Have you been 'just going along with it' for the last twenty-four hours?"

She had no reply. The sun was sinking lower, turning the ocean into a glorious, rippling sheet of chrome.

"Don't think it to death, Carly," he advised. "It'll either drive you crazy or make you depressed, neither of which are good options. Are you sorry about things already?"

"No," she said honestly. "I'm not sorry."

"Me neither. Life is a banquet. Have it now—it doesn't keep."

She was going to get her shoes and, consequently, her life back in less than a week. Presumably everything would right itself. The world would be a better place. She'd be done with the film and would never have to be in the same room with Evan ever again if she didn't want to. Unfortunately, she did want. The ransom just went up. It was going to cost. A lot. More than she ever wanted to pay. She'd get her luck back and Evan would walk away with her voice on tape and maybe a piece of her heart stuck to the bottom of his shoe.

Dark in Mexico was darker than at home. In all the times Carly had been up and down the Baja coast, it occurred to her, she'd never driven it at night. Being a city girl, she wasn't used to miles of unlit highways and the endless thick, black nothingness beyond the car's headlights.

"Nervous?" Evan asked.

Carly strained to see the moonlight glinting off the ocean to their left. They were driving north, hugging the mountainside but, since the lanes were narrow and winding, it did little to calm her nerves. That was one steep, ugly drop.

"A little." She looked out at the water again. "I've just discovered an incredible fondness for guard-rails."

"Don't worry, pretty girl," he said calmly, reaching for her hand. "I'll get you home in one piece."

After the worrisome emptiness of the coast passed, they still had to contend with the demolition derby traffic of Tijuana and then the stop-and-go lines at the border. Any hopes that they might reach home before midnight faded when the Toyota was pulled out of line by the border patrol. Evan and Carly sat in the noisy waiting room while agents and drug-sniffing dogs combed the vehicle.

"Damn it," Evan said impatiently. "If they screw with those tapes . . ."

"It'll be fine." Carly tried to reassure him, although she wasn't so sure herself. She'd heard the horror stories of innocent motorists having their cars pulled apart bolt by bolt at the slightest provocation. "I'm going to see what I can do."

"Carly, don't make this worse than it already is."

"Have a little faith, Evan," she said, patting his arm. She squared her shoulders and walked purposefully in search of the person in charge. Carly had gotten Dana out of enough scrapes to have picked up a trick or two along the way. Fifteen minutes later they got the all clear and were back on gentle U.S. pavement.

They were in San Diego proper before Evan finally swallowed his pride enough to ask what happened. "Okay, I know you're dying to tell me what happened."

"No, I'm not," she said.

"Not what?"

"Dying to tell you."

"Carly . . ." he said in an ominous rumble.

"Okay, okay," she said and smiled impishly. "I just showed 'em my stuff."

"You what?!" The truck veered out of its lane a little before Evan regained control. The driver of the car next to them hit the horn and gestured obscenely before speeding away.

"What exactly did you show them?" he demanded.

She batted her eyes innocently.

His eyes narrowed and sparked dangerously.

Carly stifled a giggle. He was so cute when he was all het up. It was hard to believe that the last time they were on a road trip she had gone out of her way not to irritate him.

"I showed them my cartoon voices," she said finally. "I told them the tapes were part of a project I was working on. It's not a cartoon, but they don't know that. Anyway, I whipped out old Ella Earthworm and Princess Ninja Dragonfire, and Greta Ground Squirrel, and a few others. Luckily the head guy has kids; he recognized them immediately. I promised to send him some eight-by-tens of the characters and a personalized message for his kids."

"Saved by Greta Ground Squirrel." Evan shook his head in disgust. "Un-fucking-believable."

"Believe it, baby." Carly blew on her nails and shined them on the sleeve of her dress before letting out a hellacious Princess Ninja Dragonfire battle yell.

"Aaaaaah-eeeeeee-yah!"

Startled, Evan lost control of the truck once more and shuddered.

Chapter Seventeen

It was late by the time they pulled up into Carly's driveway. She'd been wondering what Evan had in mind when they finally got back within the contractual confines of the U.S. and its protectorates. Was their Mexican interlude now over? Carly wanted him to stay but the thought of asking him scared the Cheez Whiz out of her.

"I want to park in the garage," Evan said. "I need to make sure the tapes are safe."

Thank you, God.

She hurried out of the truck and went to unlock the garage before he could change his mind. Five minutes later, the truck was locked in the garage and she and Evan were locked in an embrace in the kitchen.

"We need to take a shower," he said. "I feel grungy from driving."

Her left eyebrow sat up a little higher than it normally did. "You feel grungy, so we need to take a shower? Interesting logic."

He took her hand, picked up his duffel bag, and led the way to the bathroom. "It's the most efficient way to get everybody clean and naked all at once."

"I'd say you're brilliant," she said as she flipped

on the bathroom light and turned the water on, "but you'd only agree with me."

"You can pretend it was your idea if you like." He shucked off his shoes, socks, and shirt, and was peeling off his jeans and underwear. "That way you can be brilliant."

Carly kicked off her shoes and wriggled out of her dress. Steam was starting to rise from the shower. He helped her out of her bra and panties, his hands sliding over her bare skin, then stepped into the shower with her.

"Do you have a lounge chair in the backyard?" he asked. They never had gotten around to testing out the one on the condo balcony.

"Yes, I do." She poured out a dollop of liquid soap into her hand and started to lather his chest. "And no, we can't. I have neighbors I'll probably see again in this lifetime. Turn, please."

He spun around dutifully. "And they're scoping out your backyard in the middle of the night?"

Carly thought about Jensen and his hidden cameras. She had no desire to have streaming video of her bouncing moonlit tush on the Internet. "You don't know my neighbors."

"Carly?"

"Hmmm?" He had the loveliest set of buns, she thought, as she soaped their twin splendor. So delicious and utterly squeezable. Hand followed thought as she pinched his bottom.

"Ever have sex in the shower?"

"Yes." Her hands slipped around his hips to lather up his other splendid squeezable bits. "But I prefer to finish in the bedroom."

"Uh, well," he said as he suddenly slapped his

hands against the tile wall for support, "if you don't move your hands soon I'm going to finish right here."

She made him wait through a shampoo and condition before she consented to head to the bedroom. He made her sit through a very thorough towel dry before he would follow.

"I'd like to teach you about the three R's," she said, rolling a condom on him as he lay on the bed.

"Readin', 'ritin', and 'rithmetic?" He looked like yummy personified, his lean, taut body lying handsomely underneath her.

"No." She slid herself down his torso, straddled his hips, and took him inside her as slowly as possible, meting out pleasure a millimeter at a time.

A rumble of satisfaction emanated from low in his throat.

"Reelin', rockin', and rollin'," she said with a satisfied smile before she brought her mouth down onto his nipple. Her tongue made tight little circles while her hips did the same.

"How long . . ." he asked, between gasps, "do you think . . . it'll take . . . to learn all that?"

"Awhile," she said with a sinful swivel. "Maybe all night."

He pulled her mouth close to his. "I've got all night."

But he didn't have all morning. The sun was barely up and yawning when Evan kissed her goodbye. He was already showered and dressed. The smell of fresh coffee steamed up from the cup he'd placed on the nightstand for her.

"I've got to go, Carly," he said, sitting down on the edge of the bed, his hand on her shoulder. "I've got a ton of work to do before Friday."

She blinked away sleep and looked up at him. He was appallingly alert and handsome despite, or maybe because of, the long night behind them. She rubbed her cheek against his hand.

"It's going to be great," he said. He slipped his hand under the sheet, caressing her from shoulder to hip and back again.

"I know," she said. He was talking about the film, but she pretended he was referring to something else.

He pressed his mouth to hers. The kiss tasted of toothpaste and coffee, a morning kiss. She sighed and closed her eyes. She heard him whisper something unintelligible.

"What?" she asked.

"Nothing."

"Right." They were back in LA. Back to reality. Back to nothing again.

"Go to sleep," he said.

And she did because it was the easiest thing to do.

Aside from a table set for one, there is nothing more lonely than an empty bed. Several hours later, Carly opened her eyes to dead air and cold coffee. No handsome, black-haired male snoozed beside her, human, feline, or otherwise.

Time to get her cat.

"How's my big boy?" Carly cooed, squeezing a happy Odin. "Did you have any problems?"

"Nah," Dana said, sitting down on the red couch next to her. "He did do a little Crouching Tiger, Hidden Poo-Poo thing outside the laundry room door. But that was my fault; I accidentally locked him out, so he couldn't get to the litter box, poor baby."

"Sorry about that."

"No big deal," Dana said. "Anything to further the cause of romance. So tell me everything."

Carly checked her watch. In an eerie, dead-on imitation of the computerized phone lady, she said, "At the tone . . . the time will be . . . nine . . . twenty . . . and . . . ten . . . seconds. Don't you have to go to work?"

"So I'll be late. Nothing new."

Carly stalled. "I've got an audition and I've got to drop Odin off at home first."

"Just give me the highlights," Dana said expectantly.

Carly shook her head.

"What? Don't tell me nothing happened."

"Something happened. I'm just not sure what it was."

"Oh, I see," Dana said, finally grasping the situation. "Has the love bug done bit you, Tinkerbell?"

Carly looked stricken. "God, I hope not. I gotta go. Quinn'll kill me if I blow off another audition."

Carly popped Odin into his carrier and headed for the door. Dana shouldered her laptop case and followed.

"Would falling in love be so bad?" Dana asked.

"No," Carly admitted. "Falling in love is great. It's the falling-face-first-into-the-cement part that comes later that I really hate."

* * *

Carly would prefer to think that there was only one person who would be ringing her doorbell at eleven o'clock at night. But running over her list of odd friends and unpredictable family members, she really couldn't say that. She belted her robe and rose up on tiptoe to peer through the peep-hole.

The man with one red shoe was standing on her porch.

Evan must have dropped into a black hole the morning he left her house and ended up in a galaxy far, far away. It was the only explanation she could come up with for his two-day absence from her life. Granted, she could have called him but she was feeling ornery and neglected. She damn well didn't want to be fair and just. Carly wanted him to share a bit in her suffering, so she held off opening the door for five whole seconds. That ought to show him. She could play hardball, too.

"Not because of Mexico," Evan said, holding the shoe aloft.

"Oh?" she said, evenly. "Then why?"

He shrugged.

"That's it?" She mimicked the quick movement of his shoulders. "What's that supposed to mean?"

He held the shoe out. "You want it or not?"

"Yes," she said irritably, snatching the shoe from his outstretched hand and drawing him into the house. She wanted it to symbolize something, and it infuriated her that he insisted it meant nothing.

He walked straight into the kitchen to the re-frigerator.

"There's leftover spaghetti if you're interested," she said.

"I'm interested," he assured her, as he pulled the pasta out, ladled himself a large serving, and popped it into the microwave. Evan pulled her into his arms for a kiss, heating her and his dinner at the same time.

Once seated at the kitchen table, he attacked his meal as if he hadn't eaten since he'd seen her last. "Hey, this is terrific," he said, slowing down to savor his dinner. "Do you always cook this well?"

Carly beamed. No Nobel Prize winner ever felt this good.

"You have a creepy neighbor with an unhappy black dog?" he asked between bites of food.

"Yeah," she said, uneasily. "That's Jensen and Megabyte."

"He's all bark and his dog is no bite," Evan said derisively. "I ran over some kid's toy that was whizzing around your driveway and he and his dog came shooting out of nowhere. Does he think he's a ninja or something?"

"He's mostly harmless," she explained.

Unconvinced, Evan shot her a "you've got to be kidding" look. "I told him if I ever caught him within a hundred feet of your house, I'd put my fist through his face."

"That wasn't very neighborly." Not to mention an impossible restriction on Jensen, who lived across the street. Carly declined to share that little fact since, judging from the disgusted look on Evan's face, he'd probably make good on his threat.

"The guy's a perv," Evan said, pushing his empty

plate away. "Make sure you lock up at night. And close the drapes, too."

Yep, he'd definitely punch him, all right. Carly cleared away his dinner plate and switched subjects to something less violent. "Did you get much work done on the film?"

He pulled a script out of the interior pocket of his jacket and tossed it on the table. "Take a look."

She topped off the coffee she was having before he'd arrived and poured him a cup before diving into the new script.

"Thanks," he said, taking the coffee from her. "The really significant narration changes occur in the last quarter of the script. The other changes are all visual or music."

She skipped forward until she got to copy she didn't recognize. Pete and Arlene's story, it was all there. Reading it brought back the warm afternoon sitting in Pete's living room, the smell of leather and espresso, the sound of his age-roughened voice. It had been less than a week since the interview, and yet it felt like a lifetime ago. Someone else's lifetime.

"This is really good," Carly said, putting down the script.

Evan took the compliment in stride. Unlike Carly, he was used to being terrific. "You should hear the tapes of Arlene. God, Carly, they're incredible. I could easily spend a whole 'nother year just going through them, but right now I'm only concentrating on the stuff I need for the film."

"How were the pictures that Pete gave you?"

"Unbelievable. There's so much good stuff there. It's going to make such a huge difference in the film." He finished his coffee and poured himself a refill.

"If you need more changes later on," Carly said as she added cream and sugar to his cup and Evan nodded his thanks, "I don't mind coming in to do them. It wouldn't cost you anything."

"That's okay," he answered quickly. "With the stuff you're doing tomorrow night and everything I've already got in the can, I'm sure I won't need it. But thanks."

Carly had been on the losing end of enough auditions to know when she was getting the brush-off.

"What do you think of the new narration?" he asked, throwing her a bone.

Miss Congeniality, she thought miserably of her consolation prize. She looked down at the script and pretended to study it so he couldn't see her face while she glued it back together. Her opinion was the last thing he wanted, but she couldn't let the opportunity pass; he'd likely never ask again. So she made a few comments on the copy, going so far as to offer a few suggestions on the rest of the film as well.

A series of noncommittal nods and grunts was all the response he gave to her critique, which was a great deal better than the first time she'd offered an opinion on his script, when he'd cut her off at the knees. He was just humoring her, she understood that. *And yet* . . . She cringed at her own foolishness.

The thumping, rhythmic, bone-shaking waves that rattled the bedroom announced the passing of a stereo system with a car built around it as it rumbled down the quiet street. Minutes later, the only thing coming through the window was the heady smell of night-blooming jasmine. Carly lay on her stomach and looked up at Evan. "Tell me what happened at Dana's party."

Evan was leaning against a pile of pillows, a lazy, contented smile on his lips. His hair was adorably rumpled and he had that smug male "I take full credit for everyone's phenomenal orgasm" look on his face. "Sure you want to hear this?"

"Not really, but I hate having blank spots in my memory."

"Okay. After you passed out—"

She groaned. "I hate stories that start like that."

"After you passed out," he reiterated, ignoring her discomfort, "I carried you into the house and tossed you into Dana's shower."

"You undressed me?"

"It was a chore, yes, but it had to be done."

"And you were just the man to do it," she replied dryly.

"I'd like to think so." He pinched her bare bottom.

"Go on," she said, smacking his hand away.

Smirking, he resumed his story. "I wrapped you up snug as a bug and put you in the bed."

"Nice of you," she muttered.

"Wasn't it? Now where was I? Oh, yes. You opened your eyes and said, 'Oh, God, Evan, stop spinning! You're making me sick.'" He used a high, twittery voice to mimic her response.

"Hey!" she said sharply. "I do the voices."

"Just trying to add realism," he said, tweaking her

bottom again. "Anywho, you started to make a lot of groaning noises, just like the ones you're making now, and asked me to kill you."

It was too much. Carly buried her face in the pillow. He gathered her into his arms and began rubbing her back.

"I refused, of course. Then you said that I was really mean, which was a shame because you thought I was very handsome."

"Noooo," she moaned piteously into his chest.

"Wicked handsome," he whispered gleefully into her ear.

"Ooooh."

"You said if I didn't have the decency to kill you then the least I could do was to take you home. So I tossed you over my shoulder and took you home. It was the least I could do."

"Since you're so mean," she said miserably.

"Uh-huh." He pulled her up on top of him and kissed her seductively. "You still think I'm wicked handsome?"

"Yes," she said, avoiding his eyes and talking to his chin.

He placed her hands on his chest. "Then show me."

Later, it was her turn to wear the "you can thank me later, when you've found your brains" face.

The shoes were back. Time to pop champagne, thump some backs, and make a bunch of celebratory woo-hoo noises.

"There's no place like home, there's no place like home . . ." Carly murmured earnestly, looking down at her once again luck-shod feet. She clicked her heels together three times just because.

Odin watched her from his perch on the sofa arm, his tail draped along one side, curling and uncurling. He looked just like a kitty-cat clock, his eyes trailing her movements as she walked back and forth across the living room.

"I don't know," she said, coming to a stop in front of him. "Something's wrong. Something's missing."

The doorbell rang and she immediately wanted to smack herself for hoping it was Evan. That was one habit she didn't need.

"I come bearing gifts," Dana said, holding up a pizza box.

"Aren't you supposed to be working?" Carly asked, following her friend into the kitchen.

"Client lunch," Dana announced, placing the box on the kitchen table.

Carly set napkins and plates on the table. "I'm not a client. And Odin's got even less money than me, although he's less picky about whose lap he sits on."

"No, I'm the client." Dana pulled a generous slice of pizza out of the box and twirled the cheese strings around her finger until they snapped. "This is real business. The *Hog Heaven* syndication package is going out at the end of this season. I want you to voice all the spots. It's a hundred TV and a hundred radio."

Carly's pizza was halfway to her mouth before the impact of what Dana was saying hit her. Stunned, she dropped the slice on her plate. "You're kidding me."

"Would I kid you?" Dana asked, then laughed.

"Okay, I would, I have, and I probably will again, but I'm not kidding now."

"God, that's incredible!" The job would more than make up for the loss of *Mr. Bert* and *Compost Critters*. "But is it your decision to make?"

"Not really," her friend said airily. "I don't actually get to vote, but I do get a say on things that would make the people who do get to vote really, really unhappy."

"I hope you're not doing this just for me, Dana. You don't have to do it and I don't want you to screw up a good thing."

Dana banished the worries away with a wave of her hand. "Yes and no. This morning they played me a tape of the girl they want and I hated it. She's totally wrong—boring, smarmy, blah. I want smart and sassy. I want you. You are Charlie after all."

"I never thought I'd be happy to hear that," Carly laughed, her faith in the shoes restored. "You're the best, D. I can't thank you enough."

"Sure you can," Dana said, getting up to rummage through the refrigerator for drinks. "Tell me all about Mexico. I noticed you've got your shoes back, and it's not even Friday yet. Details, Tinkerbell, I need hard, sweaty details."

"You drive a hard bargain." Carly sighed, acknowledging defeat. She brought her hand up to her forehead and made an L with her thumb and index finger. "I think it's love."

Dana's eyes twinkled. "How many condoms do you have left?"

"About five, maybe less."

Dana whistled, long and low.

Carly's cheeks flushed. "It's not just about sex."

Dana looked at her, askance.

"Okay," Carly conceded, "it's a lot about sex, at least it was at first. Now it's a ton of other things as well."

"Like?"

"Like he does what he says. Evan's word is his deed. No false promises, no fillers, no additives, no kidding around. Evan's idea of lip service doesn't involve talking."

"Like good chocolate," Dana said with whole-hearted approval.

"He acts like he doesn't care," Carly continued, ignoring Dana's odd analogy. "But when I needed help with Odin, he didn't tell me I was stupid or to get over it, he just dealt with it. He seems like one thing on the outside, but inside he's something else—something better than you ever thought. You know what I mean?"

"A cream center," Dana answered, smacking her lips.

"Uh, sure. Anyway, he's smart and loyal and he never, ever gives up. His kisses taste so good I have to put my arms around him or I might float away."

"Mmmmmm, truffle," Dana replied, channeling Homer Simpson.

"Well, okay." Chocolate never made Carly feel that good, but she was glad Dana got something out of it. "He thinks I'm talented and tells me I'm not a loser and he laughs at my jokes."

"Godiva gold box!" Dana concluded. "Carly, hang on to that man no matter what. And shoot anything that gets in your way."

"There's no point," she said with a defeated

shake of her head. "How can I hang on to something I don't have?"

"Are you sure?"

"The last thing in the world Evan wants is true love. Trust me, he doesn't go down that aisle at the supermarket. His life is about making films. He doesn't need anybody. Evan's handsome, brilliant, and doing what he wants to do. He's doing just fine without it."

"There's always room for love, chocolate, and sex."

Carly shrugged. "He's with you on two out of three."

The look on Dex's face said it all when Carly walked into the studio. He looked her up and down and his normally pleasant, guileless eyes narrowed. He knew, no doubt about it. But how? There was absolutely no way afterglow lasted that long.

"Hi," she said, a little too brightly, wondering if she should give him his usual hug or not. Her left eyelid started to twitch as she recalled Quinn's reaction when she'd stopped by his office. It had fallen way short of a high five. More the verbal equivalent of the one-finger salute. He was merely frustrated with her; Dex was beyond that. Quinn got over it when she threw the *Hog* promos at him. She had nothing for Dex except the "let's just be friends" spiel.

"Hi," he said curtly. His body language said hugs were out.

Carly sniffed herself discreetly. Was she now unwittingly reeking of Eau de Evan, causing those of the hairier sex to step back and hold their breath?

"How was Mexico?" Dex asked, muting the sound on a beach volleyball competition playing on the monitor.

"Good," she answered as neutrally as possible. Now was not the time to howl in triumph and pump her fist in the air.

"I'll bet." He fiddled with the editor, avoiding her gaze.

She took a seat on the couch. This was not part of the plan. Not that she had a plan, but if she did, it wouldn't have included hurting Dex's feelings. It didn't seem fair that what made one person happy should make another person unhappy, as if there were a finite measure of happiness in the world and getting more meant someone else getting less.

"Don't be mad, Dex," she said, deciding to tackle the situation head-on.

"I'm not mad," he answered, his voice losing some of its hard edge. "I guess I'm just disappointed."

Disappointed. God, she hated that word. Her mom used it often. If Judith ever got a tattoo, that's what it would say.

"I'm sorry," Carly said.

"Why?" he asked without rancor. "What did you do wrong?"

"I don't know," she sighed. "What did I do right?"

"Everything about you is all right, sunshine." Dex sat down next to her and put his arm around her shoulders. He placed a kiss on the crown of her head. "Why do you think I'm so disappointed that you didn't pick me? Don't worry about it. Life's a beach, remember?"

"Then you die."

"No." He motioned to the monitor. "Then you watch women in tiny outfits play volleyball."

"I see," she said, giving him a quick hug.

"So you gonna marry him?" Dex asked suddenly.

"Yeah, right," she laughed. Evan had set up camp for a long weekend and Dex thought the guy was laying down concrete for a foundation. Guess Dex wasn't as good at reading scent markings as she thought he was.

He gave her a sidelong glance and then went back to watching women lunge and sweat, a slightly forlorn smile on his lips.

If Evan was surprised to find them arm in arm on the couch watching television, he didn't show it. He nodded at them like a general giving his troops permission to relax. Carly caught the briefest look pass between the men and realized that they'd just negotiated some sort of peace accord. It was eerie, this language of men, so full of unspoken posturing and physical innuendo, so full of grace and pride. So full of shit sometimes. But, damn, she thought as she stared at the surfer boy and the film stud conferring over the console, don't ya just love 'em?

Chapter Eighteen

"Pedro DaSilva, son of an Italian father and a Mexican mother, was born in the heart of Mexico's wine country on the Baja coast. Brought up to be a winemaker like his father and a good Catholic like his mother, he chose to play the saxophone . . ."

A series of photo montages played on the monitor: Pete as a barefoot child in the vineyards, a youth self-consciously posing with his saxophone, a beautiful young man playing onstage. Pete Silver's voice took up the narration, describing in awed tones the first meeting he'd ever had with Arlene. A picture of the two of them in a nightclub flashed on the screen.

Carly was riveted by the images playing on the monitor. She'd already seen some of the photographs and had been there for Pete's interview, but viewing Evan's rough cut overlaid with music and her narration was still amazing. The whole, as usual in successful creative endeavors, was much greater than the sum of its parts. Even Dex, who had claimed to have lost interest in the project, was enthusiastic about the new footage.

"I've hardly made a dent in Pete's tapes," Evan said when they broke for dinner. "So far, what's there is terrific. It's just Arlene singing and Pete on the sax. Just hours of recordings they made together through the years."

"You going to transfer it all?" Dex asked.

"That's the agreement I have with Pete. He'll let me use whatever I want so long as I archive copies of everything for him. It's no small job. A few of the tapes are in pretty bad shape."

"I'd be willing to help, if you need it," Dex offered.

"Thanks," Evan said, "but the budget's pretty dry."

"We can work something out," Dex assured him. "I can't pass up a chance to hear Arlene Barlow singing something no one's ever heard before."

Evan looked about to refuse, then nodded.

Carly sat quietly as the two men brainstormed ideas for the tapes. As their excitement grew, so did her sense of melancholy. In a little while, her participation would be over and the film would go on without her. The first time she'd see it would probably be at a screening along with a hundred other people. Getting cut from *Critters* meant the loss of a job and income. Bowing out of the Arlene Barlow project lost her nothing, but Carly clearly felt a vacuum forming that would be a lot harder to replace. Something that her shoes couldn't help her with.

The blue Toyota followed her home from the studio. The men, despite having been rivals, had gotten along better than they had at any previous session. This time Carly was the odd man out.

"A horse walks into a bar," Evan said as Carly unlocked the door to the kitchen and let them in. Once inside, he took her into his arms. He kissed the worry lines on her brow and both downturned corners of her mouth. "The bartender looks at the horse and says—"

"Why the long face?" Carly said, supplying the punch line.

He kissed her softly. "So why the long face?"

She shrugged. "Postproduction postpartum depression?"

He kissed the tip of her nose. "I've got a cure for that."

"I'm sure you do," she said, taking his hand and leading him to the bedroom. Here today, gone tomorrow. Carly was going to take it one hour at a time, one night at a time. Between the choice of nothing and a little bit of something, especially something as incredible as what she was feeling, well, she chose something. He wanted to be with her, at least for that moment, and she'd take it. She'd survived on less.

"Anyone ever tell you," he said seductively when they were finally naked under the sheets. "That you have the most gorgeous, all-time incredible, mindblowing, killer . . ."

"Yes," she said expectantly.

". . . bed in the world?" he finished.

She hit him with an expensive feather pillow.

He laughed and grabbed her, pinning her underneath him for a kiss. "You're not so bad either."

She pushed him away and pulled the sheet up over herself. "I like my bed."

"I do, too," he said seriously. "This is a great bed.

It's not tiny and wimpy like some beds. A decent size, too."

"California king," she informed him.

He reached behind to rap the mahogany head-board with his knuckles. "Solid. You'd have to really work to tear this bed apart."

She envisioned what it would take to do just that and cleared her throat. "I never thought about it that way."

"I thought about it the first time I tucked you in."

"Really?" She dreaded thinking about that first time. She could only imagine what she had looked like: rumpled, bed head, runny mascara, probably drooling.

He pulled the sheet away to expose her. "I thought you were absolutely breathtaking, lying there naked on those crisp white sheets."

"I had a robe on." She pulled the sheet back up.

"Eventually." He tugged the sheet off her and the bed, and tossed it to the floor. She squirmed under his gaze.

"Why do you do that?" he asked.

"What?"

"Get nervous when I look at you."

"Dunno." Her eyes studied the ceiling fan over her bed. It needed dusting.

"What do you see," he asked softly as he ran his fingertips lightly from the top of her head, down her neck, across her breasts, stomach, thighs, and legs, "when you look in the mirror?"

She rolled over, her back to him. "You don't want to know."

"I bet you don't see what I see." Evan snuggled up

behind her, tucking her into him the way he liked. "You want to know what I see?"

Carly sighed.

He held her tightly and whispered gently into her ear. "I see kind, and funny, and warm." His hand stroked her body tenderly. "I see a heart-stopping smile, incredible brown eyes, a mouth I love to kiss, and a woman that drives me out of my mind in bed."

She recalled the silly game she and Dana played with their fortune cookies. "Beautiful things await you," hers had read. "In bed," they'd amended with a shout. Now that it had come true, she wished she hadn't put such narrow parameters on it.

He got up early the next morning, just like when they first arrived from Mexico. His work was waiting. He had to go.

As he stood to leave, her body righted itself along with the mattress. It struck her that the dip and rise of the mattress, as a lover entered and left the bed, were probably among the happiest and saddest of sensations.

Naked, Evan headed to the kitchen to start the coffee. Odin wandered in like the changing of the guard. He jumped on the bed and sniffed Evan's pillow before kneading it vigorously and plopping himself down.

Carly listened to the hiss of hot water as Evan began his shower, and wondered if she should join him. Maybe put off his departure for a little while longer. He was in such a rush he was done before she'd even made up her mind.

"Oh, well," she said, regretting her lost opportunity.

Evan walked through the door as bare as when he left, carrying two coffee cups. He had a birthmark the shape of a crescent moon on his left hip. "What did you say?"

"Just talking to Odin."

He grunted a response and put the cups on the nightstand before he pulled on his underwear and jeans. He threw his shirt on without buttoning it and sat on the edge of the bed to drink his coffee.

Carly sat up and reached out to touch him. She ran her hands up his chest and placed a kiss on his throat before she started to button his shirt. "You're so beautiful."

He brought her hand up and kissed it. "Is that what you see?"

"Yes," she said.

He looked at her expectantly.

She gave him a melancholy smile and touched her fingers to his cheek. "You don't want to know what else I see."

He gave a short nod of understanding. "You're probably right."

"It's going to be great." She buttoned the last button of his shirt.

Carly was measuring out brown sugar when the phone rang.

"What are you doing?" Evan asked without preamble.

Her heart flew out of her chest and whizzed around the room. "I'm making cookies."

"I'll be right there," he said and hung up.

Fifteen minutes later, Even was kissing the back of Carly's neck as she doled out spoonfuls of cookie dough onto a buttered baking sheet.

"How long does it take to bake?" he asked as his hands slipped under her apron and unbuttoned her blouse.

"Twelve minutes." She sighed when his palms came in contact with her breasts. "In fifteen you can eat them."

"I can't wait," he purred in her ear.

"Time out, please." She shooed him back, popped the pan into the oven, and set the timer.

"Twelve minutes," Evan reminded her as he untied the apron and pulled it over her head. Thirty seconds later he had her backed up against the wall and was tossing her shorts and panties over his shoulder.

Odin padded into the kitchen. "Mew?" he inquired softly.

"Not now, sweetie," Carly gasped. "Why don't you go and play?"

"I am playing," Evan said, heading toward her breasts.

Carly struggled with the buttons of Evan's shirt and pushed it off his shoulders. He slid down her body.

"Eight minutes," Evan called out before his mouth touched down between her legs. He pulled her leg over his shoulder and kissed her deeply.

Eight minutes, that's how long it takes the sun's rays to travel across space before hitting the surface of the earth. How long Carly had before she could go supernova.

"Five minutes." Evan stood, dropped his jeans and underwear, and rolled on a condom.

"Five minutes!" she wailed miserably. She could do this for hours. Why, oh, why hadn't she baked a pound cake?!

He lifted her up so she could wrap her legs around him and plunged into her like a man without a minute to spare, which he was.

The room was flooded with the aromas of butter, brown sugar, and chocolate, and the sounds of desire, passion, and going-for-broke sex.

"Three minutes," Evan said breathlessly, checking the clock.

"Oh, God, Evan. Shut up!" she yelled, desperately wrapping her arms and legs tighter around him. She was on the brink of dying and he was doing math. Carly, Evan, and the cookies were all done within seconds of each other. She hoped, as she watched a delightfully half-naked Evan pull a sheet of cookies out of the oven, that she wouldn't climax every time she heard a kitchen timer ding. It would be so embarrassing.

Half-dressed, sprawled on the kitchen floor, they ate hot chocolate chip cookies and cold milk. It was with bittersweet satisfaction that Carly ate her treat. Fresh cookies had gone the way of kissless flan. Not much point if she had to kill twelve minutes all by herself.

"Want to go to the Bowl?" Evan asked suddenly.

"My arm always hurts the next day," she replied.

"Not bowling," he explained slowly, "the Hollywood Bowl. Wednesday night. They're playing tango music by Piazola. We could bring a picnic."

She looked at him suspiciously. Was he offering

to sit underneath the stars with her, sipping wine, serenaded by an orchestra? "Are you asking me on a date?"

"It would seem that way," he said as if it were a surprise to him, too.

"Yes," she said, smiling at the lug of her life as she fed him a bite of cookie. Perhaps she wasn't going to have to bake by herself after all. "I'd love to go."

It wasn't until the next morning, after the breakfast dishes were washed and put away and Evan was at the table, doing the crossword puzzle, that Carly got up the nerve to make her offer.

"I've been thinking about the film."

He nodded as if that was only right.

"I've got some money saved—"

"No," he said, cutting her off.

She sat down next to him. "You didn't even hear me out."

"I don't have to. I'm not taking your money, Carly. I'll finish this some other way."

She leaned forward. "You wouldn't be taking the money. I could just loan it to you."

He shook his head. "No."

She tried one more time. "Interest free?"

"No."

"Why not? You need the money and I'm offering. So what's the problem? Pete's tapes were an incredible windfall but you said yourself you're running on fumes. Even with Dex's help, how are you going to pay for the transfers *and* finish the film? You have to get the money from somewhere. Why not me?"

He looked her in the eye steadily. "What do you want for your money?"

"I want to help you finish the film," she said, thinking she was stating the obvious.

"Is that all?" He tapped the newspaper with his pen.

"Yes." She stared at the bouncing pen. "What else?"

He tossed the pen down. "How about a piece of the film? Or a piece of me? Isn't that how it works at the Bank of Carly?"

"What are you talking about, Evan?"

He leaned back in his chair. "Dana told me all about your interest-free 'loans' to your brother and sister."

"What does my helping Julian and Stacey with college have anything to do with the film?" she asked, dismayed by his reaction.

"You and the Mighty Bill McLeish have a lot in common," he sneered. "It's that old rule; whoever has the gold makes the rules. Well, you can't buy me or my film. They're not for sale."

Anger flared inside her chest and exploded out of her mouth. "Don't you dare compare me to your father! I don't have to pay for anybody's love or time. You're right, though, it's my gold, my rules. I can give it to whomever I want for no other reason than I feel like it. Has it ever occurred to you that someone might be motivated by something more than greed?"

"Actually," he said, his voice flat and dull, "not really."

The coldness in his voice snuffed out the remains of her anger. "I'm not trying to buy the film or take it away from you, Evan," she pleaded. "I'm trying to give it to you."

His response was as bleak as the expression on his face. "How can I believe you?"

"We're back to that again, aren't we? You won't trust me and I'll never convince you otherwise. I want to help you, but you don't want it. You want to control everyone and everything. Well, guess what? It isn't going to happen. You think that I'm going to screw up your film. Let me tell you something." She pointed a finger in his direction. "You're the one screwing up your film. No one but you and your damned pride."

The day that had started out so full of opportunity had imploded and it wasn't even noon. Foolishly, she'd gotten complacent and had stopped checking for falling anvils and trapdoors. She hadn't reckoned on the light at the end of the tunnel being an oncoming train.

"Good-bye, Carly," Evan said as he stood up and touched her cheek, his face full of disappointment and regret.

That was it. He was done playing kickball with her heart and now he was packing it up and going home, the jerk. Her jerk.

"Before you leave," Carly said, barely holding back tears, "I want you to know—"

"Don't," he said sharply with a quick shake of his head.

"Don't tell you I love you?" A rueful smile pulled at the corners of her mouth slightly. "Or don't love you?"

"All of it," he demanded. "Don't."

"Maybe your heart does what your head wants,

but mine doesn't," Carly replied sadly. She'd crashed and burned down this road before. There were no skid marks on her Highway to Heartbreak, nothing to indicate that she ever hesitated, swerved, or even tapped the brakes before flying off the road into oblivion. "Like it or not, I love you. Even though it's positively hopeless, even though it'll probably kill me. I love you, Evan, with all my foolish heart."

He held her chin in his hand and looked her in the eye. "All that misery for what? Stick with the cat, sweetheart. It's not worth it. You don't want that."

"You have no idea what I want," she said vehemently. "You don't know even know who I am. Even after all this time, you don't know me any more than you did the first time we met."

"That's not true."

"Then trust me!" She held on to her last breath, a drowning woman hoping for a lifeline.

Slowly he shook his head.

The gesture broke her will. Fat silvery drops of distilled heartache cascaded down her cheeks.

"Don't do this to yourself," he said, taking hold of her arms. "I'm not the man for you. There are a million men who'd get down on their knees for a woman like you. Pick one of them."

"There's a lot of money in movies for a talented guy like you," Carly said. "Does that mean you're willing to change the kind of films you make?"

"No."

"Don't worry," she said bitterly, swiping at the tears that were replaced as quickly as she could push them away. "I'll get over it."

"Carly . . ." He rubbed her shoulders sympathetically.

"Go away, Evan," she said, roughly shrugging his hands off. "And thanks for saving me from a really bad investment. I'll just go back to my kiddie shows and commercials; there's more money in it. I've done all the charity work I can afford for the year."

She listened to the sound of Evan's retreating footsteps, her heart hesitating along with the momentary catch in his stride just at the door, before he shook off whatever second thoughts had halted his exit. Carly wept all over the *New York Times* crossword puzzle as Evan sped away from her house for the last time.

If life had a soundtrack, the "bad guys are coming" music would have been playing long before the doorbell rang. Carly would have known to put the shields up and set phasers on "stun." As it was, she answered the door totally unaware and unarmed.

Judith Engstrom, tall, blonde, and irritable, stood on the doorstep. Over the years, disappointment had washed the blue out of her eyes, leaving them as gray and flat as nail heads.

"Mom." Carly was momentarily blinded by the sunlight gleaming off three blazingly blond heads. Squinting, she finished her roll call. "Julian. Stacey."

"Hi," her siblings said in unison.

"We need to talk," Judith said, impatiently tapping her foot.

"How are you?" Carly asked, ignoring the proclamation.

"Good." "Okay." The sibs answered, heads bobbing.

"Well, are you going to ask us in?" Judith asked.

The weekend had been a nonstop sufferfest for Carly, a pity party where the only dance partners were grief, regret, and loneliness. No amount of baking therapy or lucky-shoe intervention could loosen the strangle grip of misery on her heart. Then, in an effort to physically do what she couldn't emotionally, she set about cleaning house, erasing all trace of Evan.

"Sure," Carly said, feeling as bedraggled and wrung out as the cleaning rag in her hand. "Come on in. Check-in is not till three, but I'll make an exception this time."

Judith marched in like a mama duck with ducklings in tow. "Everything always has to be a joke with you, doesn't it?"

Odin jumped off the sofa and streaked out of the room as they entered. Wrinkling her nose, Judith sat down stiffly on the couch between her nervous charges. Carly took a seat in the rocker.

Julian and Stacey had been to her house numerous times, but her mother had visited only once before. Years ago, in her first Thanksgiving at the house, Carly had hosted the festivities and prepared a feast. Judith, predicting culinary disaster, had brought one with her. It was dueling dinners, an adult food fight with Judith's Butterball vs. Carly's free-range turkey. Julian and Stacey had filled their stomachs and cheek pouches to bursting in a nonpartisan effort to please.

Wasting no time, Judith fired her first volley. "Julian tells me that you've been kicked off your cartoon."

Her brother looked at Carly apologetically. He knew how to neutralize every video foe in existence, but he was powerless against Judith, Supreme Mom Warrior, and her arsenal of soul-grinding weapons of personal destruction. Poor kid.

Carly didn't waste ammunition returning fire.

"Stacey says that you're financing some sort of movie."

The baby of the family stared at her feet. Her self-defense strategy was the same as a possum's—freeze and maybe they won't notice you. Maybe one day she'd graduate to "run and hide."

Carly sat idling her engines.

"If you'd only finished your degree," Judith lamented. "But you wouldn't listen. Now you've lost your job—"

"A job." Carly should have let it pass but couldn't. One point for Judith.

"Another job." Judith had a long memory for shortcomings. "I knew it wouldn't last. Now your fifteen minutes are up. So what do you do? You throw your money away on some stupid movie. That's got to be the dumbest thing you've ever done!"

In another century, her mother would have happily filled up her days embroidering scarlet A's on the bodices of wayward women and attending witch burnings.

"Say something!" Judith finally snapped. "Don't just sit there like an idiot, Carly."

It was her cue to come out with guns blazing but suddenly Carly didn't have it in her to carry on fighting a useless war. Evan didn't believe that she only wanted to help him. Her mother didn't trust her to be anything but a failure. And neither of them had any faith to spare. Well, to hell with the both of them.

"I just don't care anymore, Mom," Carly said, throwing down her arms. "Keep your precious love and approval. I finally have some of my own. I don't need any good luck charms or ruby slippers. I am my own lucky charm and nothing you do can ever change that. My career is fine. More than fine. It's fabulous. It always has been and it will continue to be. Cool, huh?"

The words fell out of her mouth like gold coins. Realization hit her like a knock on the head. Her mother's constant critical nit-picking had made Carly insecure, doubtful, and anxious. But a lifetime of going to battle against Supreme Mom Warrior had earned her her stripes. Carly Beck was tough, strong, and resilient. Forget the loser crap. Carly was Princess Ninja Dragonfire. She ought to know, she did her voice.

"Thank you," Carly said, giving her mother a heartfelt smile.

Judith's eyebrows rose. "For what?"

"For being you," Carly said.

The view from the back of the restaurant was magnificent. It was an awe-inspiring sea of blue, an uninterrupted carpet of navy that undulated from one end of the room to the other. Dana had come early to secure front row seats. It was fireman day at

Sharky's, a small Mexican fast food restaurant on Vine just north of Hollywood Boulevard.

"So that's it?" Dana asked, finishing her steak tacos. "You kicked Judith out and you told Evan to *hasta* his *vista*?"

"Pretty much, yeah." Carly nibbled halfheartedly at her meal.

"You need a pick-me-up." The blonde's eyes swept across the restaurant for the hundred-thousandth time, taking in the scenery. Men sat crowded together at small tables, their broad shoulders bumping as they ate and joked. "Dial 911, make a friend."

"Nuh-uh," Carly said. "Go directly to jail, do not pass Go."

Dana shrugged. "Or you could refill our drinks and probably pick us up a dozen bed warmers on the way back. A variety pack would do nicely. Just smile, Carly, smile. You remember how."

Sighing, Carly drifted off toward the drink machines and was instantly enveloped in an invisible fog of testosterone. Despite her blue mood it was hard not to smile back at the cheerful handsome faces that caught her eye. Each and every one was certainly worthy of adulation, but not a one of them was Evan. So far, falling in love had ruined a lot of things for Carly: fresh-baked cookies, road trips, the entire country of Mexico, sleeping, eating, life in general, and now fireman day.

"I heard you're back on *Compost Critters*," Dana said when Carly came back with their drinks.

"Yeah, can you believe that? They got a bunch of hate mail from some truly pissed-off little kids, so I'm back as twins—Ella and Ellie Earthworm."

"Maybe you should get those kids to write to Evan."

"Evan has never been one to be swayed by public opinion. It would take more than a letter-writing campaign by a bunch of preschoolers to change his mind."

"Maybe he has changed his mind. Why don't you call him?"

"Don't think I haven't thought about it a million times," Carly said, shaking her head sadly. "But if he was going to have a change of heart and suddenly decide to trust me like I'm Fort Knox, I think he would have called. Or just shown up. He's never hesitated to do that before."

"Maybe it's not over," Dana offered hopefully. She wasn't above trying to give CPR to a dead romance. "I ran into Dex the other day, and he told me that listening to your voice every time they work on the film hasn't been sunshine and flowers for Evan, either."

By unspoken agreement, the film and Evan were *verboten* subjects between Carly and Dex. "He's probably just happy that it's tape and not the real thing. It was a lot easier for him to deal with me when I was reading a script that he wrote. It was me doing my own talking that he didn't like."

Dana opened her mouth to protest, but Carly waved her off.

"Love sucks," Carly said with finality. "I'm never falling in love again. And I'm never having sex again."

Dana almost choked on her drink.

"Not worth it," she explained, handing her a napkin. "And, frankly, Evan has ruined me for other men."

"Don't you think that's a bit extreme?" Dana said, alarmed.

"Sex with Evan," Carly said sadly, "was like drinking a bottle of Dom Pérignon. Some years are better than others but they're all excellent. In comparison, sex with anyone else is like having sparkling wine in a plastic cup."

Dana stared at her suffering friend with sympathy in her eyes. "Can you be more specific?"

Chapter Nineteen

Checking her booking sheet, Carly could say her life was pretty much back to its pre–shoe kidnapping level of prosperity, if not happiness. Gumby had gone back to being just an innocuous little green ball of clay, and Silver the Audi was dentless once again. Just like Quinn had said, "You're up. You're down. You're up again. Get used to it." And she finally had, trusting that there was always another job waiting.

Evan was also right, she admitted ruefully, unwilling to throw much credit his way but too honest to deny the truth. The shoes were just a magical placebo, stand-ins for her own talents and abilities. Before, it was much easier to put her faith in shoes imbued with supernatural powers than in herself. Now, she realized, she'd much rather actively pursue her future—the good, the bad, and the fugly—than just stand around waiting to win the life lottery.

The last-minute booking at TimeCode almost escaped her notice. Quinn had the one-hour promo job tacked onto the end of the following day. Nothing suspicious there except that there was no show title and no producer listed. It wasn't unusual for information to be missing on her schedule but something about it set off Carly's "woo-woo" radar. Despite her new pragmatic life view, she still put a little stock in premonitions. Some omens, like dead pigeons on the doorstep, were not to be ignored. It was late but Carly called her agent anyway.

"This better be good," Quinn answered irritably.

"It's Carly."

"Oh."

Oh? Her suspicions were growing by the second. "What's this promo session at the end of the day?"

"You called me at eleven o'clock for this?"

"What's it for, Quinn?" she pressed.

"It's a revision for your no-money documentary."

"What?"

"I told you it was a dumb idea," Quinn grumbled to someone as Carly let loose with some choice phrases of agreement.

"Carly, it's Glen," he said, breaking into her rant.

"Glen, what the hell is going on?" she demanded. "Why do I have a session with Evan?"

"It's like this," Glen explained gently. "He called Quinn—"

"Like he should have the first time," Quinn yelled in the background.

"Hush," Glen scolded his partner. "Anyway, Carly," he continued sweetly, "Evan needed a revision and he thought maybe this was the best way to do it."

"I'll bet," she sneered. "Whose idea was it not to put his name down on my booking sheet?"

"Mine," Glen admitted guiltily.

"Dumb idea," Carly and Quinn said at the same time.

"I think he misses you," Glen explained.

"Good," was Carly's heated reply. "He can miss me even more tomorrow!"

"You've reached Evan McLeish. Leave your name and number and I'll get back to you as soon as possible."

Beeeeeep!

"No," she said.

"What do you mean, 'no'?" Evan said, picking up the phone.

"No. As in N for never, O for over my dead body."

"You can't say no."

"What do you mean I can't say no?" she snapped. "You don't run my life. I can say no all I like and you can't stop me! No, no, no, no. See?"

"But I booked you!"

"Well, I'm unbooking me."

"You have to do this, Carly," he argued. "Otherwise I can't finish."

"How tragic," she replied lightly.

"I thought you cared about this film."

"I do. But I offered to help you once and you threw it back at me. I care, but not that much."

"I'm not asking for favors. I'm paying you this time."

"That's exactly why I'm not doing it."

"Wait a minute! First you get mad because I can't pay you, now you're mad because I want to pay you."

"Exactly."

"Exactly nothing. That makes no sense."

"You said I can't buy you," Carly raged. "Well, you can't buy me, either!"

"Now you're being petty."

"Well, you're a sneak." She stabbed the air with her finger as if he was right in front of her. "You went behind my back."

He let out a derisive snort. "When is booking with your agent going behind your back? I thought that was his job."

"Evan, why didn't you just ask me? Not my agent. Me."

"I'm asking you now," he growled.

"Too late." Carly hung up at the beginning of what sounded like an agonized scream on the other end of the phone.

Glen, Dana, Dex, and a few others were all on her answering machine when Carly got home the next day. A whole Greek chorus entreating her to do Evan's revision. Traitors, every last one of them. Carly was definitely taking them all off the cookie list. They could eat freshly baked rocks, for all she cared.

"Mew." Odin stared up at her, hope shining in his eyes.

"If this is about the film," Carly said, stooping to scratch the cat behind the ears. "I don't want to hear it."

She started by phoning the grossest offender of all.

"Rudolph, here."

"Dad, how could you?"

"How could I what?" he asked innocently. A little too innocently. A television could be heard in the background.

"You know what I'm talking about." Carly stood in front of the fireplace mantel and glared at her father's picture. "How could you let Evan put you up to this? You don't even like him."

"Still don't," he agreed. "But I think you should do the revision, Carly. Have you seen the film?"

"I am no longer involved with the production at this time," she said brusquely.

"That's an official statement, if I've ever heard one."

"No comment."

"Evan mentioned you'd had a difference of opinion."

"That's one way to put it. It's my opinion that Evan is a jackass. It's his opinion that he is a god."

Beck laughed in response.

"It's not funny, Dad."

"Yeah, I know, baby," he chuckled. "It's just that I've been having the same argument with my editor for years."

"Then you see what I mean," she said, relieved that he'd come back from the dark side.

"Except my editor doesn't answer my home phone."

"Once!"

"Early morning on a weekday."

"That's neither here nor there," she huffed.

"Absolutely correct." In the background, Arlene Barlow started singing. "You need to put your feelings aside, Carly. Watch the film. It's worth going the extra mile for."

Carly heard the murmur of her own voice in the

background. "You're watching it right now, aren't you?"

"Evan sensed I needed a little convincing before I would agree to call you. It's a terrific documentary and you are absolutely perfect on it. I think you're really going to regret it if you don't do this fix."

"I already regret it," she grumbled, her anger tamed slightly by his compliments.

"Aw, Carly," he wheedled, "be the better person and do it. It's the professional thing to do."

She made a stubborn face.

"Then you can tell that sonofabitch to go to hell."

"Dad!"

"That's what I always tell my editor," he said with a smile in his voice. "Does my ego a world of good. Of course, my editor never answered my home phone."

"Once!"

The road to Studio A Hell was paved with the good intentions of anyone Evan could coerce, cajole, or command into supporting his cause. Carly was besieged by friends and associates to do the session. Ultimately she gave in partly out of frustration, but mostly out of a desire to do the "professional thing," as Beck had advised. At least that's what she tried to convince herself before she got behind the mic. Now, staring through the glass at Evan, she realized that professional ethics had very little to do with it. She was there simply because she missed him.

Despite going cold turkey, she was still hopelessly addicted to Evan. The single act of falling in love had irrevocably changed her, forever bonding her

to him as surely as any narcotic. Her hard-won in-
dependence was a tenuous thing, more fiction than
fact. One sip of Evan and she'd be enraptured once
again, spellbound and witless.

"Hello, my name is Carly and I'm an Evanoholic,"
she whispered, her voice barely audible. "You see,
folks, it all started with a pair of red shoes . . ."

"What was that?" Dex asked, his voice blaring
through the speakers.

She winced. Her eardrums curled in on themselves for protection. "Could you turn that down?"

"Sorry," Dex apologized, the volume much lower
this time. "What did you say?"

"Nothing. Just practicing."

Evan looked up from his laptop to look at her, his
face impassive, eyes guarded. They'd been coldly
civil to each other from the minute Carly entered
the studio, like estranged parents trying to make it
work for the sake of the child.

"Ready?" Evan asked her.

She nodded.

"We're just going to re-record the highlighted
parts of the script. Dex will play what we've got so
you can match the voice."

They worked for a solid hour, picking out a
phrase here and a word there. Carly subtly changed
the shading and emphasis of each read as directed
by Evan, who honed each take like an obsessive-
compulsive piano tuner, jotting down copious
notes between reads. As the time slowly ran out, so
did Carly's patience. As far as she could see, the
changes were so minor as to be basically immater-
ial. Evan was either trying to make her crazy out of
spite or he was nuts himself.

"Okay, McLeish," Carly said, challenging him when she got out of the booth. "What was that all about?"

"What was what all about?" Evan asked as he shut his laptop.

"Oh, please!" Carly threw her hands up in frustration. "We just spent an hour re-recording lines that sound exactly the same as they did originally."

"To you, maybe," he said. "But that's my call, isn't it?"

"Oh-ho!" she cried. "So it's a power play, is it? You hounded me mercilessly and browbeat everyone I knew just to get me to do this. What an ego you've got."

He raised his brows. "Sounds like you're the one with the ego. I have better things to do than hound you."

"I was so mad, I kicked everyone off the cookie list. I hope you're happy now."

"Delirious," he said pleasantly.

Dex was not as pleased. "You kicked me off the cookie list?"

"Yes," Carly said, turning to Dex, crossing her arms across her chest. "You've been sleeping with the enemy."

"Excuse me?" Evan sputtered indignantly.

"One call!" Dex wailed. "One measly call and I'm off the cookie list. Don't you think that's a little harsh?"

"Cookies are for friends," Carly explained. Her eyes gave him the once-over before kicking him to the curb. "True friends."

"I'm a true friend," Dex pleaded. "I'm as friendly as they get!"

"Wait a goddamn minute!" Evan barked. "When did I become the enemy?"

"No more cookies!" Carly insisted, her words rising above the others and exploding like firecrackers.

The studio door flew open and an irate engineer stood at the threshold, angrily shaking his fist. "I'm trying to record next door and I can hear you better than the people in my own booth! Now shut the hell up or take it outside!"

Chastened, heads bowed, they stared at their feet as the engineer stomped out of the room. Yelling in the control room was a studio faux pas—it wasn't soundproofed.

"How about pancakes?" Dex whispered, after a few moments. "Do I still get pancakes?"

"To hell with the goddamn pancakes!" Evan roared at Dex and then turned his bellowing toward Carly. "What is this 'enemy' crap? Why do you have to make everything so personal?"

"Better than being a cold sonofabitch like you, Evan."

"Do I still get my pancakes?"

"No!" Evan stormed at Dex. "No pancakes ever! Don't even ask. In fact, don't even think about Carly's pancakes. Wipe them completely from your mind."

"You don't own her pancakes!" Dex said defiantly.

"Leave my pancakes alone, both of you!" Carly grabbed her briefcase. "And you, Evan, go to hell!"

He gathered himself up to his full height and leaned into Carly's face. "Is that any way to talk to the man you love?"

There was no thought to the action, just movement, fast, quick, and deadly. The violent collision between boot tip and bone would, no doubt, leave a bruise on Evan's shin for weeks.

Evan was shouting expletives just as the other engineer crashed through the door once again. The sight of Evan yelling and hopping around on one leg stopped him in his tracks. But it was Carly, who looked like a Valkyrie with a bad case of road rage, that made him step back.

"Aaaaaah-eeeeeee-yah!" Carly yelled and swept out of the room.

It was early December when the invitation for the screening arrived in the mail. Carly had sat on her front step wearing Evan's sweatshirt that she'd never returned from the night of Odin's rescue, and looked at the card for a long, long time before retreating into the house. The scorching heat of summer had passed, leaving the grass on the hills a chamois yellow, the brush a rusty gray. Fall, ushered in by the blustery Santa Anas, was ending its reign with a small Pacific storm or two, sluicing down the streets and icing the peaks of distant mountains. Christmas lights and decorations adorned streetlights, storefronts, and palm trees. Bikinis were put away and snowboards replaced surfboards. The world had gone on and so, in her own way, had Carly.

The doorbell no longer had the power to send her pulse skipping. She'd stopped looking for Evan's truck in her driveway whenever she returned home, at least most of the time. Everyone, while not totally forgiven, had been reinstated on the cookie list. Like the city after an earthquake, Carly had dusted herself off and rebuilt. Superficially all was as it was before her world had suffered its emotional catastrophe, but there was no changing the fact that the earth had shifted and she along with it. Fault lines lay buried within her heart, deep fractures that no amount of prettying up would ever fix.

Carly scraped up a thin smile before she entered the lobby of the movie theater. It was a night of ironies. This was the same theater where she and Evan had first met. And she was wearing the shoes that had kicked everything off. They were no longer lucky, per se, but they were still a darned cute pair of shoes.

She was outfitted in a long red velvet dress that seemed to flow over her body when she moved, clinging and caressing like a fabric familiar. The day had been spent at the spa and hairdresser getting scrubbed, polished, clipped, and detailed down to the last fingernail and hair follicle. Her skin was luminous, her smile dazzled with gem-quality brilliance, even her elbows and earlobes were award-winning. This was Carly's last stand, and she was going to go out looking like a million bucks, even if she had to spend nearly that much to get there.

"Marry me?"

Carly met the dancing brown eyes with a smile. "Hello, Raymond. I'm glad you could come."

"Only for you," he said, happily accepting a kiss. He was in his winter wear: a white turtleneck, light blue golf pants, cream Hush Puppies. "So what do you say?"

"I say this city is full of women; why settle for just one?"

"But you're worth a million women," he said, turning up the charm.

"See the tall blonde in the tiny black dress over there?" Carly pointed to Dana, who was standing by the refreshments table.

"The looker?" Raymond's eyes widened with interest.

"Tell her Tinkerbell sent you. You're just her type."

"Don't say?" he murmured as he walked across the lobby.

"Are you sure that was wise?"

The Intruder Alert signal went off in her head, and she was glad that Evan was standing behind her so she had time to erase the stricken look on her face. "They were meant for each other."

Evan came around and faced her. He was wearing the suit he'd worn for their ill-fated liaison. He looked like the prototype for handsome. Whereas Carly had spent days in heavy remodeling, he probably only had to take a shower and iron a shirt. Men don't have to try to look good, they only have to clean up. Women not only have to clean up, they also have to erect a whole new persona while they're at it.

"Hey, pretty girl," he said.

"Hey, yourself." She congratulated herself for not wincing at the pet name.

"How are you?" His eyes searched her face for clues.

"Fine," she lied, trying her best to look like it was true. "How about you?"

"All right."

He looked it, so he must be. "Is Pete Silver here?"

"No, he's lying low. He figures the world will be beating a path to his door soon enough."

A friend came up to say hello to Evan, and Carly saw her opportunity to slip away. He must have felt her desire to leave, and put his hand on her arm. It was like closing a circuit. Currents of emotion suddenly ran riot through her insides. One touch and all her strength and resolve fell away. One touch and Carly was ready to bawl mournfully like a motherless calf lost on the winter prairie. She broke away and fled to the safety of the women's room while Evan called after her.

"Lisa & Chuckie" had been crossed out in favor of "Kristin & Chuckie" and then "Amanda & Chuckie." Carly stood facing the stall door and wondered how a man who would willingly choose to go by the name "Chuckie" should be so wildly popular with the ladies. She blew her nose on a wad of toilet paper and threw it down the toilet. It was one of those automatic types, so she had to sit down and stand up again to get it to flush. She sat and stood for the third time and wondered if things could get any worse.

"Carly?" It was Dana. "I know it's you, Carly. I recognize the shoes."

"Shit."

"You okay?" The tips of Dana's own shoes became visible under the stall door. She was wearing five-inch stilettos that made her legs come up to Carly's armpits. Carly tried not to be too bitter about that.

"No."

"You want me to come in there?"

"No!"

"You want me to wait for you?"

"No. I just want to stay here for a while. Okay? I'll be fine. Go watch the film."

Dana's feet squirmed for a moment, then disappeared. "I'll be around if you need me."

Carly waited until she knew the documentary had started before she emerged from the bathroom. Through the closed theater doors, she could hear Arlene singing. She melted into a crowd of latecomers and entered the theater, grabbing the closest seat to the door she could find. An incredibly young Arlene Barlow sang an a cappella version of "Fly Me to the Moon" as the opening credits ended. Arlene's tattered birth certificate appeared on the screen and Carly's narration started up.

"Angela Arlene Barlow was the only daughter, and third of four children, born to Ed and Carol Barlow . . ."

New pictures and music accompanied her words as Arlene's life unfolded on the screen. Evan had done a masterful job. Even though she was familiar with most of the elements and had read the script dozens of times, the final product was still enthralling. It was great, just as Evan had predicted.

"She wanted to go home, so I took her home. It was spring. She liked spring."

Pete's emotion-choked voice followed her as she slipped out of the theater and into the night.

Chapter Twenty

Los Angeles covers over four thousand square miles, most of it paved. Carly wanted to drive, to do nothing but drive, to join the endless strands of head and taillights, like diamonds and rubies strung across the city. She circumnavigated the city in a huge loop, hitting five freeways in under an hour before deciding to finally head for home. Masochistically picking at her wounds, she looked for Evan's truck as she drove down her street. It wasn't there, of course.

She prayed earnestly that love was like some terrible disease that, if contracted and hopefully survived, a person could thereafter count on lifelong immunity. Walking into her kitchen, she knew that she couldn't handle falling in love more than once in her life. She had serious doubts about whether she'd live through the first bout.

"Mrrew?"

"From now on," she said, picking Odin up as she entered the living room, "I'm sticking with the cat."

"Mrrew," he answered righteously.

The answering machine light was blinking. Automatically, she hit the play button.

"Aye carumba!" Dana's voice leapt from the machine. A piano tinkled in the background. "Coproducer, Carly! He gave you coproducer credit. What do you say to that, huh?"

The piano music stopped and a crackly voice wheezed, "Marry me!" before starting up again. Carly wasn't sure if Raymond was talking to her or Dana.

"I gotta go. Call me back or else I'm coming over there!"

Dazed, Carly headed to the bedroom to think and change out of her clothes. The thought that Evan had named her coproducer had yet to truly make an impact. Like lightning without thunder, it was only half real to her. She'd just stepped out of her dress and had barely begun to assimilate the facts when the blast came. But it wasn't thunder. Three times, in quick, impatient bursts, the doorbell echoed through the house.

"Damn it, Dana." She threw on her robe and headed for the door. Not bothering to check the peephole, Carly shouted as she threw open the door, "just use your key if you can't wait!"

"I don't have a key."

Evan McLeish was standing on her front step, the patio light gleaming silver off his black hair and casting half his face in shadow.

"I—I thought I was expecting someone else," she stammered, blindly reaching for words as her heart crashed around her chest. "I mean . . . I wasn't expecting *you*."

He noted her state of semi-undress and scowled.

Carly got ahold of herself and squared her shoulders. "What are you doing here?"

"I was in the neighborhood." It was his standard reply but not his standard look. He was so picture perfect and so at ease at the screening; now his jacket and tie were gone and he seemed more than a little scattered. "Can I come in?"

Too startled and confused for either fight or flight, Carly hesitated for a moment, then backed away from the door and followed him into the kitchen. Once there, he turned and stared at her intently, freezing her in place with his unblinking gaze.

"You're beautiful, Carly," he said reverently. Breaking his trance, he closed his eyes for a long moment, as if to rest them from such a glittering vision, before turning his attention back to her. "Just when I think I'm over how beautiful you are, you turn your head a certain way, or you laugh, or you smile like you just remembered something wonderful, and it hits me all over again like an atom bomb."

She looked away. Of all the things she expected him to say, that wasn't it. She wanted to say that she'd never get used to looking at him no matter how old she got. But she wasn't going to make that offering; instead she changed the subject.

"Thanks for my credit. Both of them."

"You don't have to thank me," he said, clenching his jaw. "You deserved it. I couldn't have done it without you."

"Was that so painful to say?"

He shrugged. "It's the truth."

"Thanks anyway." She waited for him to explain why he was there, but he didn't. "Looks like you got your funding."

"Yeah," he answered with a halfhearted laugh. "You'll never guess who financed me."

She shook her head.

"My mom." He noted her surprise and nodded. "I know. She had money from a business she used to own. She told my dad the same thing you told me. She was going to do what she wanted with her money and she wanted to put it into the film."

"She loves you a lot." Carly didn't point out that she loved him a lot, too.

"I think I still have a bruise," he said, motioning toward his shin.

"Good." She still had one hand on her heart. "You deserved it."

He shrugged. Was he agreeing, denying, apologizing? She couldn't tell. For her, Evan was as hard to crack as the thorniest *New York Times* crossword, and unlike the puzzle, there were never any answers waiting for her the following week.

Stumped, she asked again, "What are you doing here, Evan?"

"I want us to get back together, Carly. I want things back the way they were." His words were threaded with weariness and a certain amount of disgruntled resignation.

"Oh?" was Carly's arch reply. The man was tired, but not so tired he couldn't still make demands. Idly, she picked a cat hair off the collar of her robe. "Why?"

"Why?" Dismayed, he blinked like she was suddenly reading off the wrong script. He prompted her again. Take two was a little less beleaguered, a bit more forceful. "I said, I want things back the way they were."

"I know," she said, refusing to pick up her cues. "And I said, why?"

He closed his eyes and screwed up his face as if he was in the throes of some personal agony. Once he'd finished wrestling with whatever it was that was bothering him, he opened his eyes again and began to speak slowly. "Because you're miserable—"

"Who said I was miserable?!" she snapped. It was God's truth but she didn't have to agree with him.

He ticked off a list on his fingers. "Your friends, your family, your agent—"

She pushed his hands away before he ran out of fingers. "What are you? Stalking me?"

"No more than you're stalking me," he accused.

"When have I ever stalked you? I haven't seen you in weeks."

"No, but you've been driving me nuts for months," he said, grabbing the sides of his head and starting to pace. "Whenever I work on the film, there you are. Every time I get in the car, you're coming out of the radio. When I turn on the TV, Ella Freaking Earthworm starts telling me I should be a good and loyal friend and, hey, kids, don't forget to recycle whenever possible. If that's not against the law, then it damn well should be!"

"None of that is my fault."

"Damn it," he said, waving his arms, pushing aside any arguments. "I miss you, Carly. I want us to be together."

Missing her, that was good start but not enough. "Together as what? Friends, lovers, significant others?"

"Whatever you want to call it," he said as he slid down into the chair. His hair was disheveled and jutting out in clumps.

Carly sat down next to him and placed her hands

on the painted tabletop. "I told you before, Evan. I want it all."

"Fine," he grumbled. "We'll get married."

"Wow, that's as romantic as a jury summons. Ever thought about asking instead of telling?"

"You're killing me, Carly." He moaned wearily, a tortured sound from deep within his soul. "You know, I used to be a reasonable man. I knew what I was doing. I got things done. I was in control. Then you and your shoes came along and kicked the crap out of everything. What I want to know is, how can I still miss you every day when I dream of you every night? Huh? Where's the justice in that?"

She watched as the unaffected, stony-faced man she had grown to know started slowly banging his head on the table. Odin seized the opportunity to start nibbling on the shoelaces of Evan's good black shoes. Evan was an unhappy, pathetic wreck, a wrinkled paper cutout of his old self. And it was all because of her. Her moment of glory was at hand but it wasn't nearly as satisfying as she had predicted.

"Stop doing that, Evan. You'll give yourself a headache."

He sat up and stared at the ceiling. Odin had left a trail of cat spit on one shoe and moved on to the other one. "I already have a headache," he said morosely. "Are you going to marry me?"

"No."

"No?!" He surged out of his chair, sending the cat shooting out of the room. "But you *love* me."

"Yep, you've definitely got me there," Carly admitted ruefully. However, she no longer was interested in a second-place finish. She deserved more. "But it's still not everything."

"I don't get it," he railed, his arms raised, appealing to the universe for mercy. "I *am* giving you everything! I want to marry you. You can produce my films for the rest of my life. I *trust* you! What more is there?!"

Carly stood and grabbed him roughly by the collar, staring him hard in the eye.

"I want this." She kissed him like Jesus was coming and there wasn't much time. She threw her life into that kiss, past, present, and future, all she had, and all she hoped to have. Every unspoken hope and desire was represented in that passionate meeting of lips.

"I want you to love me," she said fiercely against his mouth, punctuating her words with an angry shake that snapped his head back, before she released him. "Nothing more, and not a damn thing less."

Like a man fearing eternal damnation, Evan, mumbling and shaking his head, staggered out of the house. Carly knew he wouldn't be back; it was over for good this time. Loud, guttural cries of anguish and grief rose thickly in her throat.

A dog's halfhearted warning yip followed by a man's shout and squeal of pain interrupted Carly mid-wail. A moment later Evan came striding back into the house wearing a look of ragged desperation. He was gingerly flexing the fingers of his right hand; in his left he held a pair of night-vision goggles.

"Get your car keys," he commanded, throwing the goggles on the counter. Then, spotting her purse, he began to rummage through it. "Never mind, I'll do it."

"W-what's going on?" she hiccuped, following in his wake. She dragged her sleeve hastily across her cheeks, leaving streaks of makeup on the chenille.

He hooked her elbow as he headed toward the back door. Along the way, he stopped briefly to top off Odin's water and pour kibble into his food dish until it was flowing down the sides.

"What's the matter? Where are we going?" Carly asked as he propelled her out the back door and to the passenger side of the Audi.

"Don't argue with me, Carly, please," he urged as he wiped the remainder of her tears away with his thumbs and kissed her cheeks, her eyes, her mouth. "Can you do that for me, just this once? Please?"

Carly had never heard him beg while fully clothed before. Speechless, she got in the car.

"Thank you," he said gratefully before closing her door. He got behind the wheel and peeled out of the driveway, heedless of the laws of physics or the state of California.

"I'm not arguing," Carly said awhile later as they roared past the other cars on the freeway. She had affected a gentle and reassuring demeanor. Like an animal naturalist in the wild, she didn't want to rile the herd, "but can I ask where we're going?"

"We're going to Vegas." The grinding action of his jaw belied the calmness of his voice.

"Vegas." From the determined look on his face, she knew he wasn't kidding. Maybe she had finally succeeded in making him crazy.

"We're getting married."

Grasping the sides of her car seat, she braced herself. She had promised not to argue but . . .

"Why?"

"Why?!" he howled in agony. Coyotes far and wide pricked up their ears and returned his mournful call. "Because you want everything! You can't stop arguing with me and I love you. You're an actress and I love you. You interfere in my film and I love you. You believe in lucky shoes, for chrissake, and I love you. Because I damn well *love* you! Are you happy now?"

"Yes!" she crowed and threw her arms around him to plant delirious kisses on the side of his face. "I love you, Evan. You're irritating and egotistical and grumpy and the biggest pain in the butt I've ever met and I love you."

He relaxed visibly, his hunched shoulders melted, and the dark indigo of his eyes softened to powder blue. The furrows on his brow receded, and his lips eased, the corners curling up in a subtle smile. Even his grip loosened on the steering wheel, but his foot was still solidly pressed against the gas pedal.

"You forgot to mention how mean I am," Evan noted.

He tried to put his stern face back on but it fell under a big fat kiss from Carly. With a contented sigh, she sat blissfully back in her seat, put her feet up on the dashboard, and crossed her ankles. Her robe fell away to reveal her bare legs. Evan glanced at her and the car skittered.

"Carly?" he asked, regaining control of the Audi.
"Hmmm?"
"What are you wearing besides that robe?"
"Just my shoes."
Evan let out another howl, triumphant this time,

and pointed the car toward the nearest freeway exit. "Roll the seat back, pretty girl. We're gonna need some space."

She watched as a familiar cockeyed grin spread slowly across his face.

"Well, hell." She stared at her feet and laughed. Maybe those shoes were lucky after all.